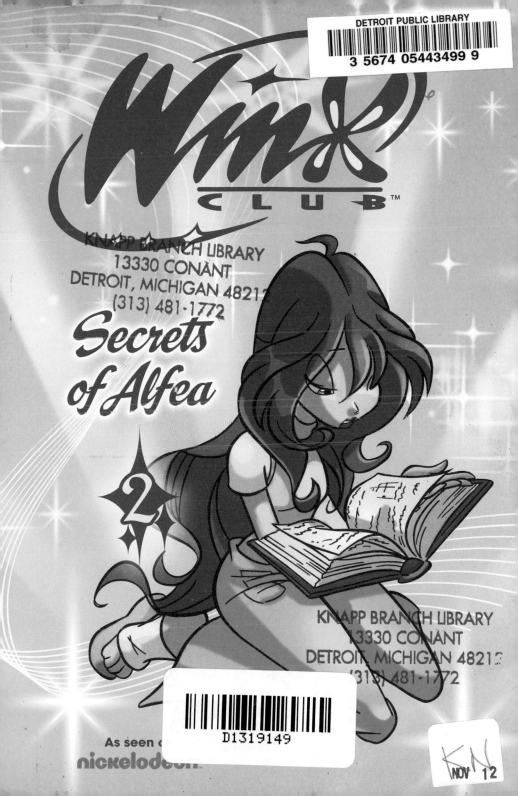

Winx CLUB™

Secrets of Alfea

2

As seen on **nickelodeon**

Winx Club
Volume 2

Winx Club ©2003–2012 Rainbow S.r.l. All Rights Reserved. Series
created by Iginio Straffi www.winxclub.com

Designer • Fawn Lau
Letterer • John Hunt
Editor • Amy Yu

Printed in China

Published by VIZ Media, LLC
P.O. Box 77010
San Francisco, CA 94107

10 9 8 7 6 5 4 3 2 1
First printing, July 2012

www.vizkids.com
www.viz.com

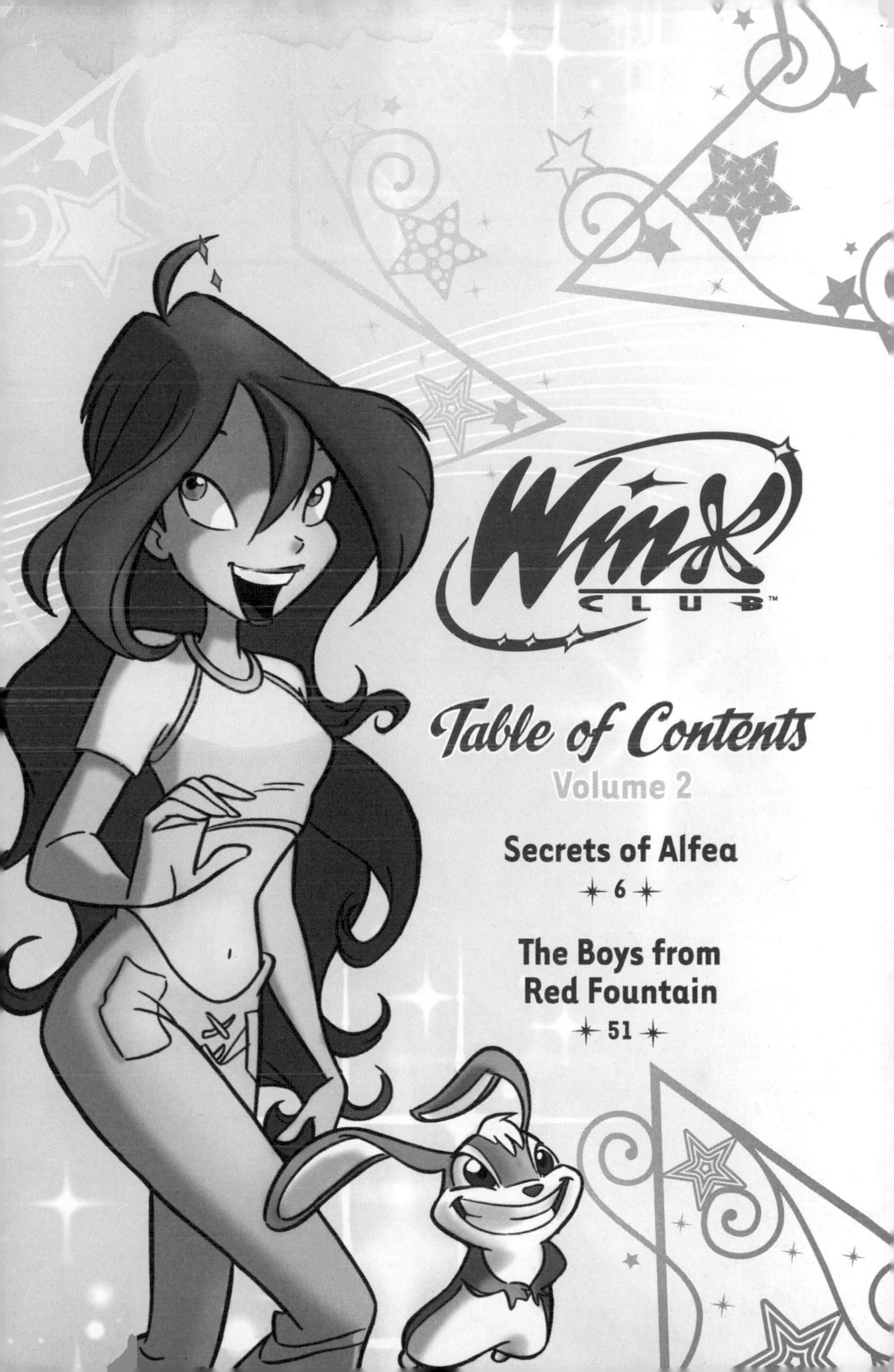

Winx Club™

Table of Contents

Volume 2

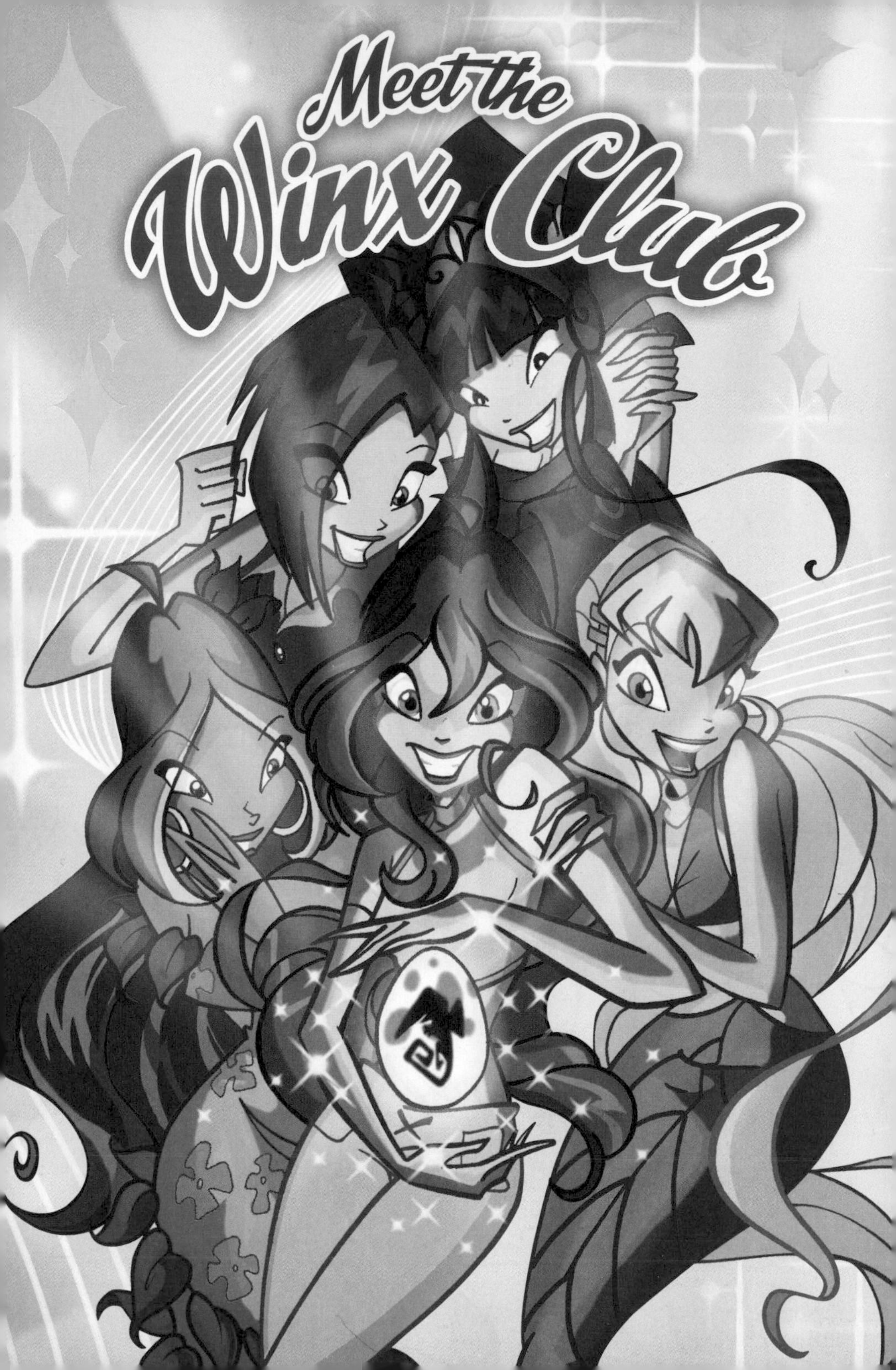
Meet the
Winx Club

Bloom

Raised on Earth, **BLOOM** had no idea she had magical powers until a chance encounter with Stella. Intelligent and loyal, she is the heart and soul of the Winx Club.

Stella

A princess from Solaria, **STELLA** draws her power from sunlight. Optimistic and carefree, she introduces Bloom to the world of Magix.

Tecna

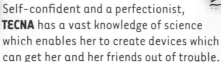

Self-confident and a perfectionist, **TECNA** has a vast knowledge of science which enables her to create devices which can get her and her friends out of trouble.

Musa

MUSA draws power from the music she plays. She has a natural talent for investigating, and she's got a keen eye for details.

Flora

FLORA draws her powers from flowers, plants and nature in general. Sweet and thoughtful, she tends to be the peacemaker in the group.

Stormy
Icy
Darcy

Their Foes

THE TRIX are an evil trio of witches from Cloudtower Academy who battle the Winx Club regularly.

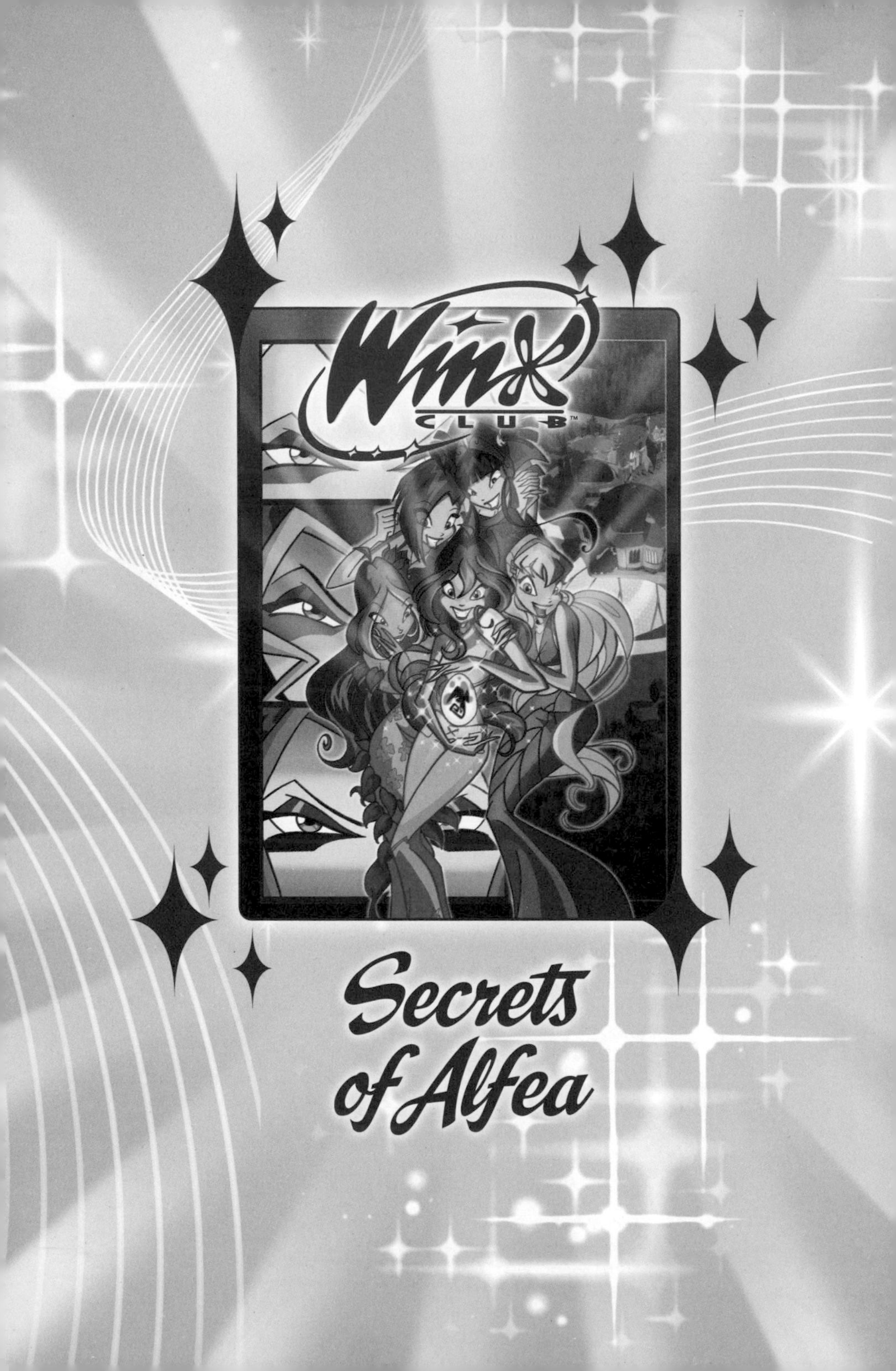
Winx
CLUB™

Secrets of Alfea

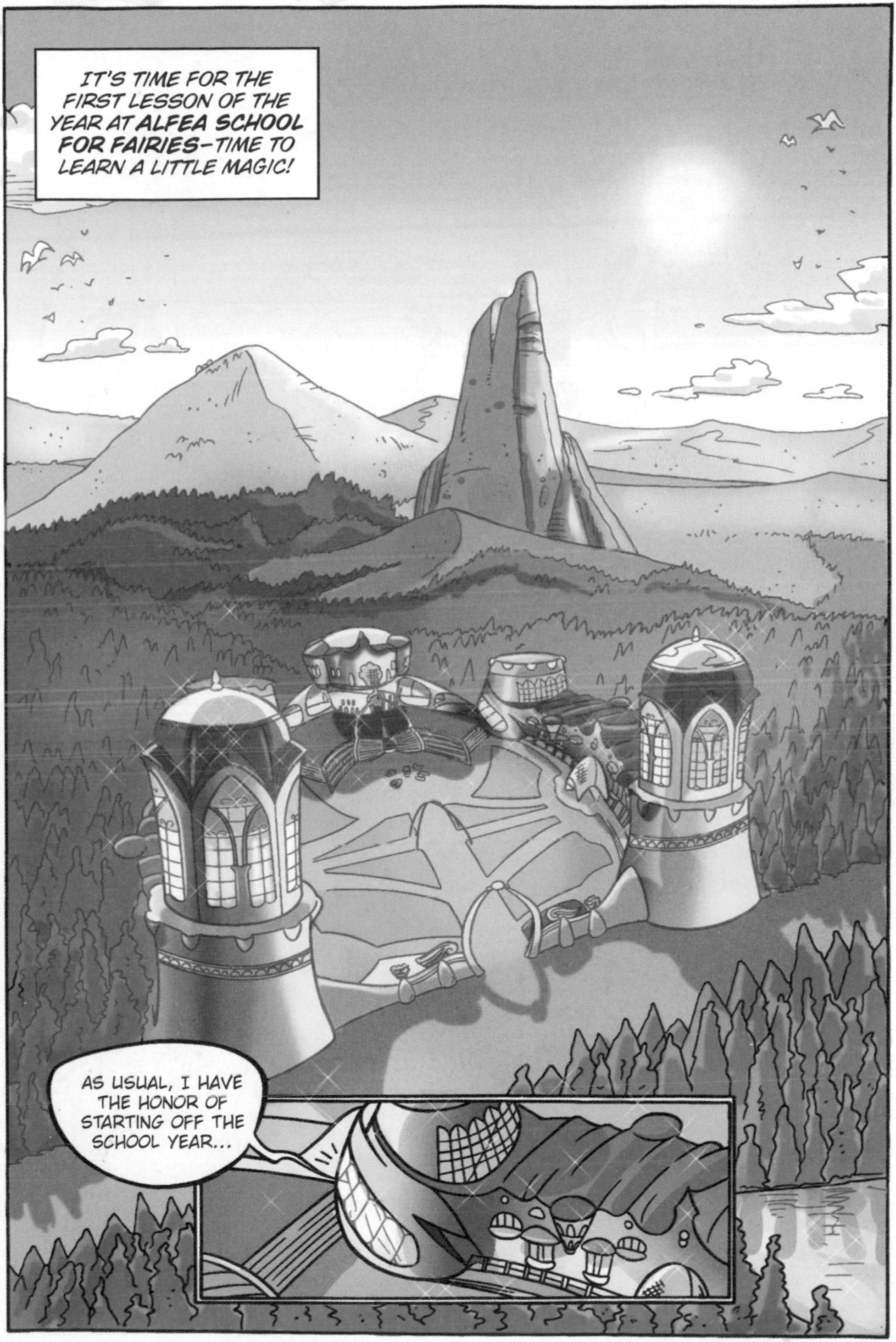
IT'S TIME FOR THE FIRST LESSON OF THE YEAR AT ALFEA SCHOOL FOR FAIRIES—TIME TO LEARN A LITTLE MAGIC!
AS USUAL, I HAVE THE HONOR OF STARTING OFF THE SCHOOL YEAR...

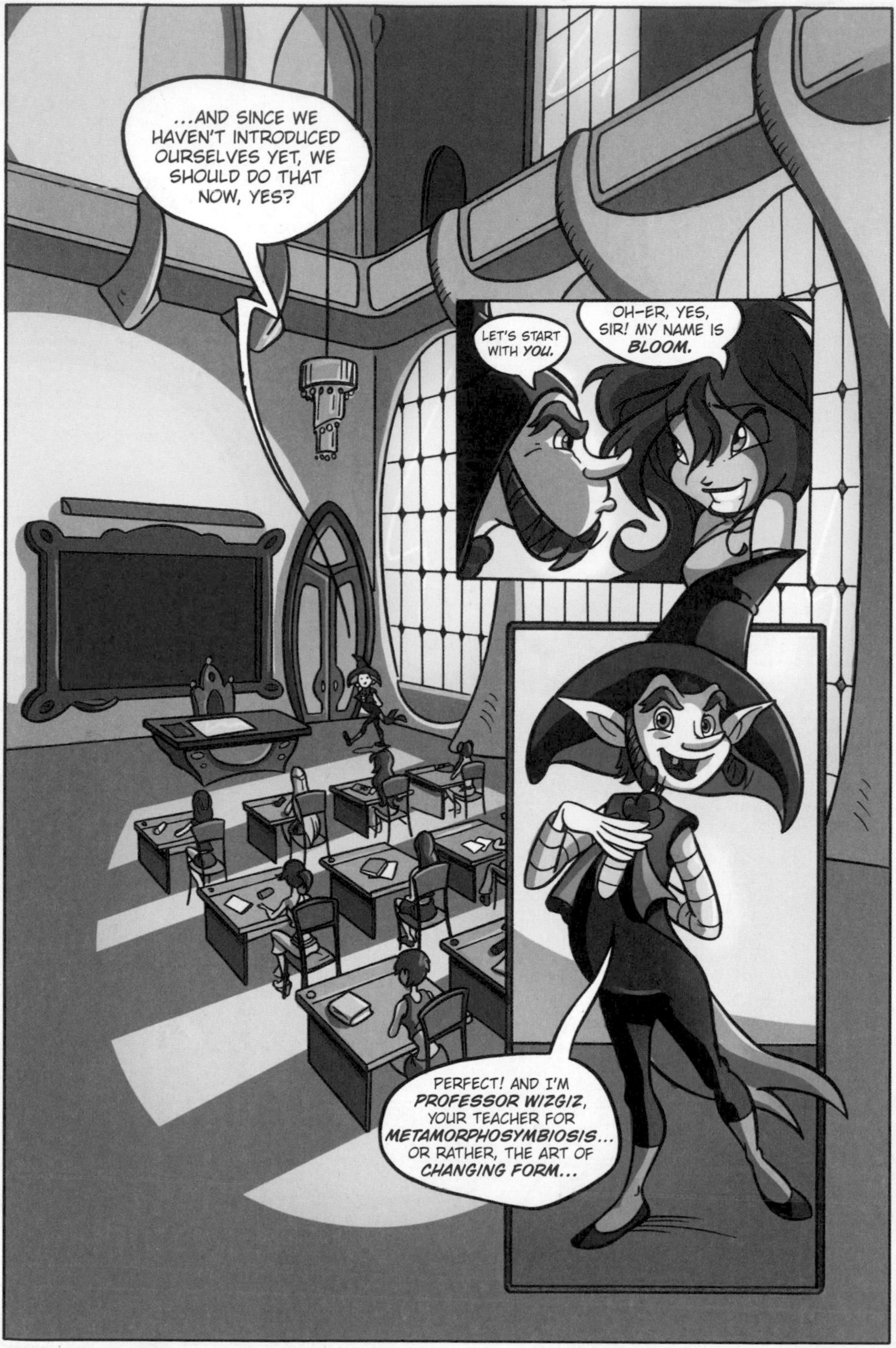
...AND SINCE WE HAVEN'T INTRODUCED OURSELVES YET, WE SHOULD DO THAT NOW, YES?
LET'S START WITH *YOU.*
OH-ER, YES, SIR! MY NAME IS *BLOOM.*
PERFECT! AND I'M *PROFESSOR WIZGIZ,* YOUR TEACHER FOR *METAMORPHOSYMBIOSIS...* OR RATHER, THE ART OF *CHANGING FORM...*

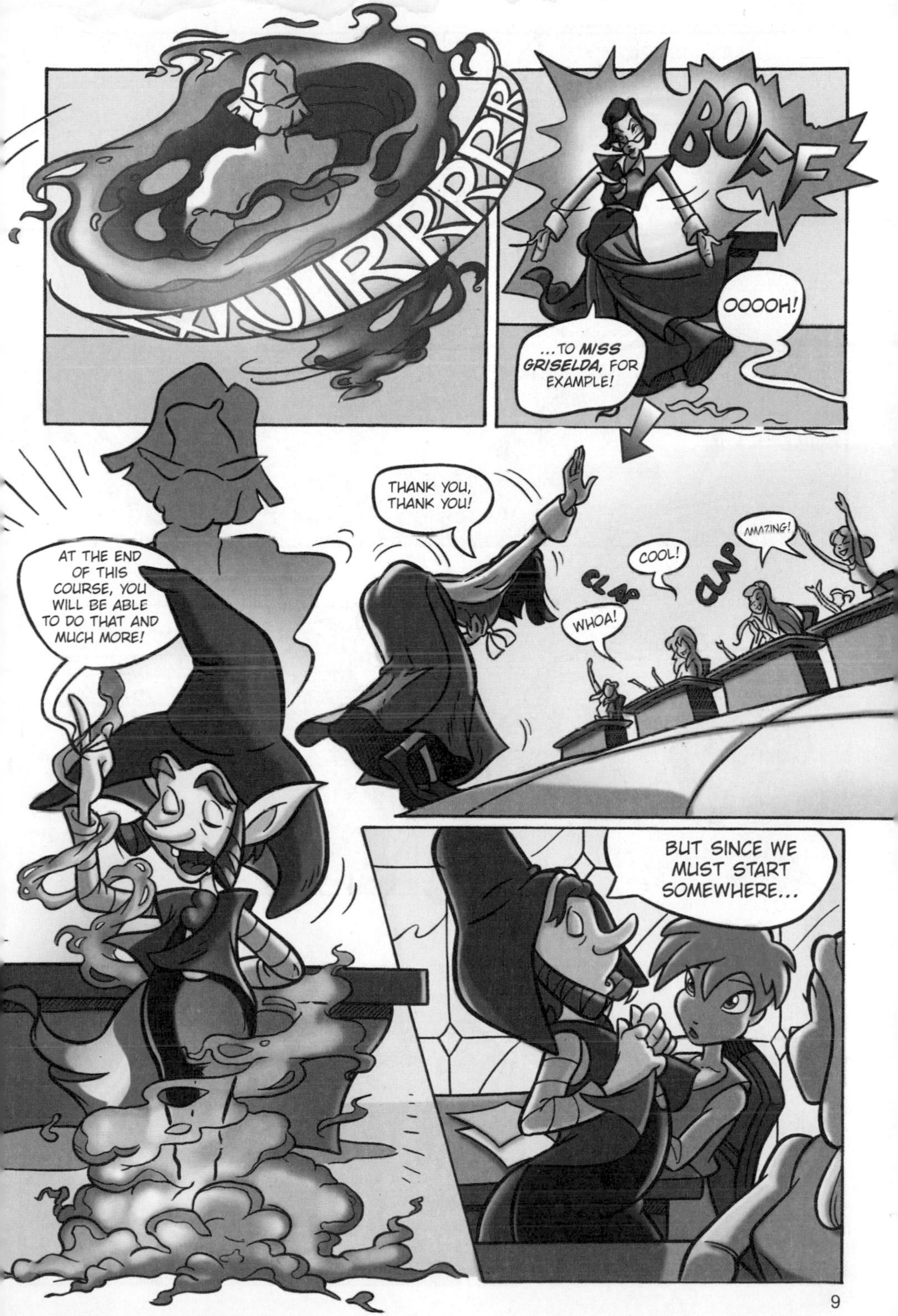
SKWIRRRRR
BOFF
...TO MISS GRISELDA, FOR EXAMPLE!
OOOOH!
THANK YOU, THANK YOU!
CLAP
CLAP
WHOA!
COOL!
AMAZING!
AT THE END OF THIS COURSE, YOU WILL BE ABLE TO DO THAT AND MUCH MORE!
BUT SINCE WE MUST START SOMEWHERE...

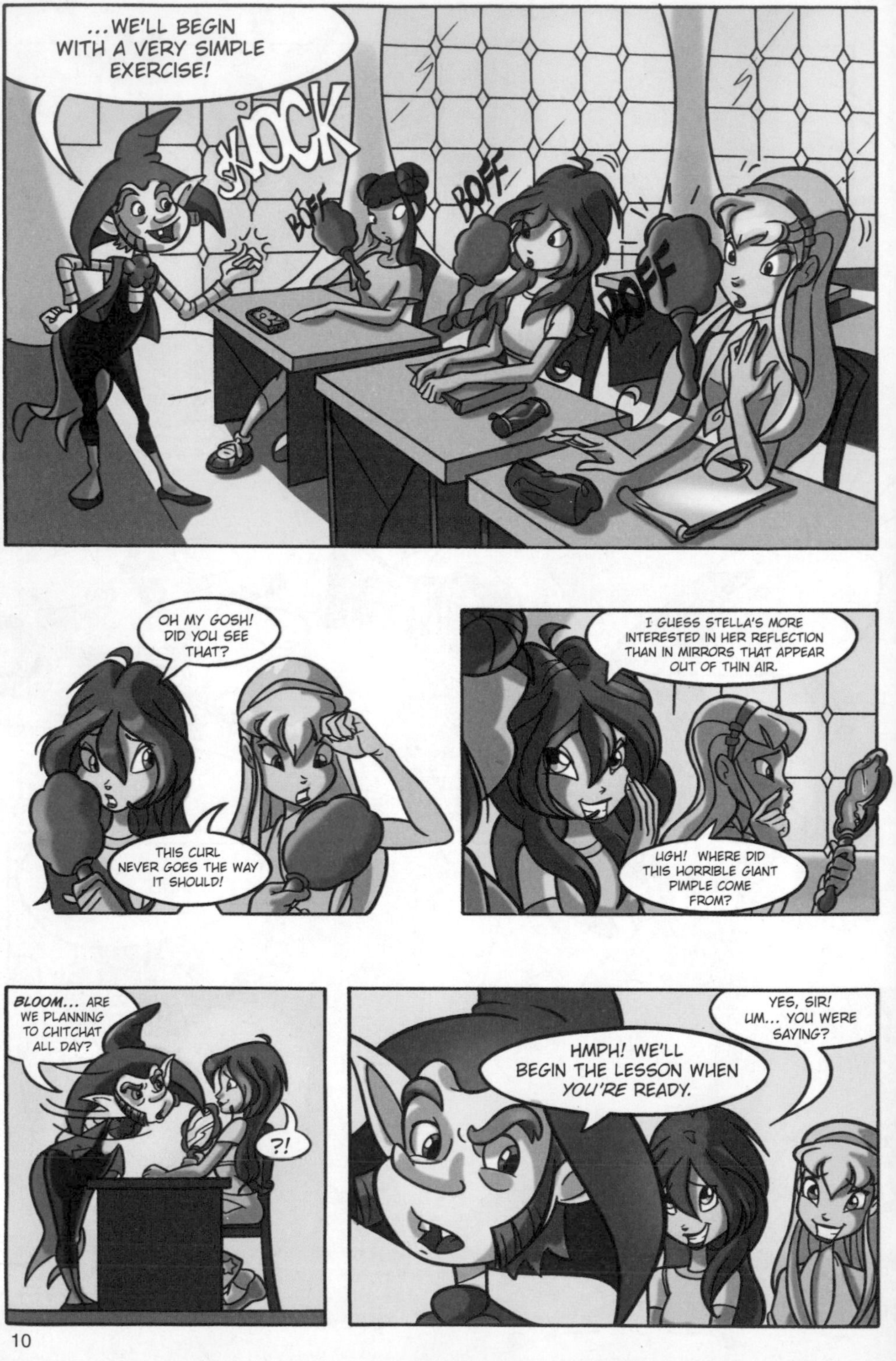

...WE'LL BEGIN WITH A VERY SIMPLE EXERCISE!
SHOCK
BOFF
BOFF
BOFF
OH MY GOSH! DID YOU SEE THAT?
THIS CURL NEVER GOES THE WAY IT SHOULD!
I GUESS STELLA'S MORE INTERESTED IN HER REFLECTION THAN IN MIRRORS THAT APPEAR OUT OF THIN AIR.
UGH! WHERE DID THIS HORRIBLE GIANT PIMPLE COME FROM?
BLOOM... ARE WE PLANNING TO CHITCHAT ALL DAY?
?!
HMPH! WE'LL BEGIN THE LESSON WHEN YOU'RE READY.
YES, SIR! UM... YOU WERE SAYING?

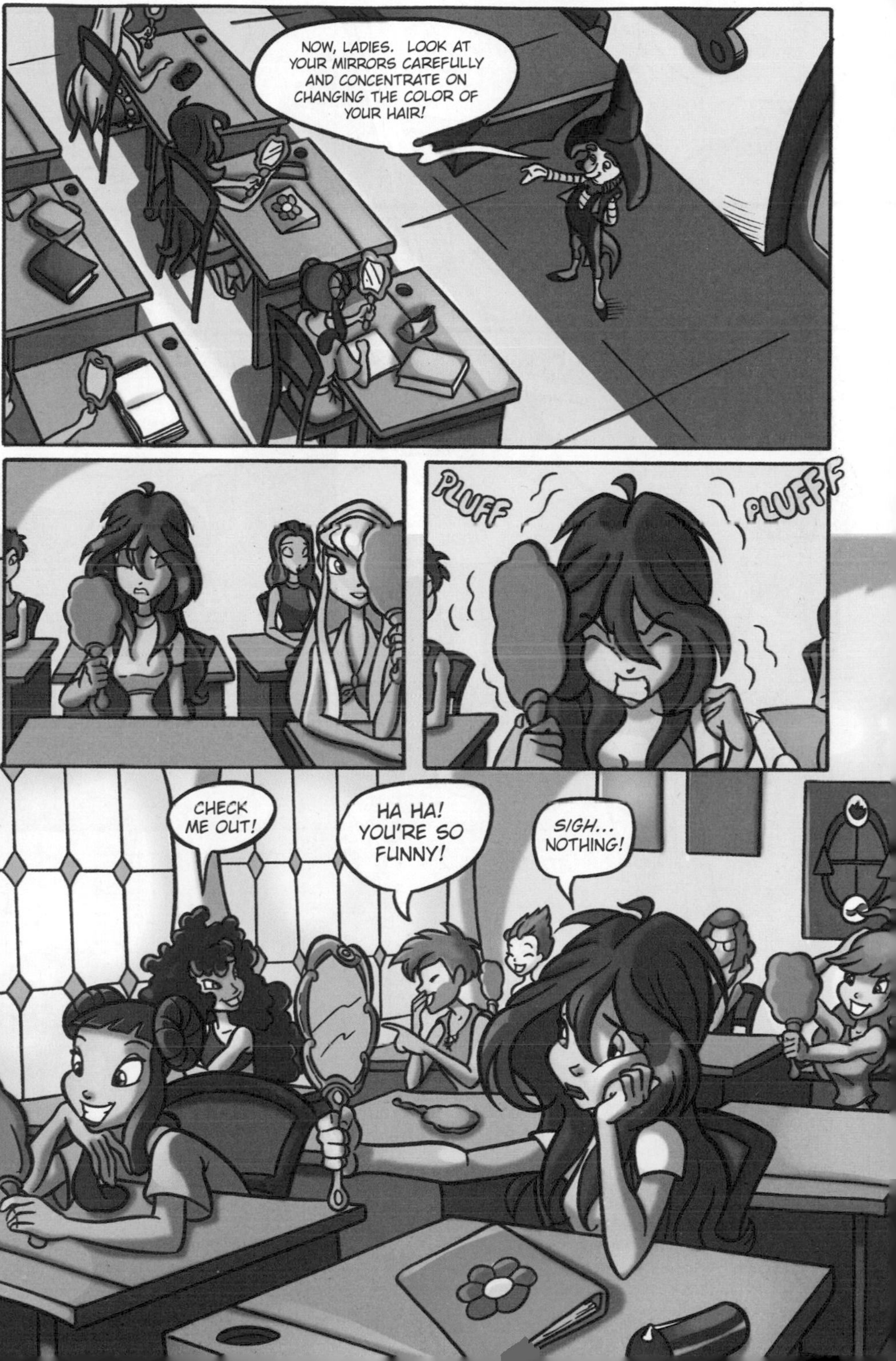
NOW, LADIES. LOOK AT YOUR MIRRORS CAREFULLY AND CONCENTRATE ON CHANGING THE COLOR OF YOUR HAIR!
PLUFF
PLUFFF
CHECK ME OUT!
HA HA! YOU'RE SO FUNNY!
SIGH... NOTHING!

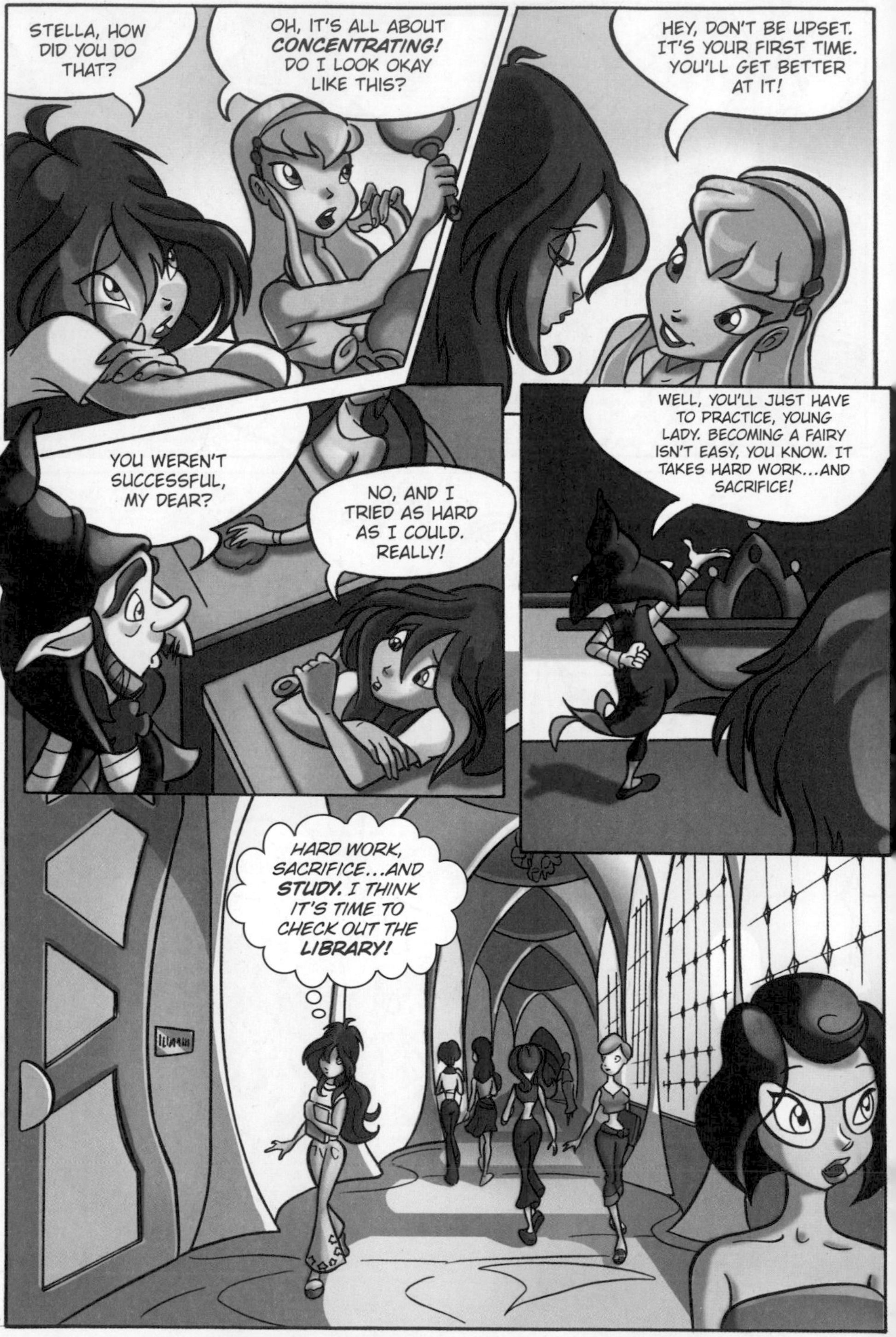
STELLA, HOW DID YOU DO THAT?
OH, IT'S ALL ABOUT CONCENTRATING! DO I LOOK OKAY LIKE THIS?
HEY, DON'T BE UPSET. IT'S YOUR FIRST TIME. YOU'LL GET BETTER AT IT!
YOU WEREN'T SUCCESSFUL, MY DEAR?
NO, AND I TRIED AS HARD AS I COULD. REALLY!
WELL, YOU'LL JUST HAVE TO PRACTICE, YOUNG LADY. BECOMING A FAIRY ISN'T EASY, YOU KNOW. IT TAKES HARD WORK...AND SACRIFICE!
HARD WORK, SACRIFICE...AND STUDY. I THINK IT'S TIME TO CHECK OUT THE LIBRARY!

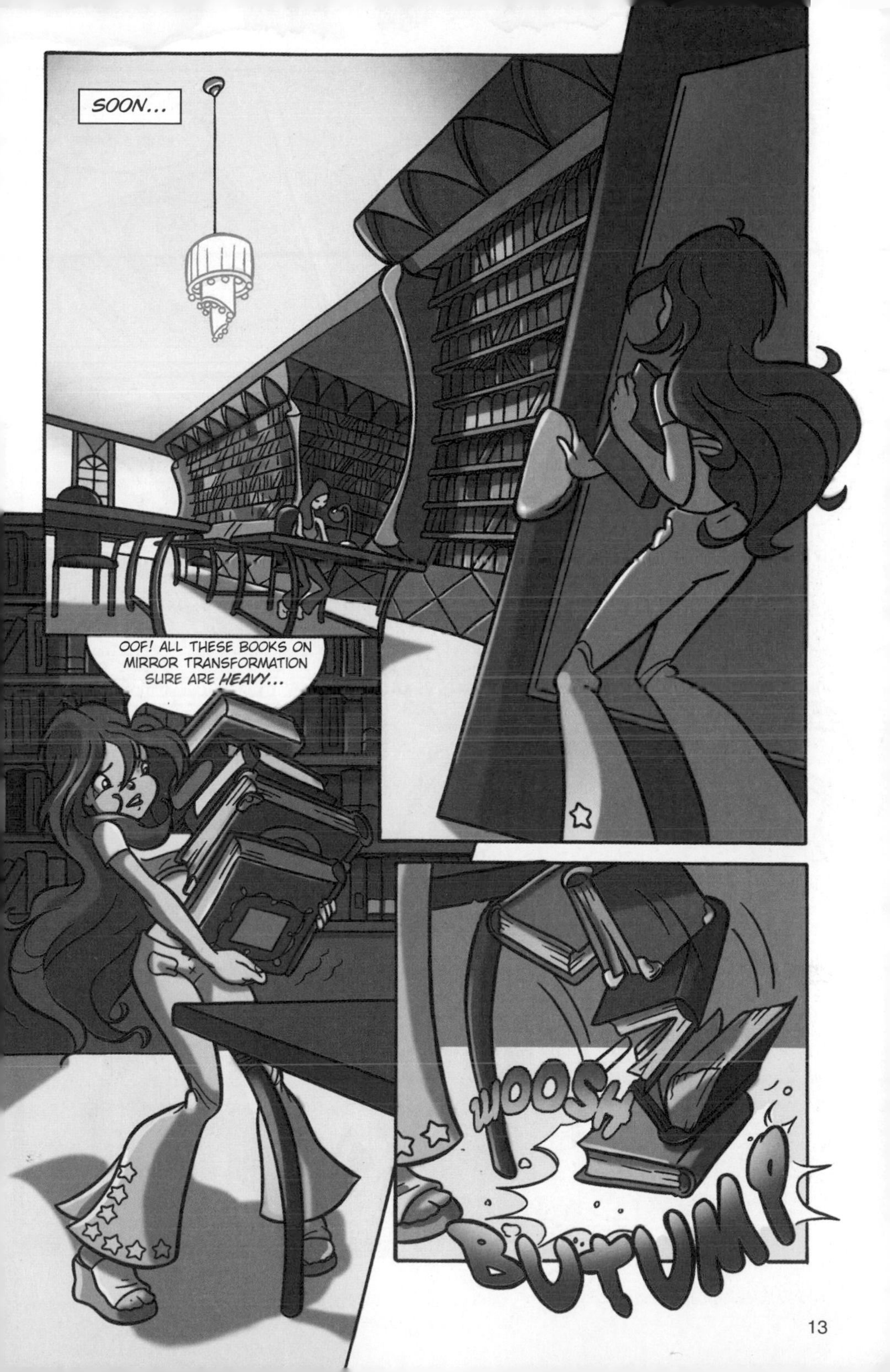
SOON...
OOF! ALL THESE BOOKS ON MIRROR TRANSFORMATION SURE ARE HEAVY...
WOOSH
BUTUMP

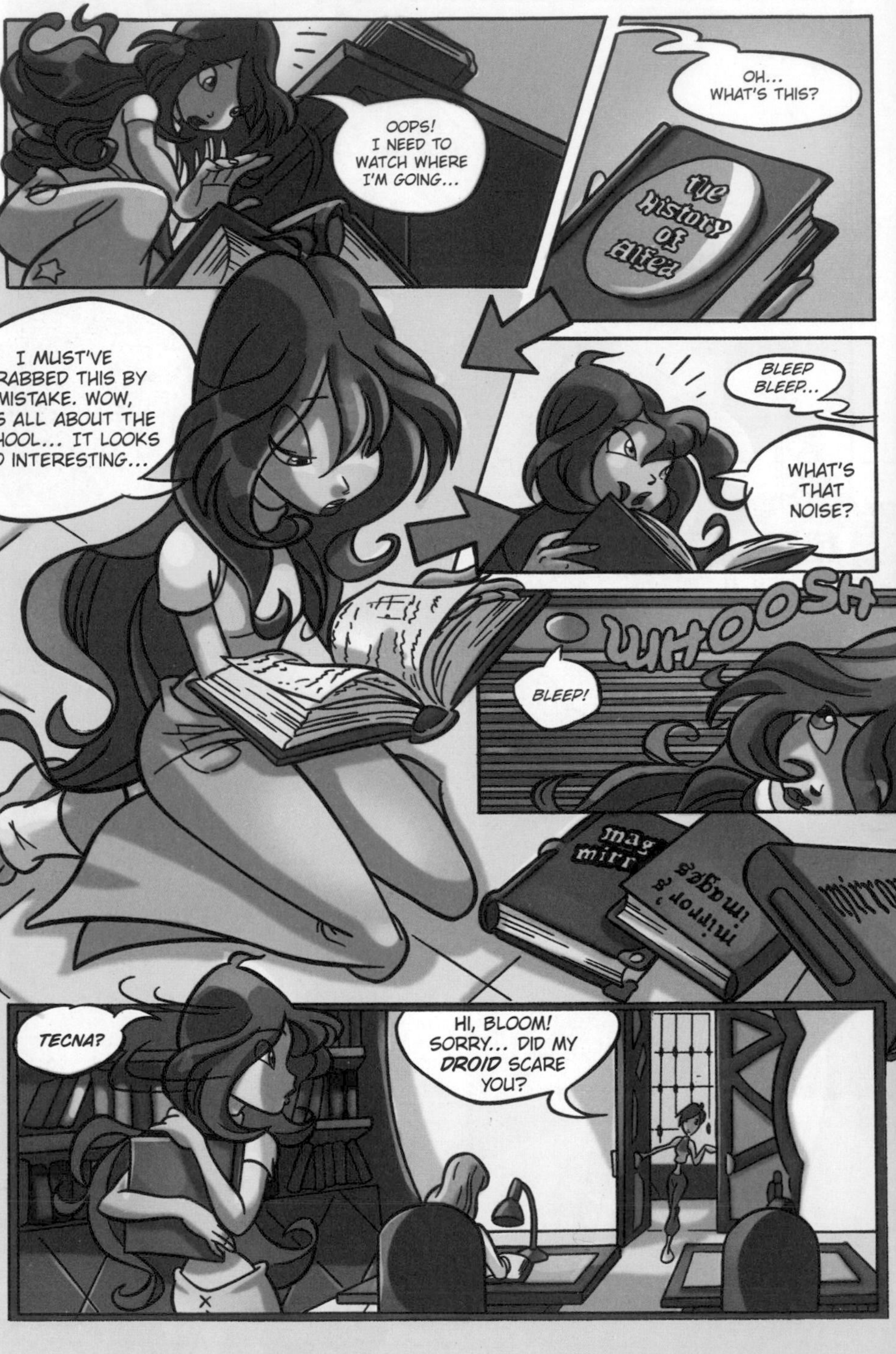

OOPS! I NEED TO WATCH WHERE I'M GOING...
OH... WHAT'S THIS?
the history of Alfea
I MUST'VE GRABBED THIS BY MISTAKE. WOW, IT'S ALL ABOUT THE SCHOOL... IT LOOKS SO INTERESTING...
BLEEP BLEEP...
WHAT'S THAT NOISE?
WHOOOSH
BLEEP!
TECNA?
HI, BLOOM! SORRY... DID MY DROID SCARE YOU?

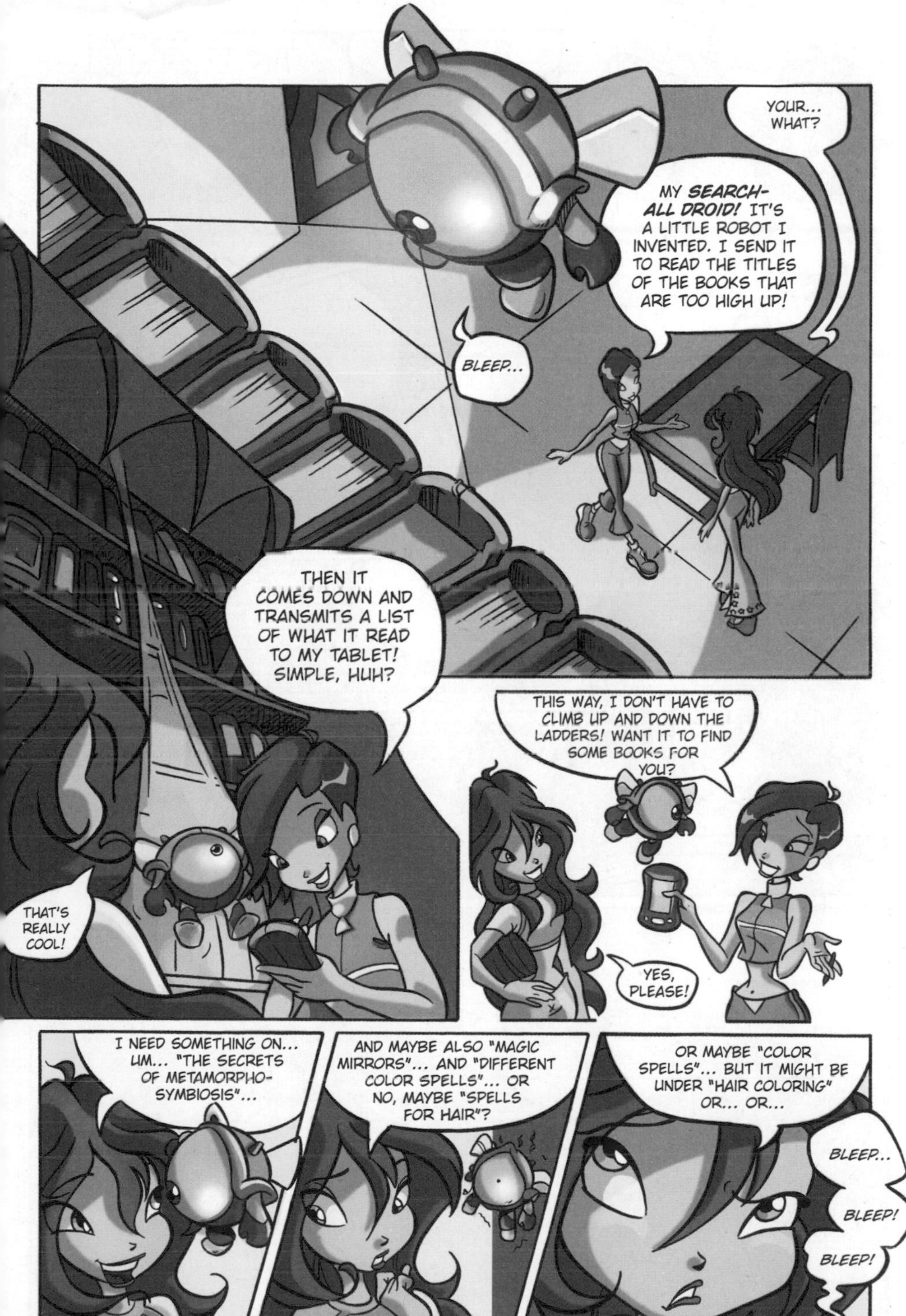
YOUR... WHAT?
MY SEARCH-ALL DROID! IT'S A LITTLE ROBOT I INVENTED. I SEND IT TO READ THE TITLES OF THE BOOKS THAT ARE TOO HIGH UP!
BLEEP...
THEN IT COMES DOWN AND TRANSMITS A LIST OF WHAT IT READ TO MY TABLET! SIMPLE, HUH?
THAT'S REALLY COOL!
THIS WAY, I DON'T HAVE TO CLIMB UP AND DOWN THE LADDERS! WANT IT TO FIND SOME BOOKS FOR YOU?
YES, PLEASE!
I NEED SOMETHING ON... UM... "THE SECRETS OF METAMORPHO-SYMBIOSIS"...
AND MAYBE ALSO "MAGIC MIRRORS"... AND "DIFFERENT COLOR SPELLS"... OR NO, MAYBE "SPELLS FOR HAIR"?
OR MAYBE "COLOR SPELLS"... BUT IT MIGHT BE UNDER "HAIR COLORING" OR... OR...
BLEEP...
BLEEP!
BLEEP!

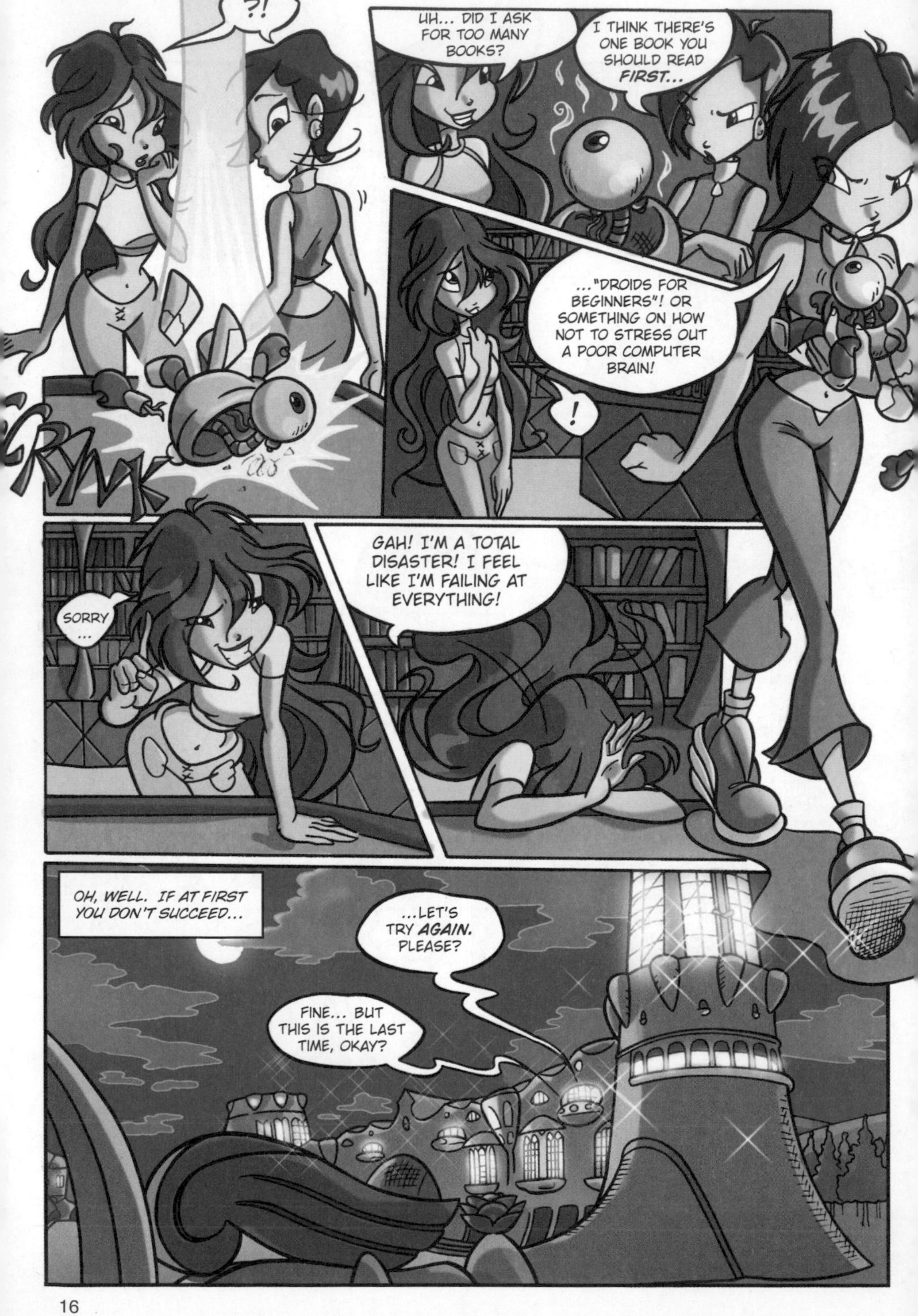
?!
GRYNK
UH... DID I ASK FOR TOO MANY BOOKS?
I THINK THERE'S ONE BOOK YOU SHOULD READ FIRST...
..."DROIDS FOR BEGINNERS"! OR SOMETHING ON HOW NOT TO STRESS OUT A POOR COMPUTER BRAIN!
!
SORRY ...
GAH! I'M A TOTAL DISASTER! I FEEL LIKE I'M FAILING AT EVERYTHING!
OH, WELL. IF AT FIRST YOU DON'T SUCCEED...
...LET'S TRY AGAIN. PLEASE?
FINE... BUT THIS IS THE LAST TIME, OKAY?

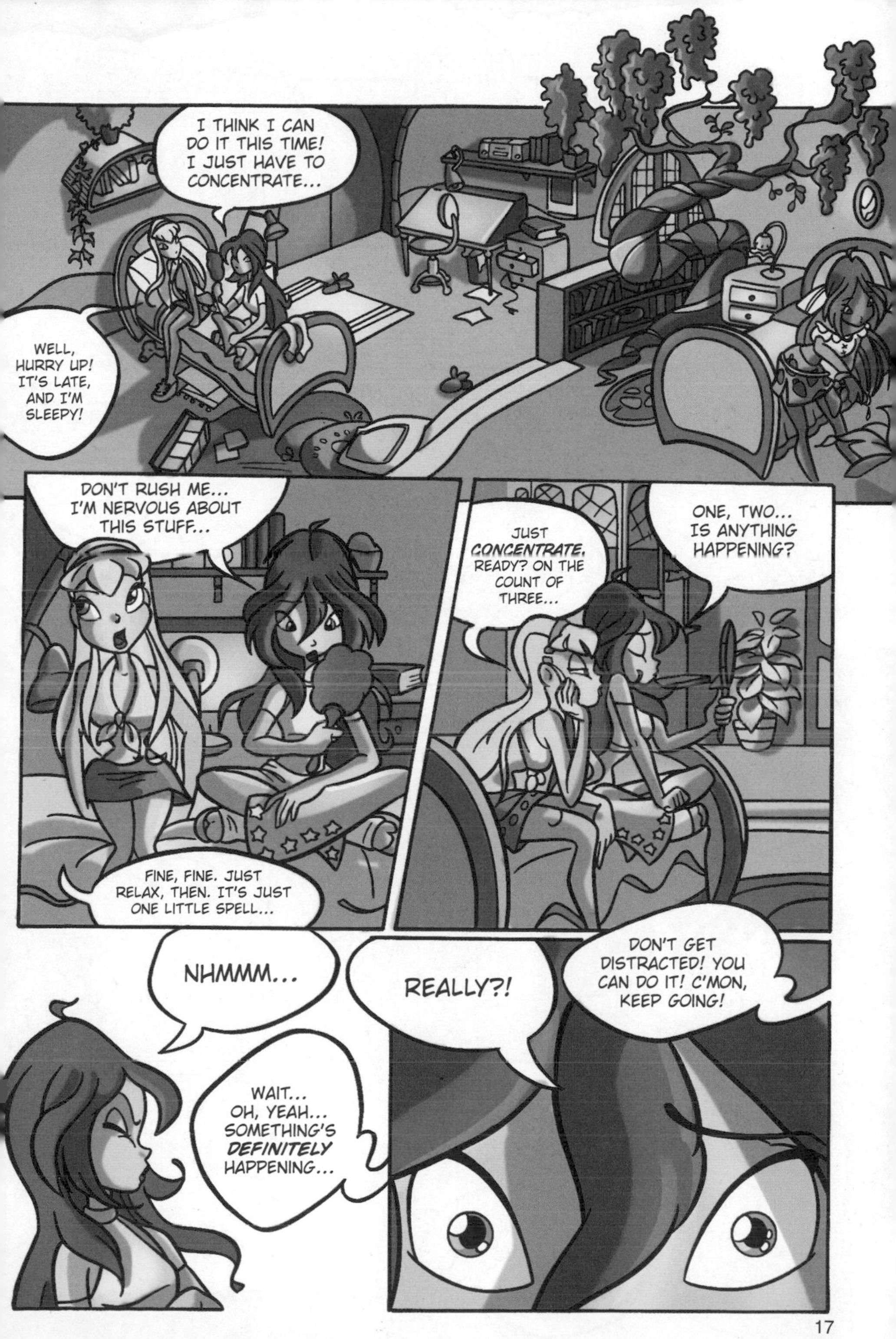
I THINK I CAN DO IT THIS TIME! I JUST HAVE TO CONCENTRATE...
WELL, HURRY UP! IT'S LATE, AND I'M SLEEPY!
DON'T RUSH ME... I'M NERVOUS ABOUT THIS STUFF...
FINE, FINE. JUST RELAX, THEN. IT'S JUST ONE LITTLE SPELL...
JUST ***CONCENTRATE.*** READY? ON THE COUNT OF THREE...
ONE, TWO... IS ANYTHING HAPPENING?
NHMMM...
WAIT... OH, YEAH... SOMETHING'S ***DEFINITELY*** HAPPENING...
REALLY?!
DON'T GET DISTRACTED! YOU CAN DO IT! C'MON, KEEP GOING!

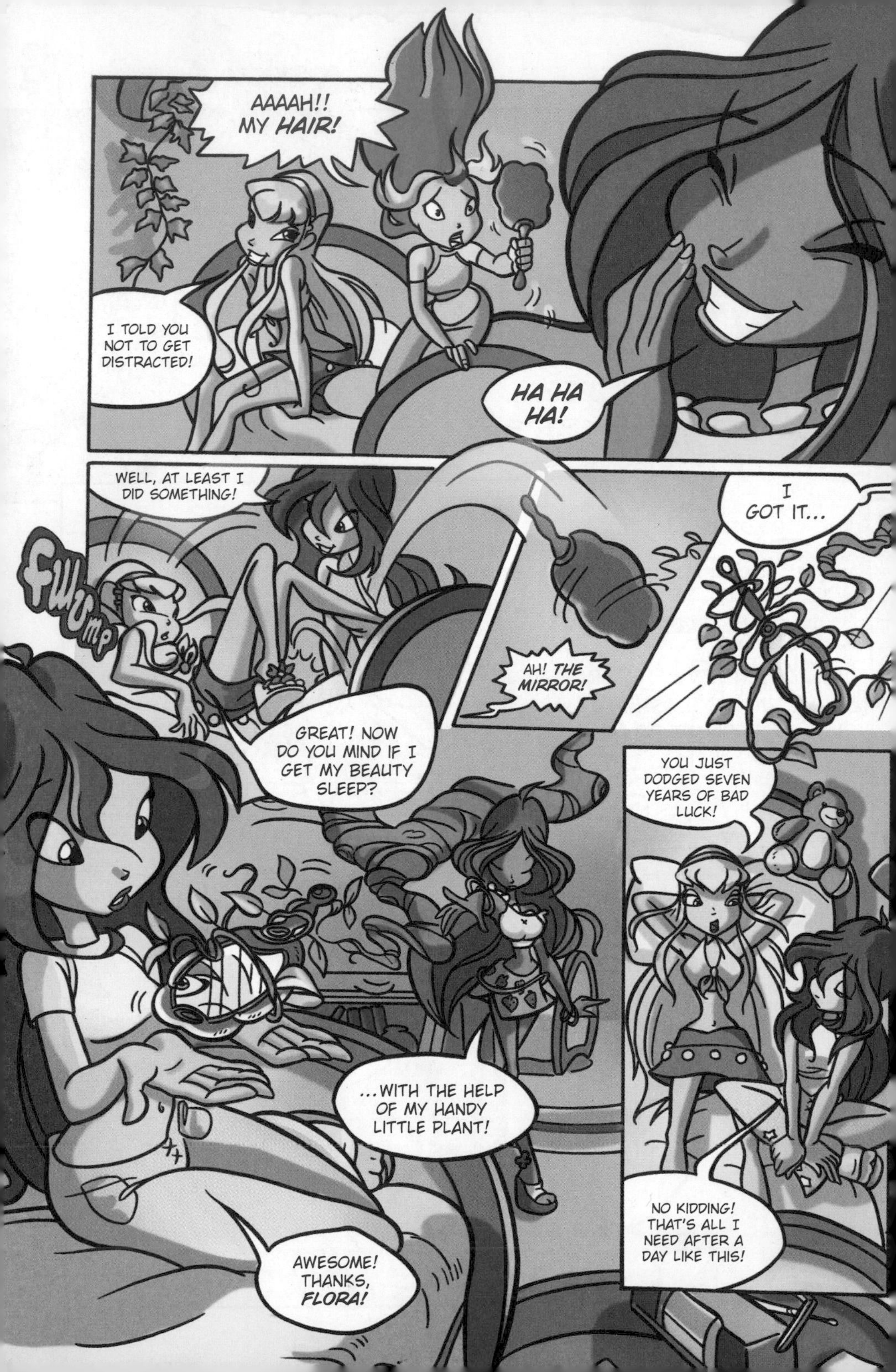
AAAAH!! MY HAIR!
I TOLD YOU NOT TO GET DISTRACTED!
HA HA HA!
WELL, AT LEAST I DID SOMETHING!
FWUMP
AH! THE MIRROR!
I GOT IT...
GREAT! NOW DO YOU MIND IF I GET MY BEAUTY SLEEP?
...WITH THE HELP OF MY HANDY LITTLE PLANT!
AWESOME! THANKS, FLORA!
YOU JUST DODGED SEVEN YEARS OF BAD LUCK!
NO KIDDING! THAT'S ALL I NEED AFTER A DAY LIKE THIS!

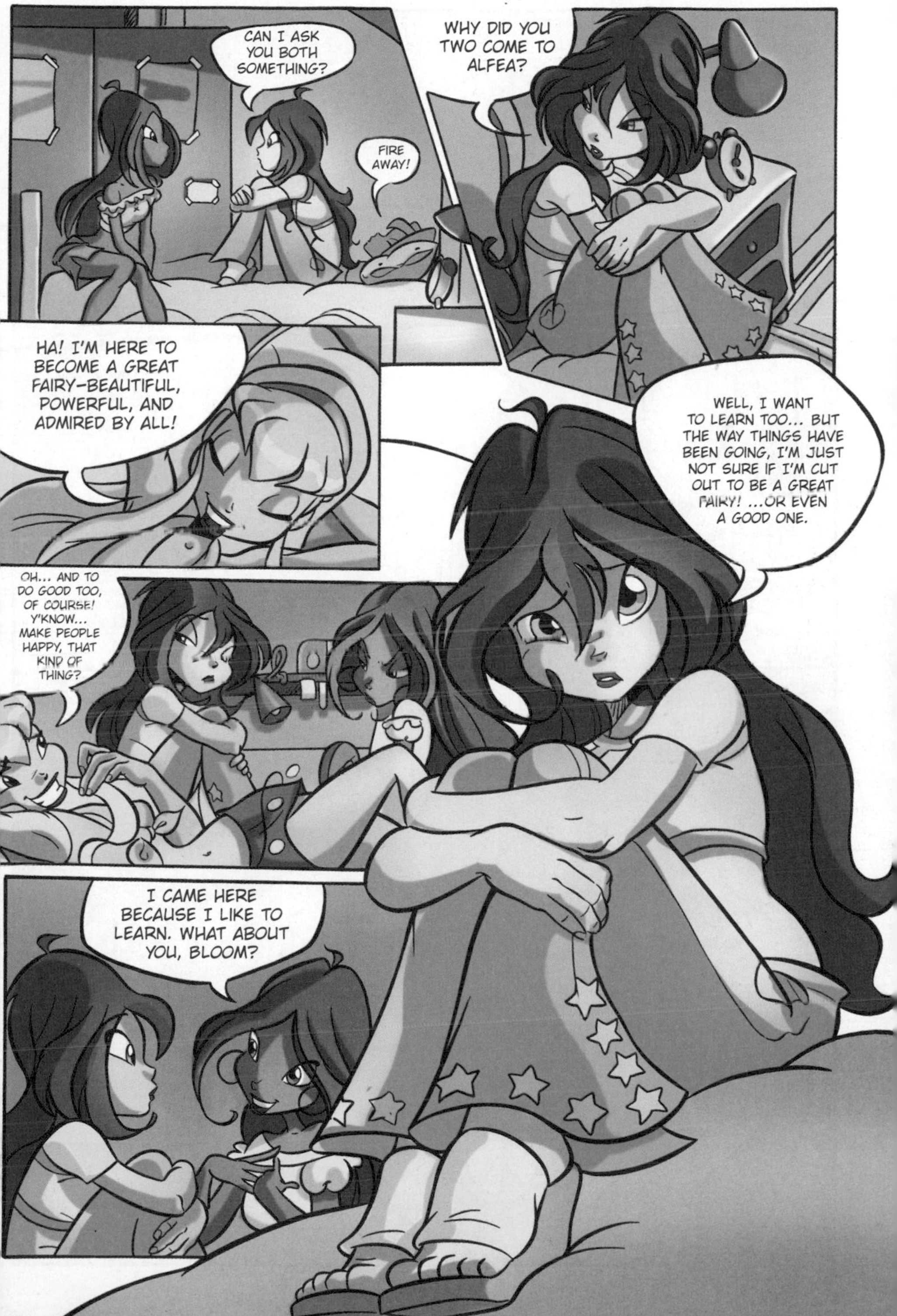
CAN I ASK YOU BOTH SOMETHING?
FIRE AWAY!
WHY DID YOU TWO COME TO ALFEA?
HA! I'M HERE TO BECOME A GREAT FAIRY–BEAUTIFUL, POWERFUL, AND ADMIRED BY ALL!
OH... AND TO DO GOOD TOO, OF COURSE! Y'KNOW... MAKE PEOPLE HAPPY, THAT KIND OF THING?
I CAME HERE BECAUSE I LIKE TO LEARN. WHAT ABOUT YOU, BLOOM?
WELL, I WANT TO LEARN TOO... BUT THE WAY THINGS HAVE BEEN GOING, I'M JUST NOT SURE IF I'M CUT OUT TO BE A GREAT FAIRY! ...OR EVEN A GOOD ONE.

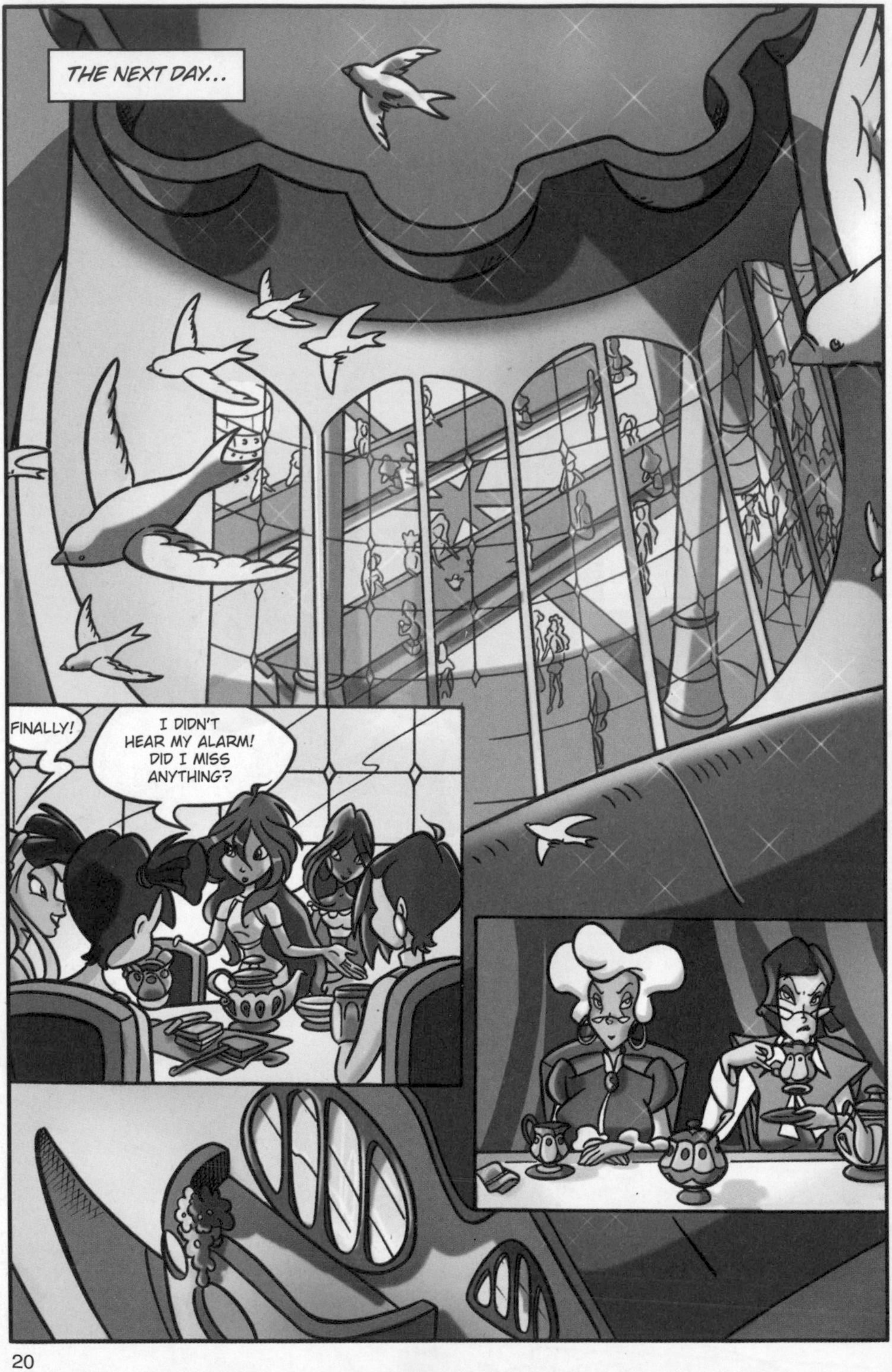
THE NEXT DAY...
FINALLY!
I DIDN'T HEAR MY ALARM! DID I MISS ANYTHING?

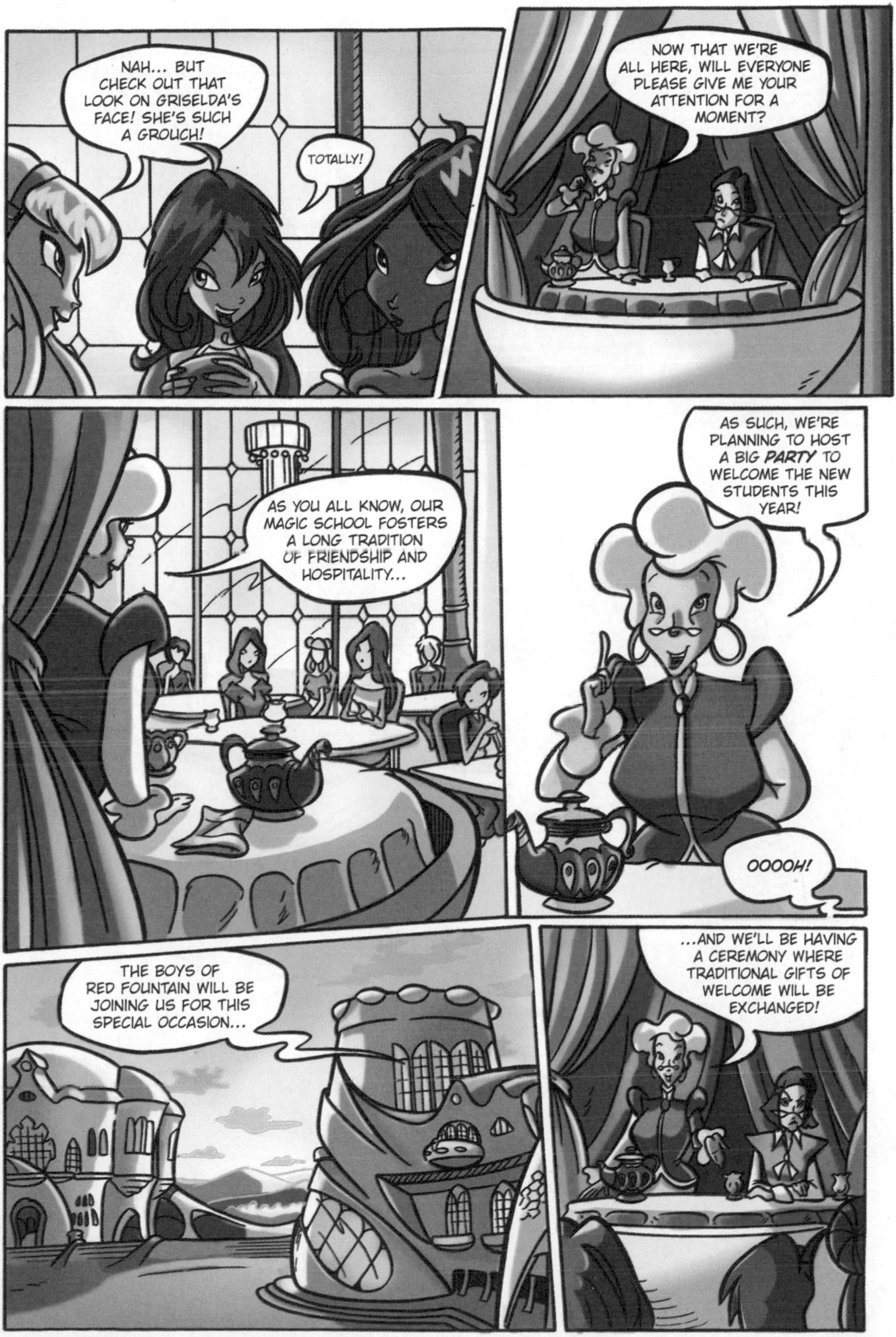
NAH... BUT CHECK OUT THAT LOOK ON GRISELDA'S FACE! SHE'S SUCH A GROUCH!
TOTALLY!
NOW THAT WE'RE ALL HERE, WILL EVERYONE PLEASE GIVE ME YOUR ATTENTION FOR A MOMENT?
AS YOU ALL KNOW, OUR MAGIC SCHOOL FOSTERS A LONG TRADITION OF FRIENDSHIP AND HOSPITALITY...
AS SUCH, WE'RE PLANNING TO HOST A BIG PARTY TO WELCOME THE NEW STUDENTS THIS YEAR!
OOOOH!
THE BOYS OF RED FOUNTAIN WILL BE JOINING US FOR THIS SPECIAL OCCASION...
...AND WE'LL BE HAVING A CEREMONY WHERE TRADITIONAL GIFTS OF WELCOME WILL BE EXCHANGED!

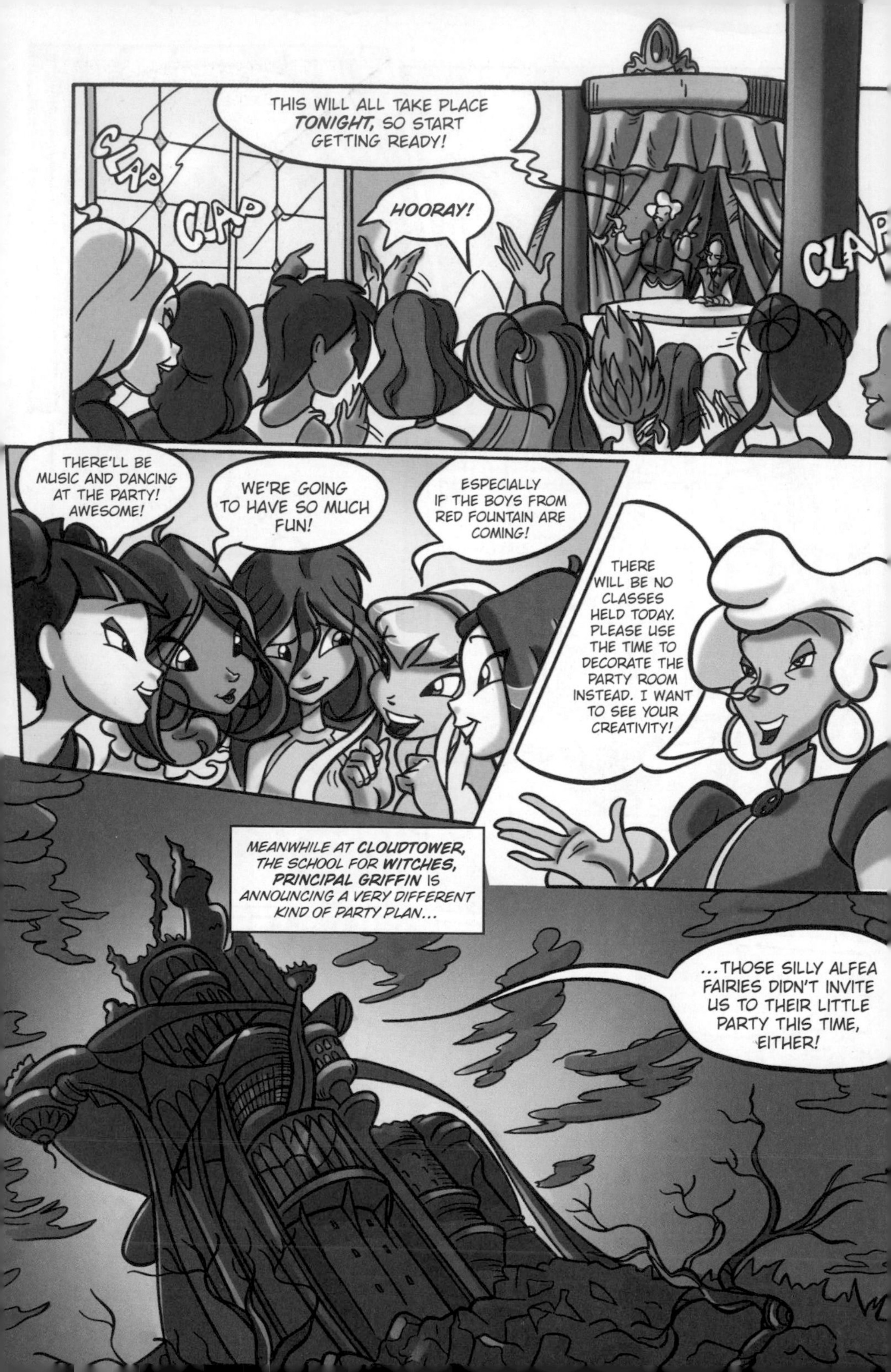
THIS WILL ALL TAKE PLACE TONIGHT, SO START GETTING READY!
CLAP
CLAP
HOORAY!
CLAP
THERE'LL BE MUSIC AND DANCING AT THE PARTY! AWESOME!
WE'RE GOING TO HAVE SO MUCH FUN!
ESPECIALLY IF THE BOYS FROM RED FOUNTAIN ARE COMING!
THERE WILL BE NO CLASSES HELD TODAY. PLEASE USE THE TIME TO DECORATE THE PARTY ROOM INSTEAD. I WANT TO SEE YOUR CREATIVITY!
MEANWHILE AT CLOUDTOWER, THE SCHOOL FOR WITCHES, PRINCIPAL GRIFFIN IS ANNOUNCING A VERY DIFFERENT KIND OF PARTY PLAN...
...THOSE SILLY ALFEA FAIRIES DIDN'T INVITE US TO THEIR LITTLE PARTY THIS TIME, EITHER!

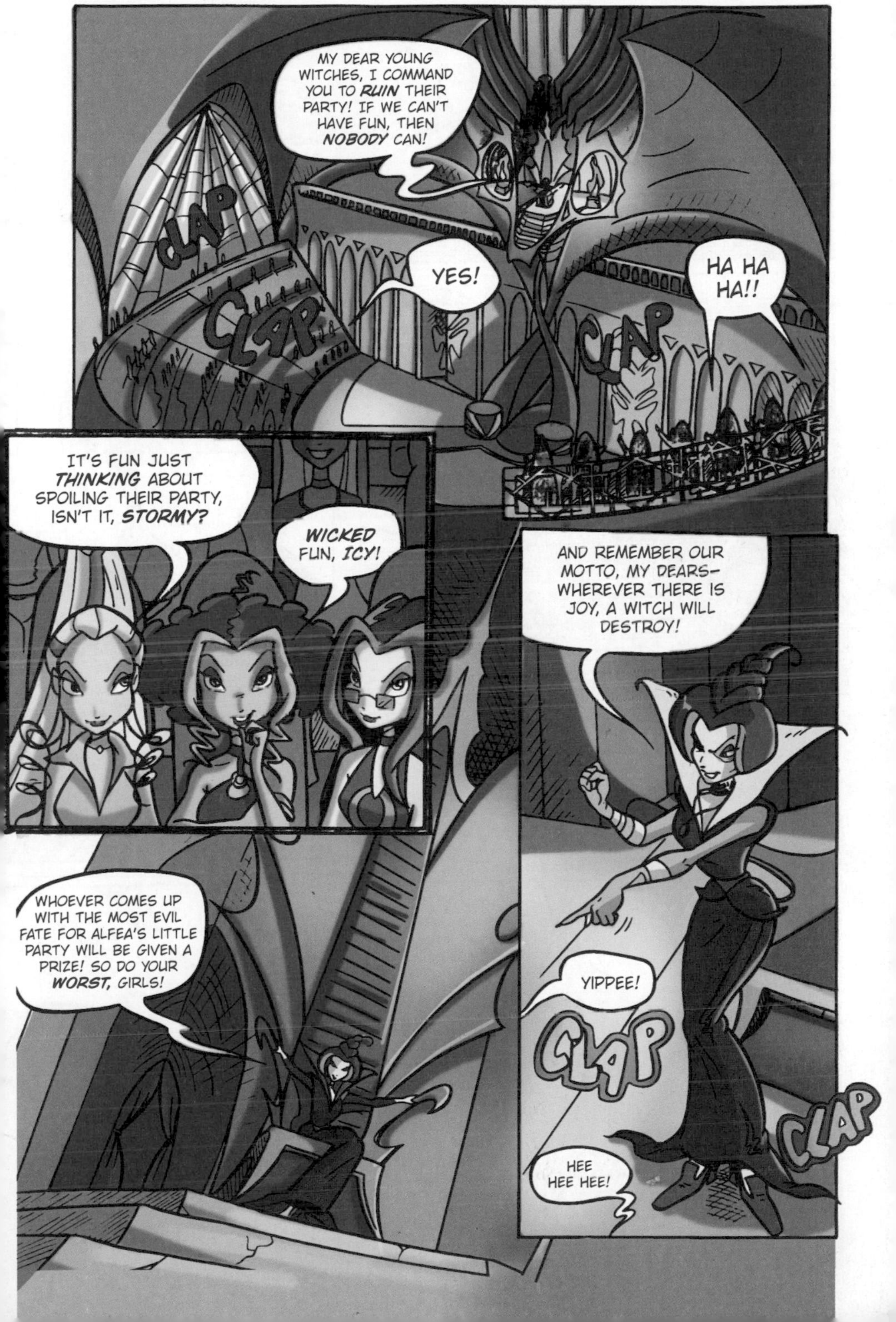
MY DEAR YOUNG WITCHES, I COMMAND YOU TO RUIN THEIR PARTY! IF WE CAN'T HAVE FUN, THEN NOBODY CAN!
CLAP
CLAP
YES!
CLAP
HA HA HA!!
IT'S FUN JUST THINKING ABOUT SPOILING THEIR PARTY, ISN'T IT, STORMY?
WICKED FUN, ICY!
AND REMEMBER OUR MOTTO, MY DEARS– WHEREVER THERE IS JOY, A WITCH WILL DESTROY!
WHOEVER COMES UP WITH THE MOST EVIL FATE FOR ALFEA'S LITTLE PARTY WILL BE GIVEN A PRIZE! SO DO YOUR WORST, GIRLS!
YIPPEE!
CLAP
CLAP
HEE HEE HEE!

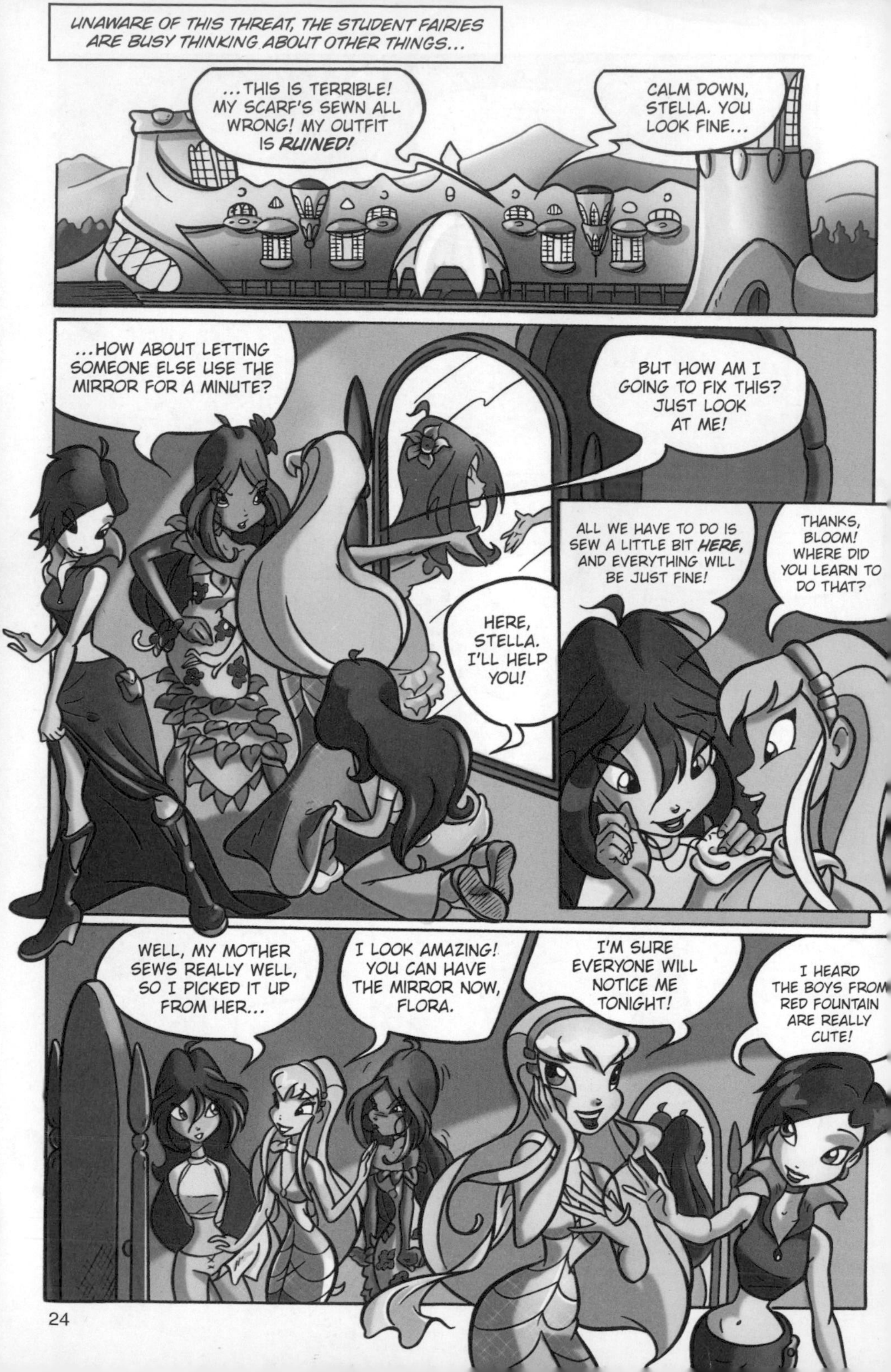
UNAWARE OF THIS THREAT, THE STUDENT FAIRIES ARE BUSY THINKING ABOUT OTHER THINGS...
...THIS IS TERRIBLE! MY SCARF'S SEWN ALL WRONG! MY OUTFIT IS *RUINED!*
CALM DOWN, STELLA. YOU LOOK FINE...
...HOW ABOUT LETTING SOMEONE ELSE USE THE MIRROR FOR A MINUTE?
BUT HOW AM I GOING TO FIX THIS? JUST LOOK AT ME!
HERE, STELLA. I'LL HELP YOU!
ALL WE HAVE TO DO IS SEW A LITTLE BIT *HERE,* AND EVERYTHING WILL BE JUST FINE!
THANKS, BLOOM! WHERE DID YOU LEARN TO DO THAT?
WELL, MY MOTHER SEWS REALLY WELL, SO I PICKED IT UP FROM HER...
I LOOK AMAZING! YOU CAN HAVE THE MIRROR NOW, FLORA.
I'M SURE EVERYONE WILL NOTICE ME TONIGHT!
I HEARD THE BOYS FROM RED FOUNTAIN ARE REALLY CUTE!

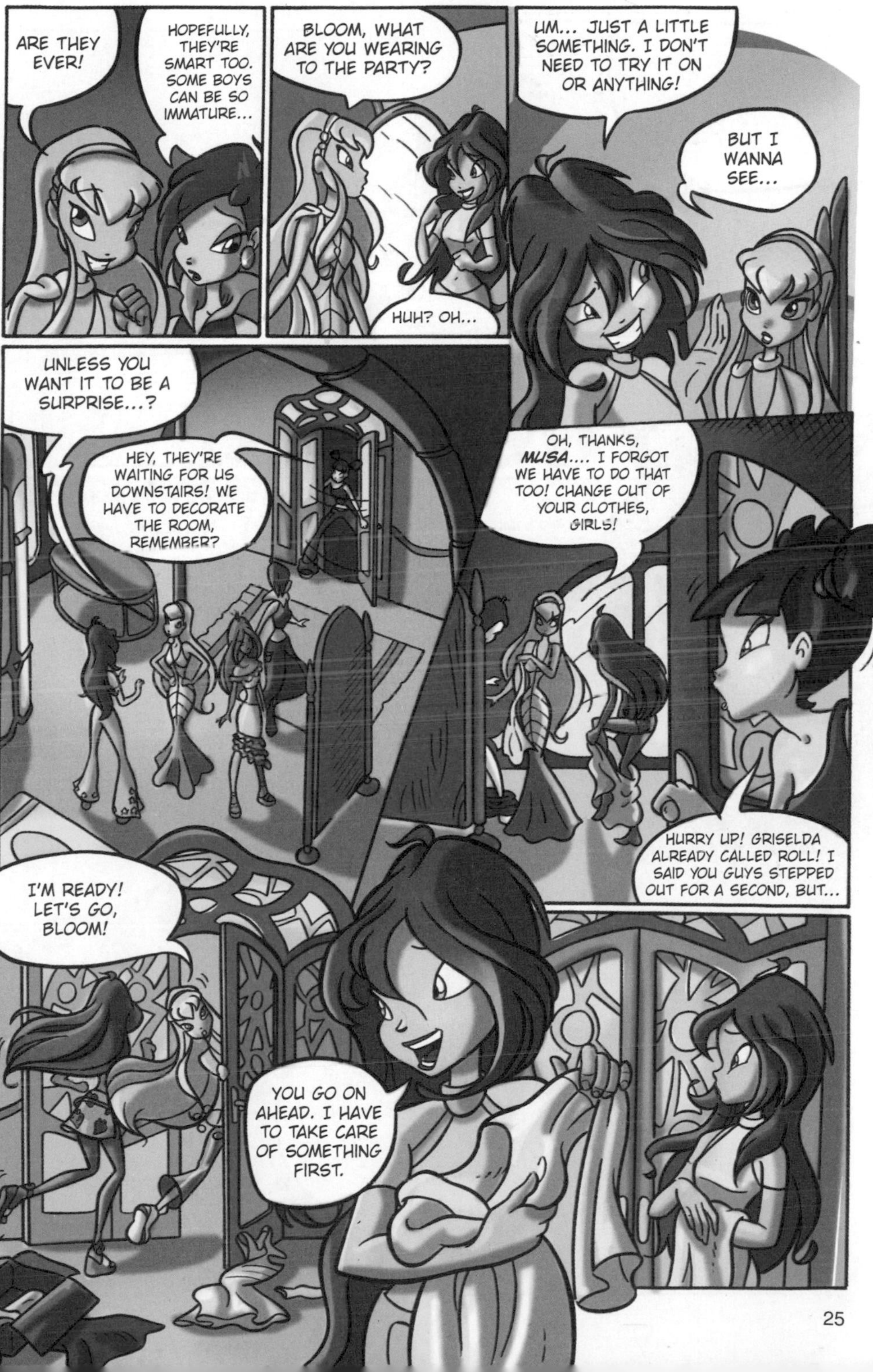
ARE THEY EVER!
HOPEFULLY, THEY'RE SMART TOO. SOME BOYS CAN BE SO IMMATURE...
BLOOM, WHAT ARE YOU WEARING TO THE PARTY?
HUH? OH...
UM... JUST A LITTLE SOMETHING. I DON'T NEED TO TRY IT ON OR ANYTHING!
BUT I WANNA SEE...
UNLESS YOU WANT IT TO BE A SURPRISE...?
HEY, THEY'RE WAITING FOR US DOWNSTAIRS! WE HAVE TO DECORATE THE ROOM, REMEMBER?
OH, THANKS, MUSA.... I FORGOT WE HAVE TO DO THAT TOO! CHANGE OUT OF YOUR CLOTHES, GIRLS!
HURRY UP! GRISELDA ALREADY CALLED ROLL! I SAID YOU GUYS STEPPED OUT FOR A SECOND, BUT...
I'M READY! LET'S GO, BLOOM!
YOU GO ON AHEAD. I HAVE TO TAKE CARE OF SOMETHING FIRST.

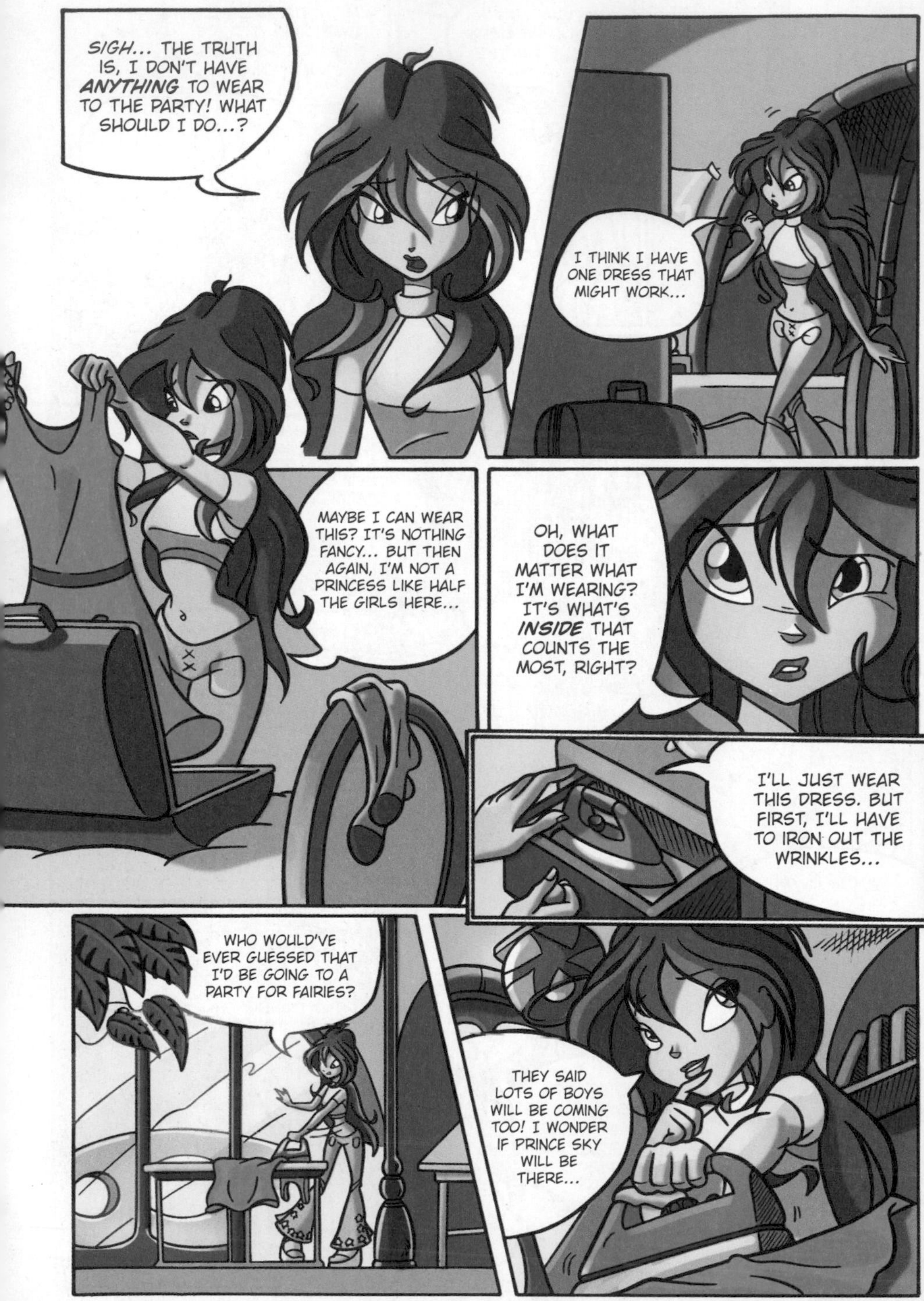
SIGH... THE TRUTH IS, I DON'T HAVE ANYTHING TO WEAR TO THE PARTY! WHAT SHOULD I DO...?
I THINK I HAVE ONE DRESS THAT MIGHT WORK...
MAYBE I CAN WEAR THIS? IT'S NOTHING FANCY... BUT THEN AGAIN, I'M NOT A PRINCESS LIKE HALF THE GIRLS HERE...
OH, WHAT DOES IT MATTER WHAT I'M WEARING? IT'S WHAT'S INSIDE THAT COUNTS THE MOST, RIGHT?
I'LL JUST WEAR THIS DRESS. BUT FIRST, I'LL HAVE TO IRON OUT THE WRINKLES...
WHO WOULD'VE EVER GUESSED THAT I'D BE GOING TO A PARTY FOR FAIRIES?
THEY SAID LOTS OF BOYS WILL BE COMING TOO! I WONDER IF PRINCE SKY WILL BE THERE...

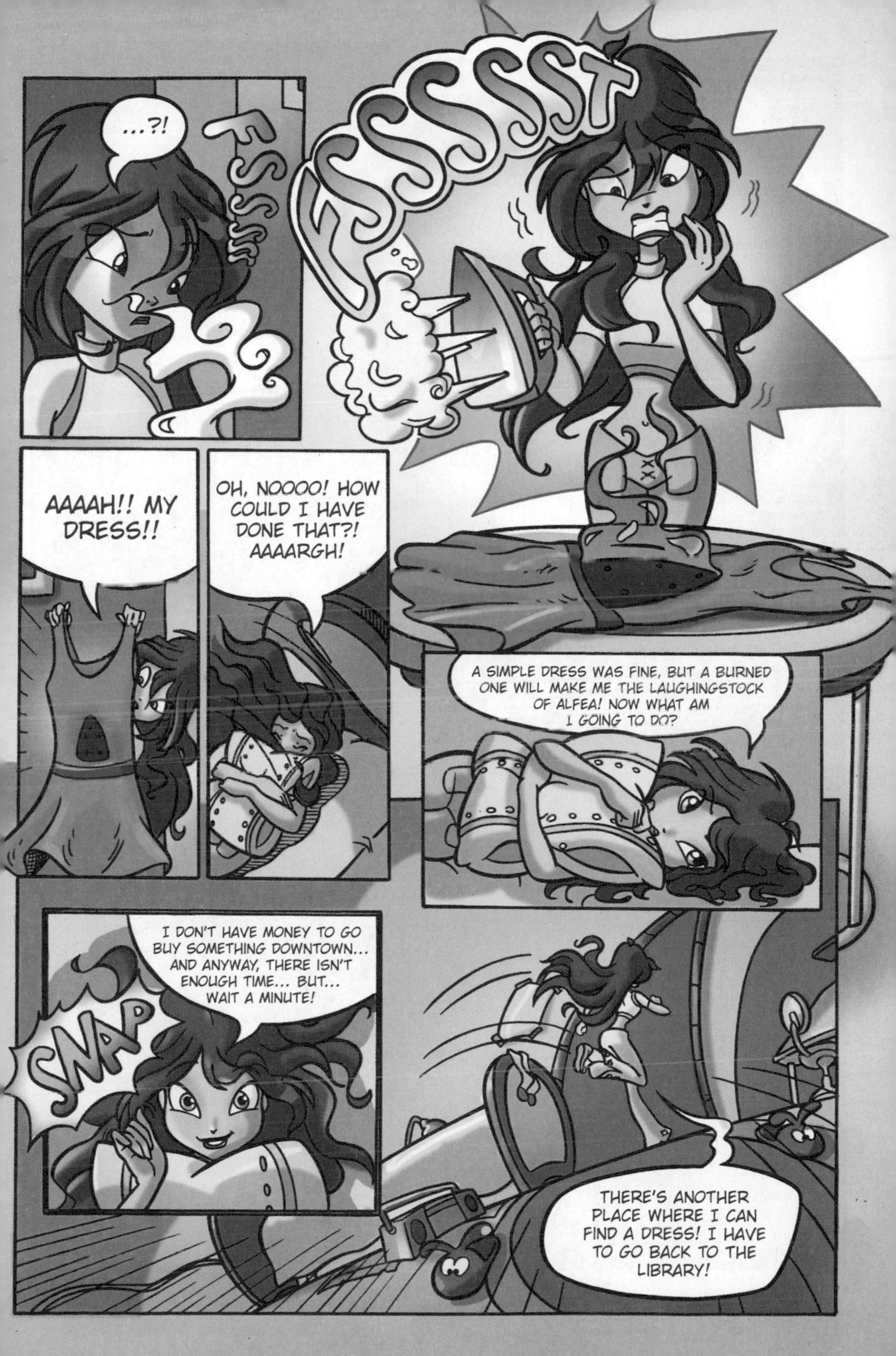
...?!
FSSS
FSSSST
AAAAH!! MY DRESS!!
OH, NOOOO! HOW COULD I HAVE DONE THAT?! AAAARGH!
A SIMPLE DRESS WAS FINE, BUT A BURNED ONE WILL MAKE ME THE LAUGHINGSTOCK OF ALFEA! NOW WHAT AM I GOING TO DO?
I DON'T HAVE MONEY TO GO BUY SOMETHING DOWNTOWN... AND ANYWAY, THERE ISN'T ENOUGH TIME... BUT... WAIT A MINUTE!
SNAP
THERE'S ANOTHER PLACE WHERE I CAN FIND A DRESS! I HAVE TO GO BACK TO THE LIBRARY!

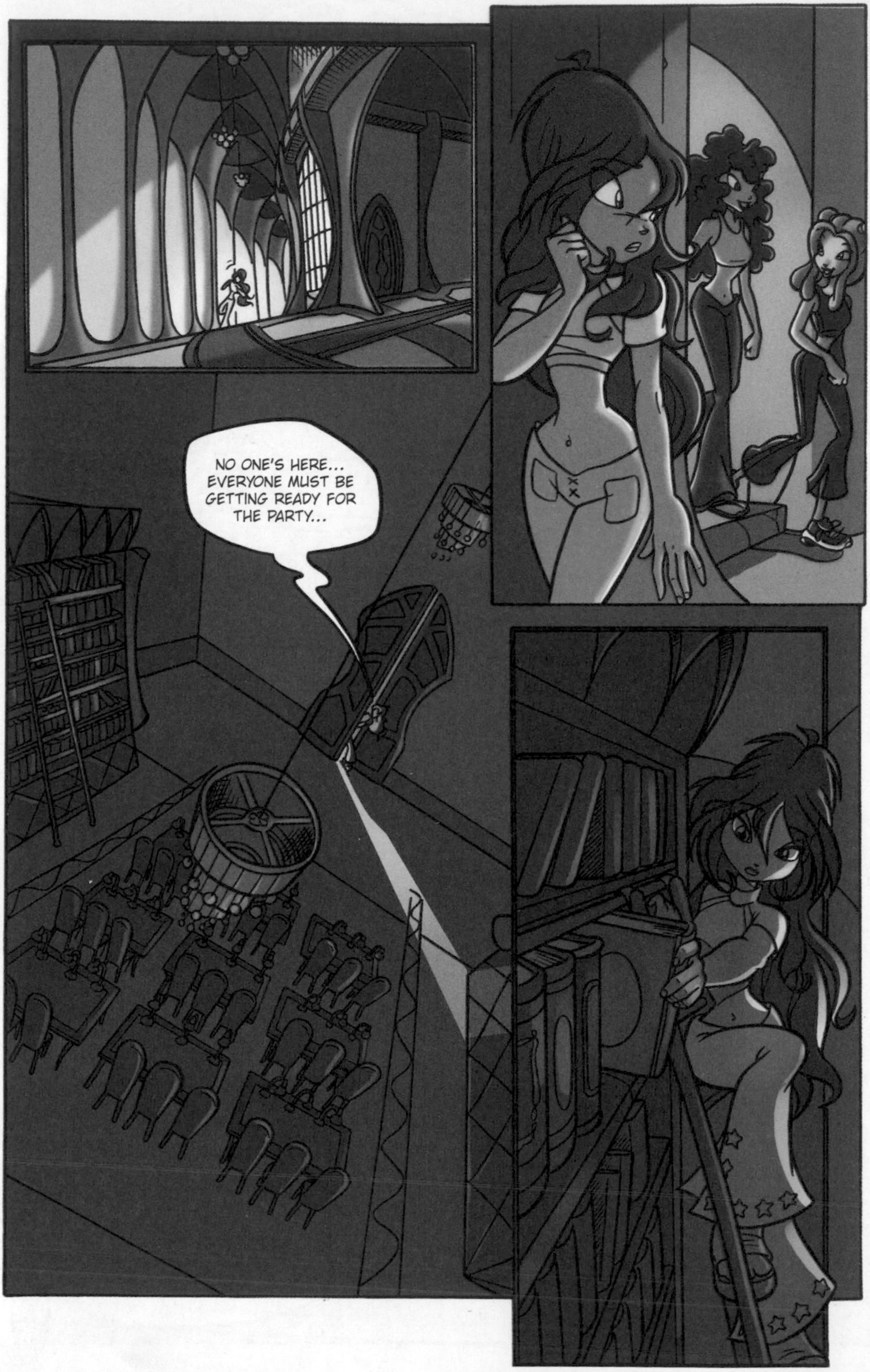
NO ONE'S HERE... EVERYONE MUST BE GETTING READY FOR THE PARTY...

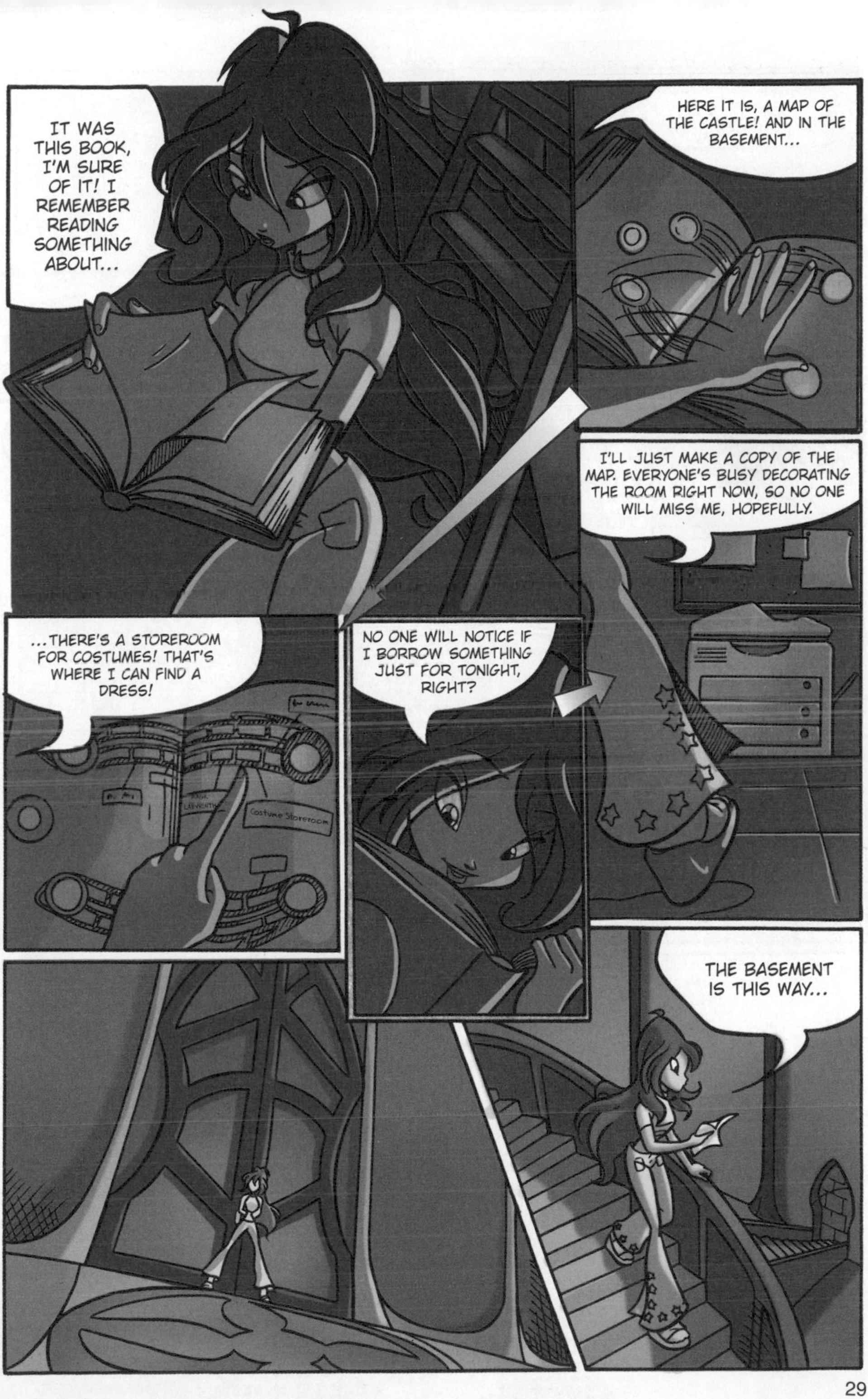
IT WAS THIS BOOK, I'M SURE OF IT! I REMEMBER READING SOMETHING ABOUT...
HERE IT IS, A MAP OF THE CASTLE! AND IN THE BASEMENT...
...THERE'S A STOREROOM FOR COSTUMES! THAT'S WHERE I CAN FIND A DRESS!
Costume Storeroom
NO ONE WILL NOTICE IF I BORROW SOMETHING JUST FOR TONIGHT, RIGHT?
I'LL JUST MAKE A COPY OF THE MAP. EVERYONE'S BUSY DECORATING THE ROOM RIGHT NOW, SO NO ONE WILL MISS ME, HOPEFULLY.
THE BASEMENT IS THIS WAY...

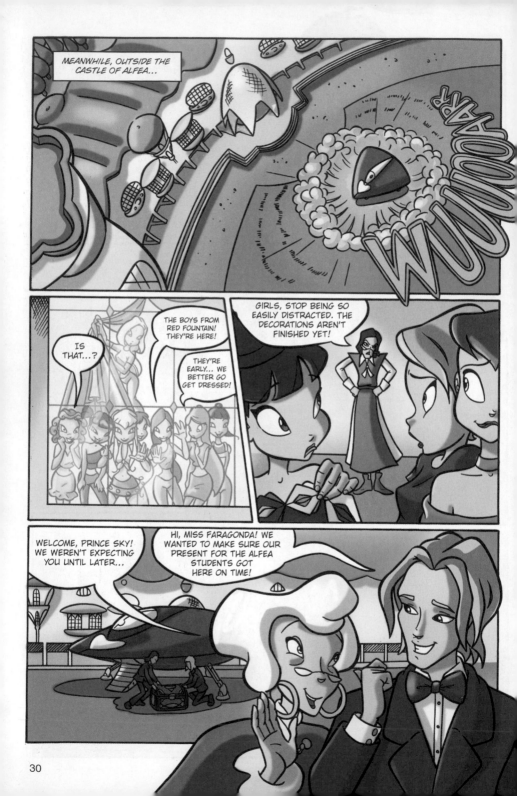

MEANWHILE, OUTSIDE THE CASTLE OF ALFEA...

WHOOOAAR

WUMM

IS THAT...?

THE BOYS FROM RED FOUNTAIN! THEY'RE HERE!

THEY'RE EARLY... WE BETTER GO GET DRESSED!

GIRLS, STOP BEING SO EASILY DISTRACTED. THE DECORATIONS AREN'T FINISHED YET!

WELCOME, PRINCE SKY! WE WEREN'T EXPECTING YOU UNTIL LATER...

HI, MISS FARAGONDA! WE WANTED TO MAKE SURE OUR PRESENT FOR THE ALFEA STUDENTS GOT HERE ON TIME!

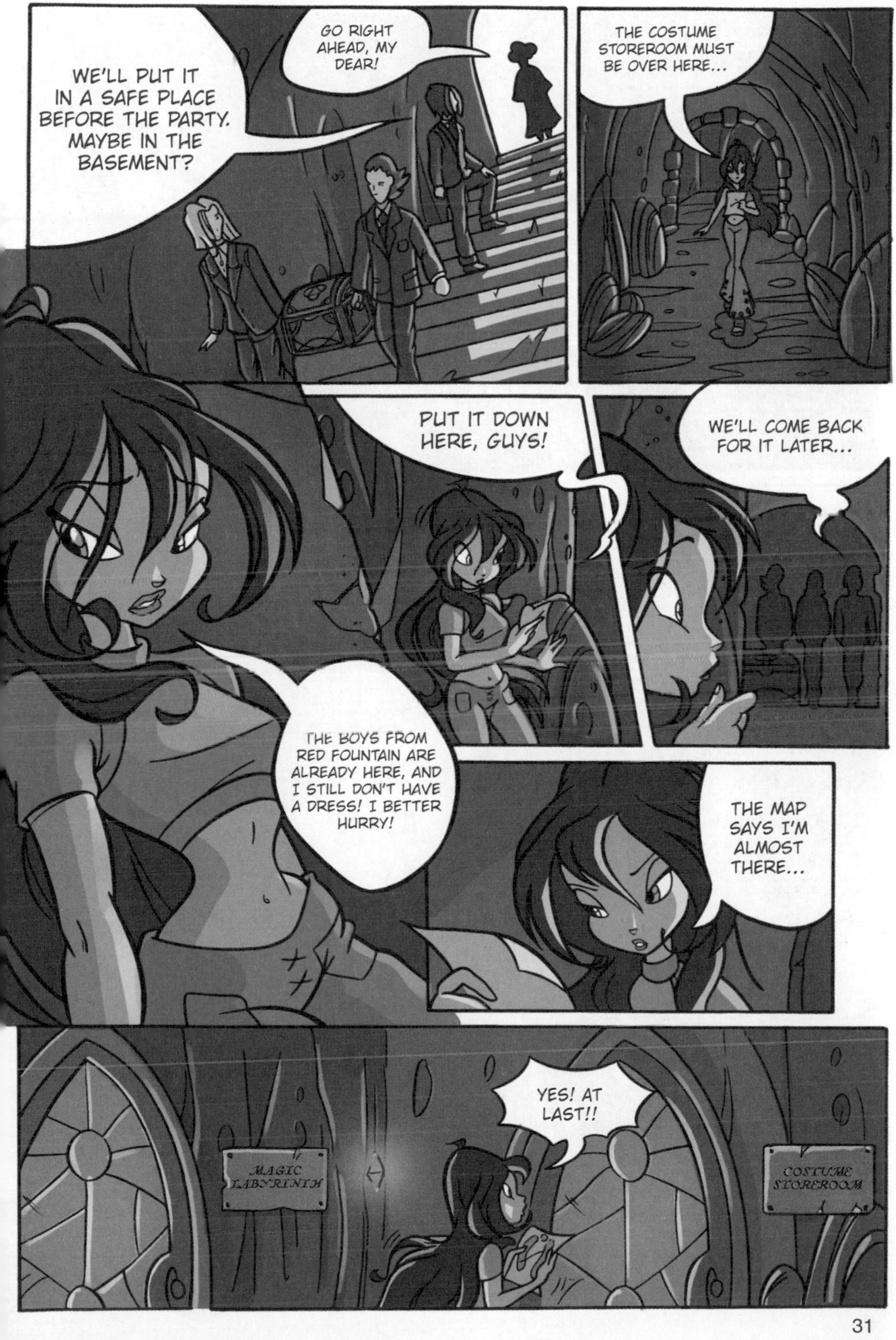
WE'LL PUT IT IN A SAFE PLACE BEFORE THE PARTY. MAYBE IN THE BASEMENT?
GO RIGHT AHEAD, MY DEAR!
THE COSTUME STOREROOM MUST BE OVER HERE...
PUT IT DOWN HERE, GUYS!
WE'LL COME BACK FOR IT LATER...
THE BOYS FROM RED FOUNTAIN ARE ALREADY HERE, AND I STILL DON'T HAVE A DRESS! I BETTER HURRY!
THE MAP SAYS I'M ALMOST THERE...
YES! AT LAST!!
MAGIC LABYRINTH
COSTUME STOREROOM

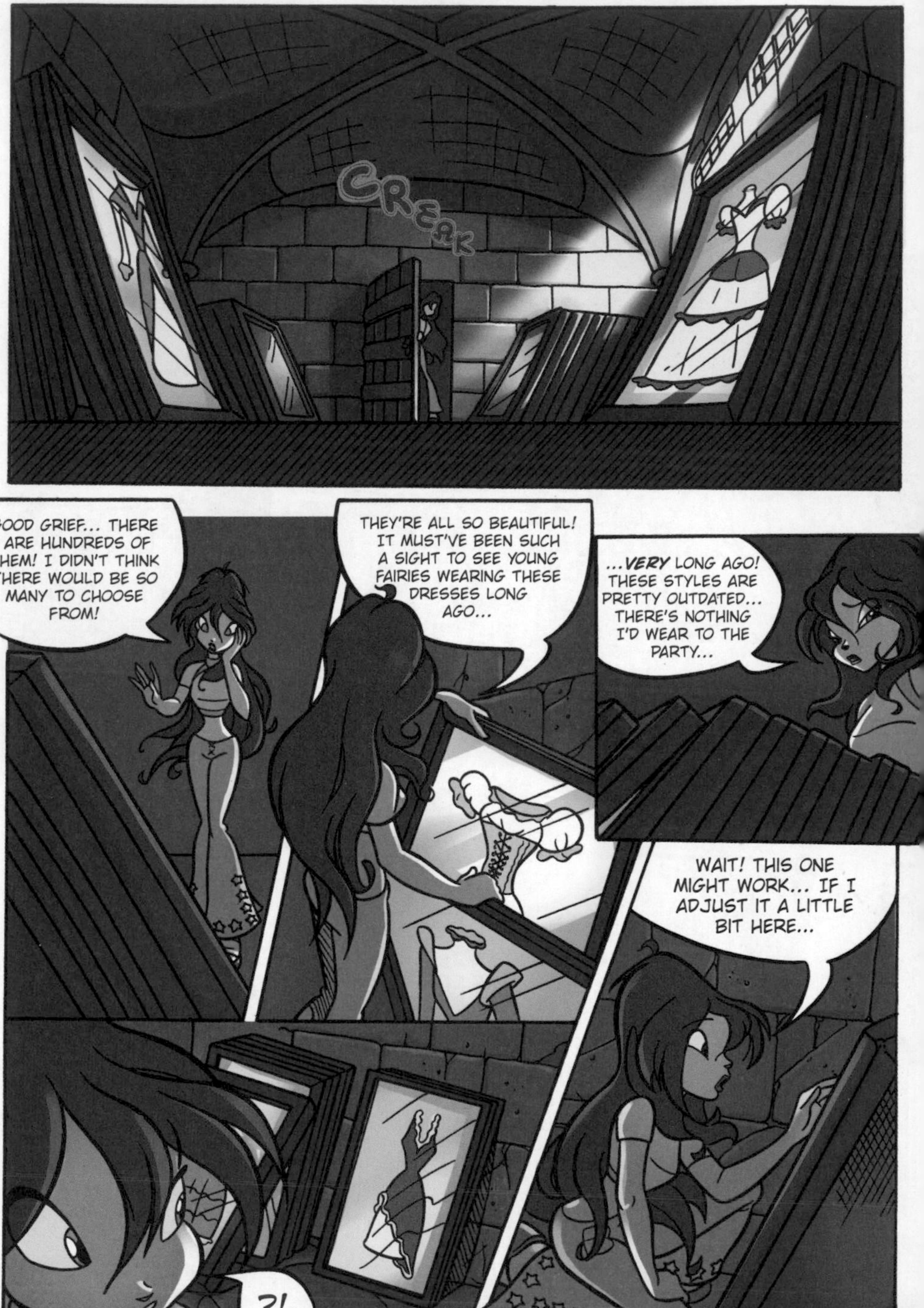
CREAK
GOOD GRIEF... THERE ARE HUNDREDS OF THEM! I DIDN'T THINK THERE WOULD BE SO MANY TO CHOOSE FROM!
THEY'RE ALL SO BEAUTIFUL! IT MUST'VE BEEN SUCH A SIGHT TO SEE YOUNG FAIRIES WEARING THESE DRESSES LONG AGO...
...VERY LONG AGO! THESE STYLES ARE PRETTY OUTDATED... THERE'S NOTHING I'D WEAR TO THE PARTY...
WAIT! THIS ONE MIGHT WORK... IF I ADJUST IT A LITTLE BIT HERE...
?!

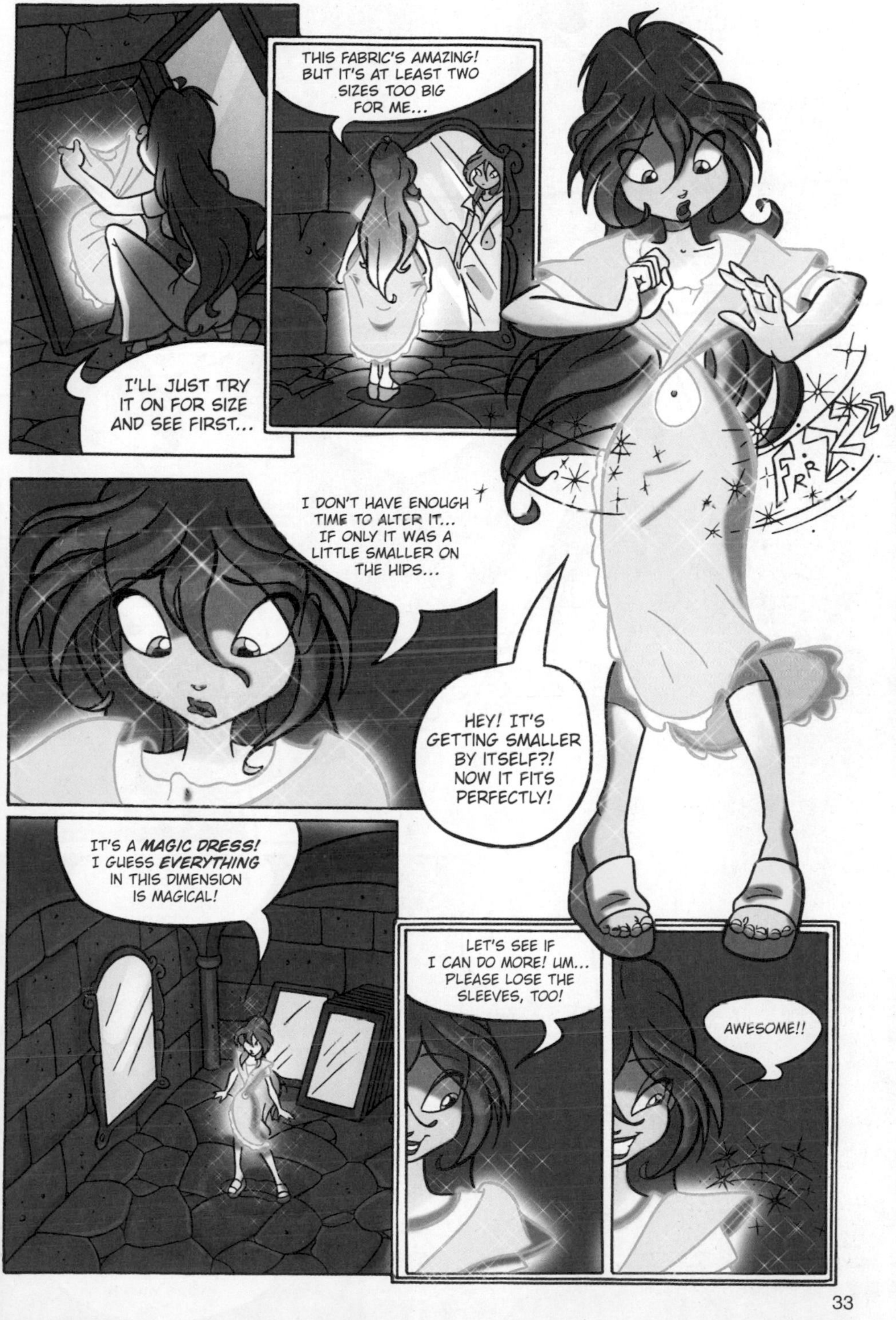
I'LL JUST TRY IT ON FOR SIZE AND SEE FIRST...
THIS FABRIC'S AMAZING! BUT IT'S AT LEAST TWO SIZES TOO BIG FOR ME...
I DON'T HAVE ENOUGH TIME TO ALTER IT... IF ONLY IT WAS A LITTLE SMALLER ON THE HIPS...
FRRRZZZ
HEY! IT'S GETTING SMALLER BY ITSELF?! NOW IT FITS PERFECTLY!
IT'S A MAGIC DRESS! I GUESS EVERYTHING IN THIS DIMENSION IS MAGICAL!
LET'S SEE IF I CAN DO MORE! UM... PLEASE LOSE THE SLEEVES, TOO!
AWESOME!!

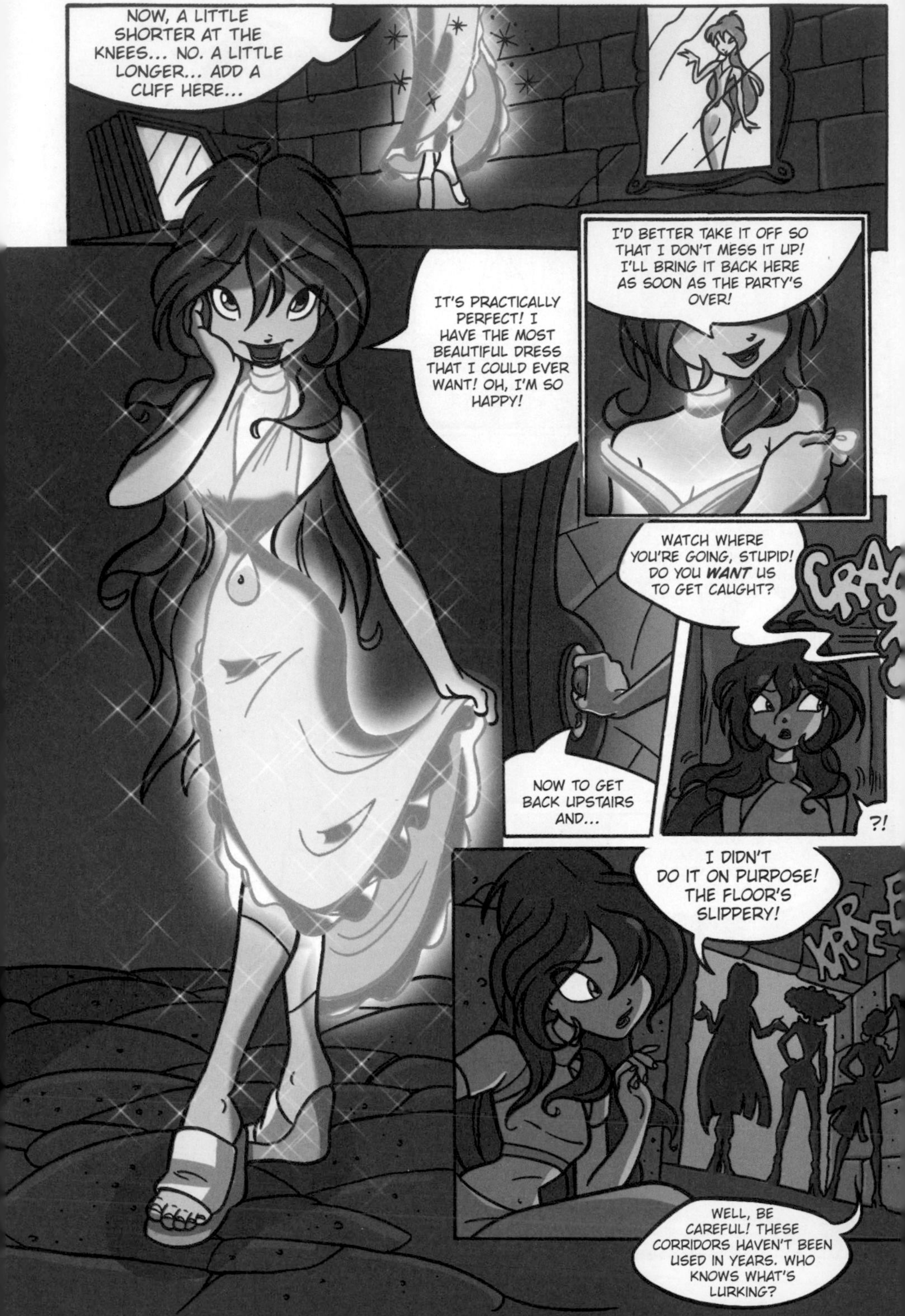
NOW, A LITTLE SHORTER AT THE KNEES... NO. A LITTLE LONGER... ADD A CUFF HERE...
IT'S PRACTICALLY PERFECT! I HAVE THE MOST BEAUTIFUL DRESS THAT I COULD EVER WANT! OH, I'M SO HAPPY!
I'D BETTER TAKE IT OFF SO THAT I DON'T MESS IT UP! I'LL BRING IT BACK HERE AS SOON AS THE PARTY'S OVER!
NOW TO GET BACK UPSTAIRS AND...
WATCH WHERE YOU'RE GOING, STUPID! DO YOU ***WANT*** US TO GET CAUGHT?
?!
I DIDN'T DO IT ON PURPOSE! THE FLOOR'S SLIPPERY!
WELL, BE CAREFUL! THESE CORRIDORS HAVEN'T BEEN USED IN YEARS. WHO KNOWS WHAT'S LURKING?

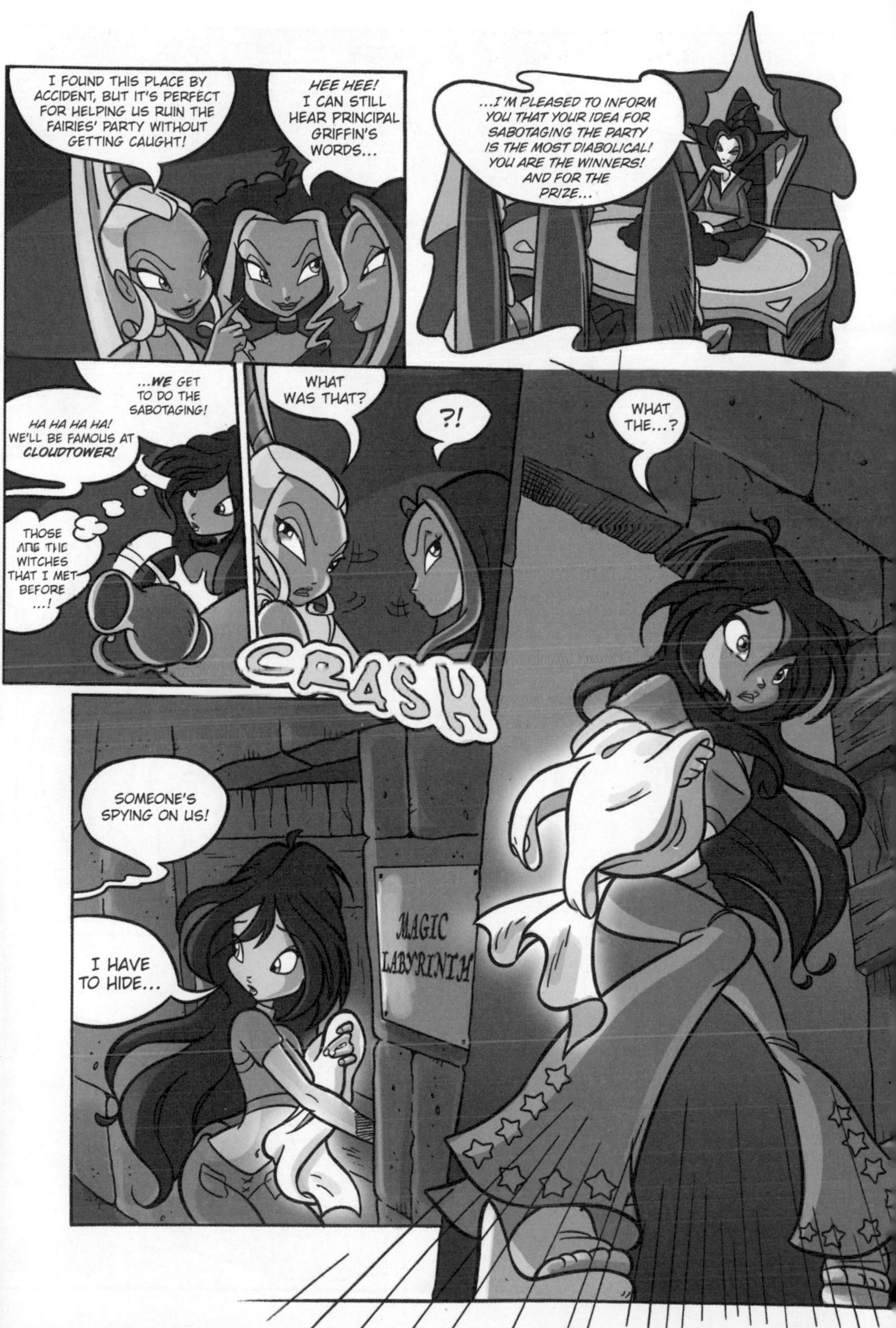
I FOUND THIS PLACE BY ACCIDENT, BUT IT'S PERFECT FOR HELPING US RUIN THE FAIRIES' PARTY WITHOUT GETTING CAUGHT!
HEE HEE! I CAN STILL HEAR PRINCIPAL GRIFFIN'S WORDS...
...I'M PLEASED TO INFORM YOU THAT YOUR IDEA FOR SABOTAGING THE PARTY IS THE MOST DIABOLICAL! YOU ARE THE WINNERS! AND FOR THE PRIZE...
...WE GET TO DO THE SABOTAGING!
HA HA HA HA! WE'LL BE FAMOUS AT CLOUDTOWER!
THOSE ARE THE WITCHES THAT I MET BEFORE ...!
WHAT WAS THAT?
?!
WHAT THE...?
CRASH
SOMEONE'S SPYING ON US!
I HAVE TO HIDE...
MAGIC LABYRINTH

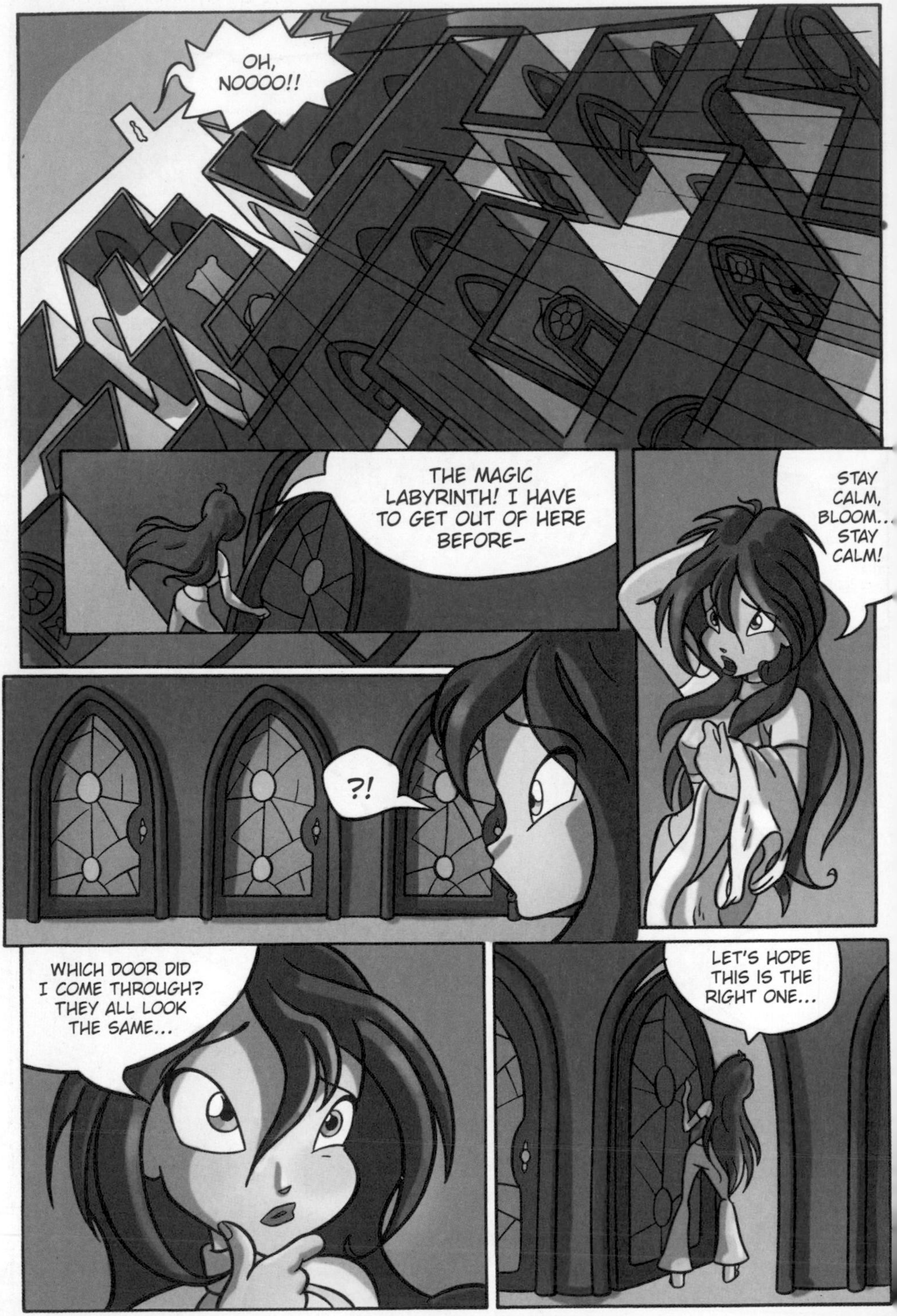
OH, NOOOO!!
THE MAGIC LABYRINTH! I HAVE TO GET OUT OF HERE BEFORE–
STAY CALM, BLOOM... STAY CALM!
?!
WHICH DOOR DID I COME THROUGH? THEY ALL LOOK THE SAME...
LET'S HOPE THIS IS THE RIGHT ONE...

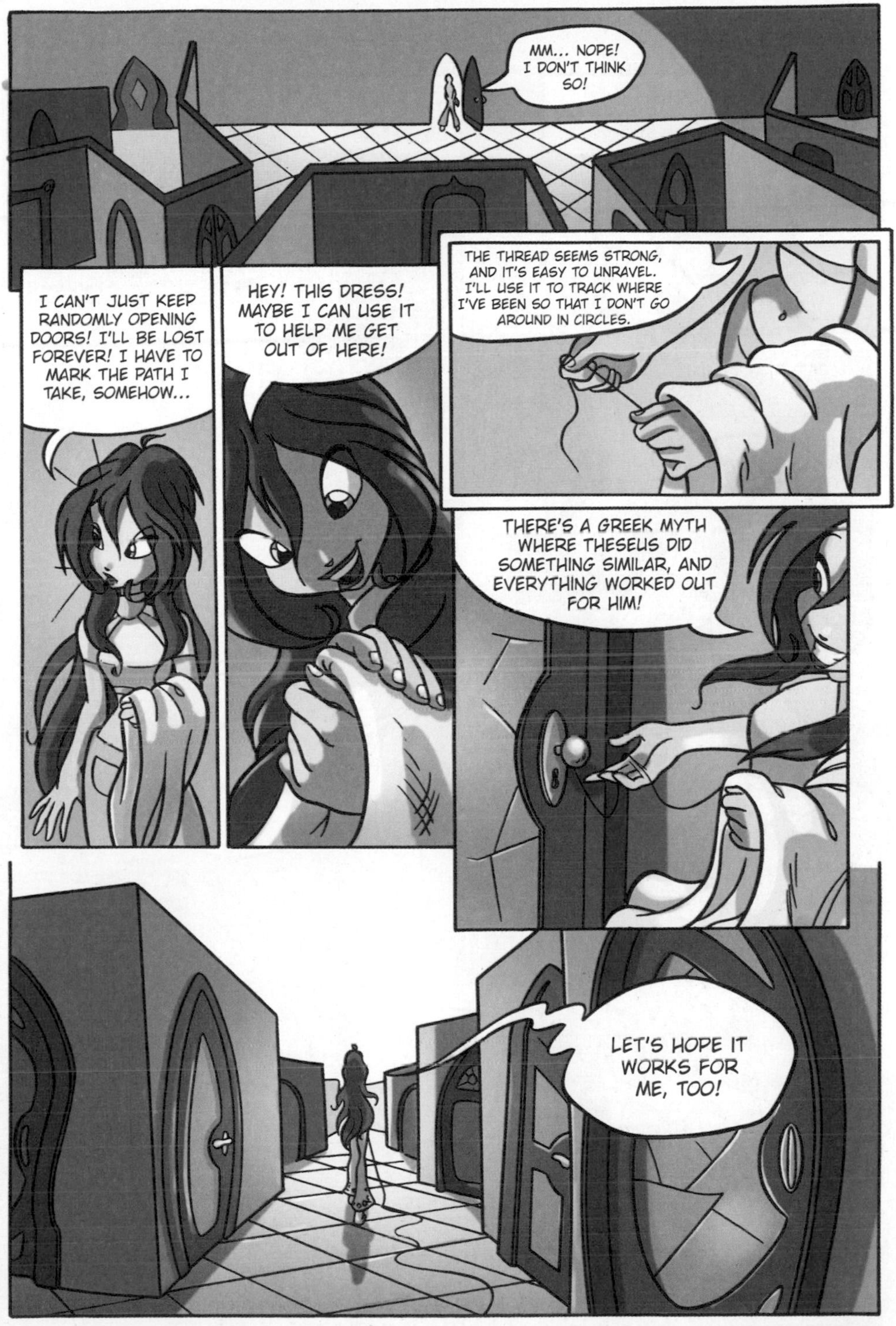
MM... NOPE! I DON'T THINK SO!
I CAN'T JUST KEEP RANDOMLY OPENING DOORS! I'LL BE LOST FOREVER! I HAVE TO MARK THE PATH I TAKE, SOMEHOW...
HEY! THIS DRESS! MAYBE I CAN USE IT TO HELP ME GET OUT OF HERE!
THE THREAD SEEMS STRONG, AND IT'S EASY TO UNRAVEL. I'LL USE IT TO TRACK WHERE I'VE BEEN SO THAT I DON'T GO AROUND IN CIRCLES.
THERE'S A GREEK MYTH WHERE THESEUS DID SOMETHING SIMILAR, AND EVERYTHING WORKED OUT FOR HIM!
LET'S HOPE IT WORKS FOR ME, TOO!

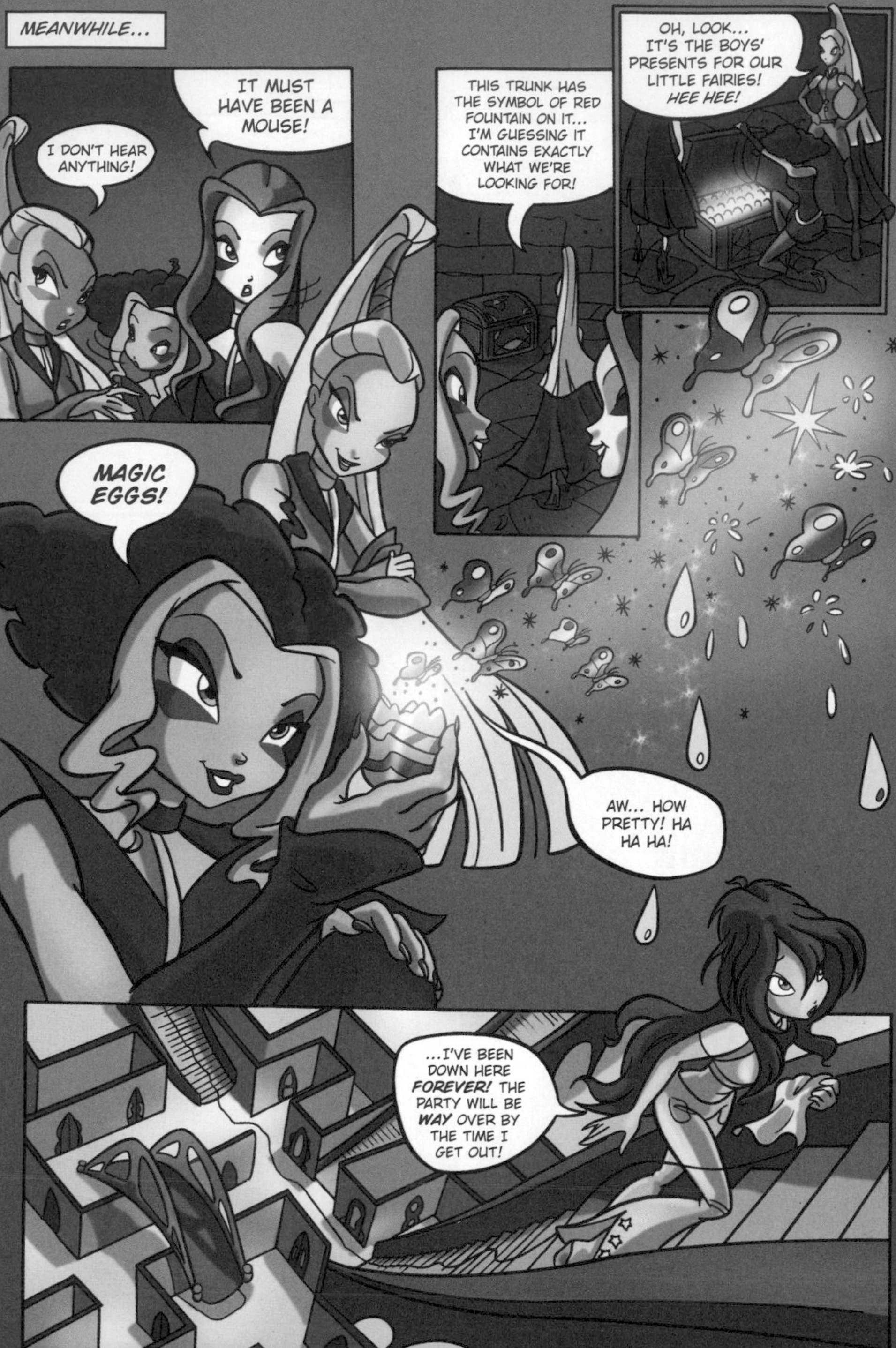
MEANWHILE...
I DON'T HEAR ANYTHING!
IT MUST HAVE BEEN A MOUSE!
THIS TRUNK HAS THE SYMBOL OF RED FOUNTAIN ON IT... I'M GUESSING IT CONTAINS EXACTLY WHAT WE'RE LOOKING FOR!
OH, LOOK... IT'S THE BOYS' PRESENTS FOR OUR LITTLE FAIRIES! HEE HEE!
MAGIC EGGS!
AW... HOW PRETTY! HA HA HA!
...I'VE BEEN DOWN HERE FOREVER! THE PARTY WILL BE WAY OVER BY THE TIME I GET OUT!

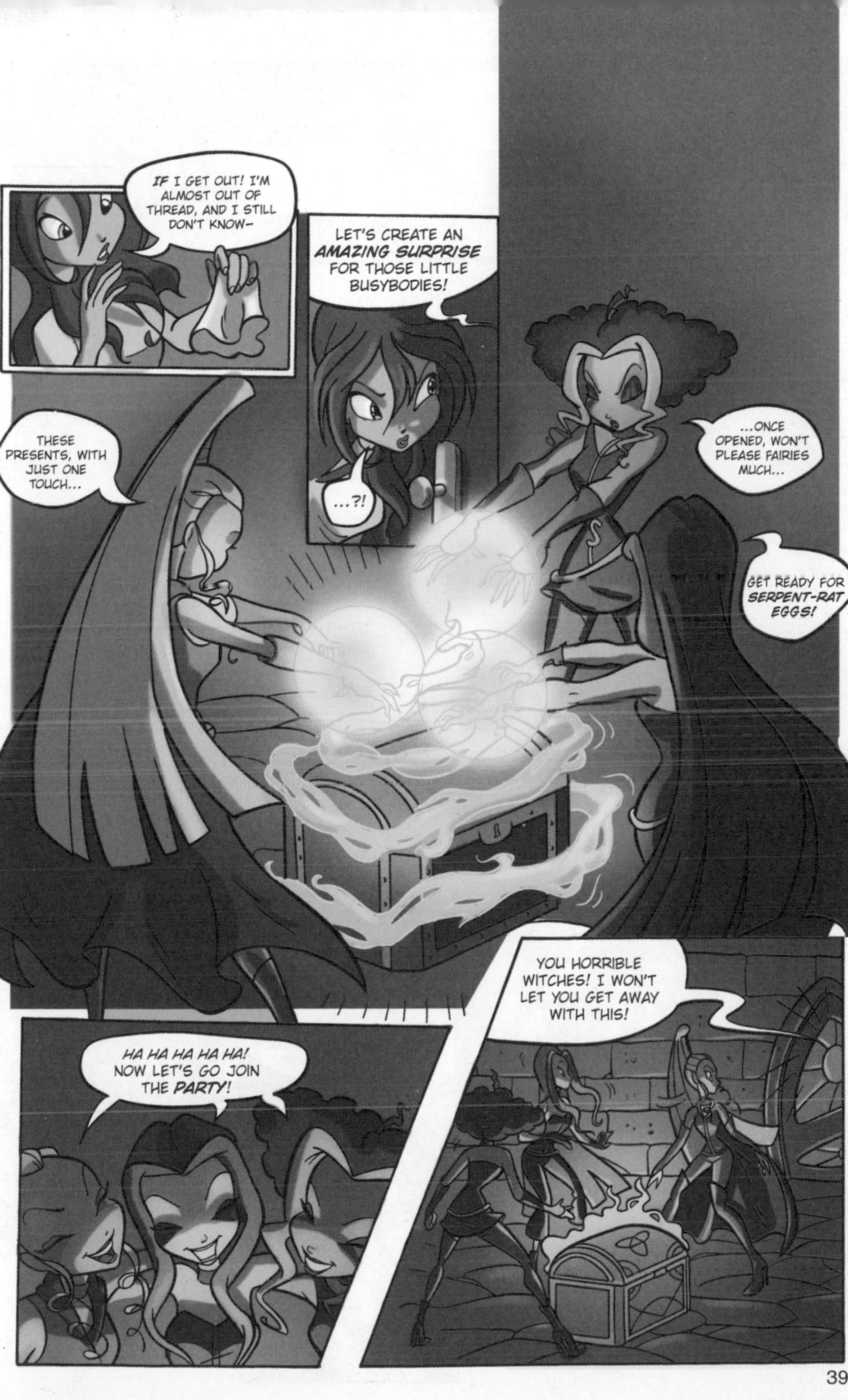
IF I GET OUT! I'M ALMOST OUT OF THREAD, AND I STILL DON'T KNOW–
LET'S CREATE AN AMAZING SURPRISE FOR THOSE LITTLE BUSYBODIES!
...?!
THESE PRESENTS, WITH JUST ONE TOUCH...
...ONCE OPENED, WON'T PLEASE FAIRIES MUCH...
GET READY FOR SERPENT-RAT EGGS!
HA HA HA HA HA! NOW LET'S GO JOIN THE PARTY!
YOU HORRIBLE WITCHES! I WON'T LET YOU GET AWAY WITH THIS!

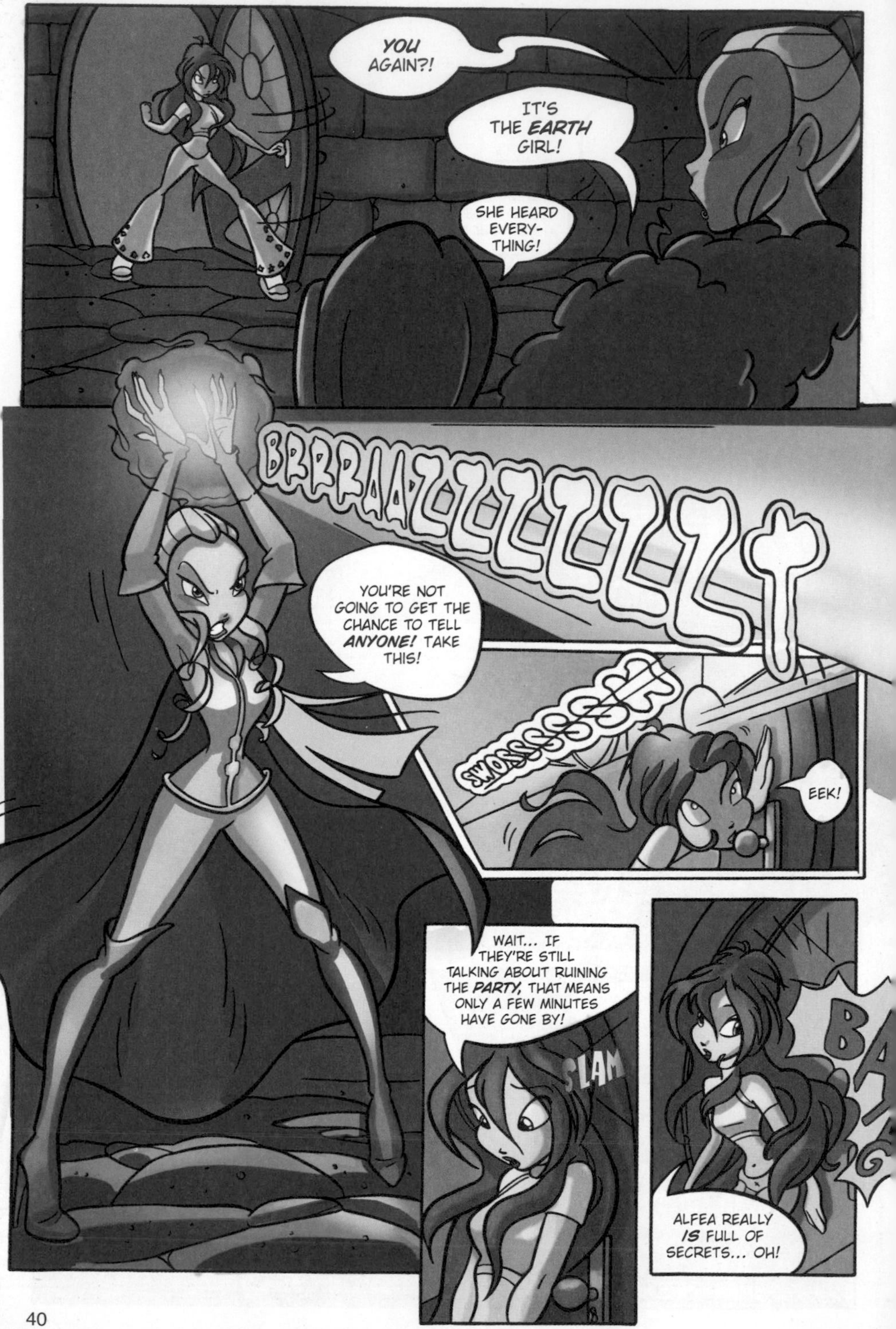
YOU AGAIN?!
IT'S THE EARTH GIRL!
SHE HEARD EVERYTHING!
BRRRAAZZZZZZZZT
YOU'RE NOT GOING TO GET THE CHANCE TO TELL ANYONE! TAKE THIS!
SWOSSSSSSH
EEK!
WAIT... IF THEY'RE STILL TALKING ABOUT RUINING THE PARTY, THAT MEANS ONLY A FEW MINUTES HAVE GONE BY!
SLAM
ALFEA REALLY IS FULL OF SECRETS... OH!

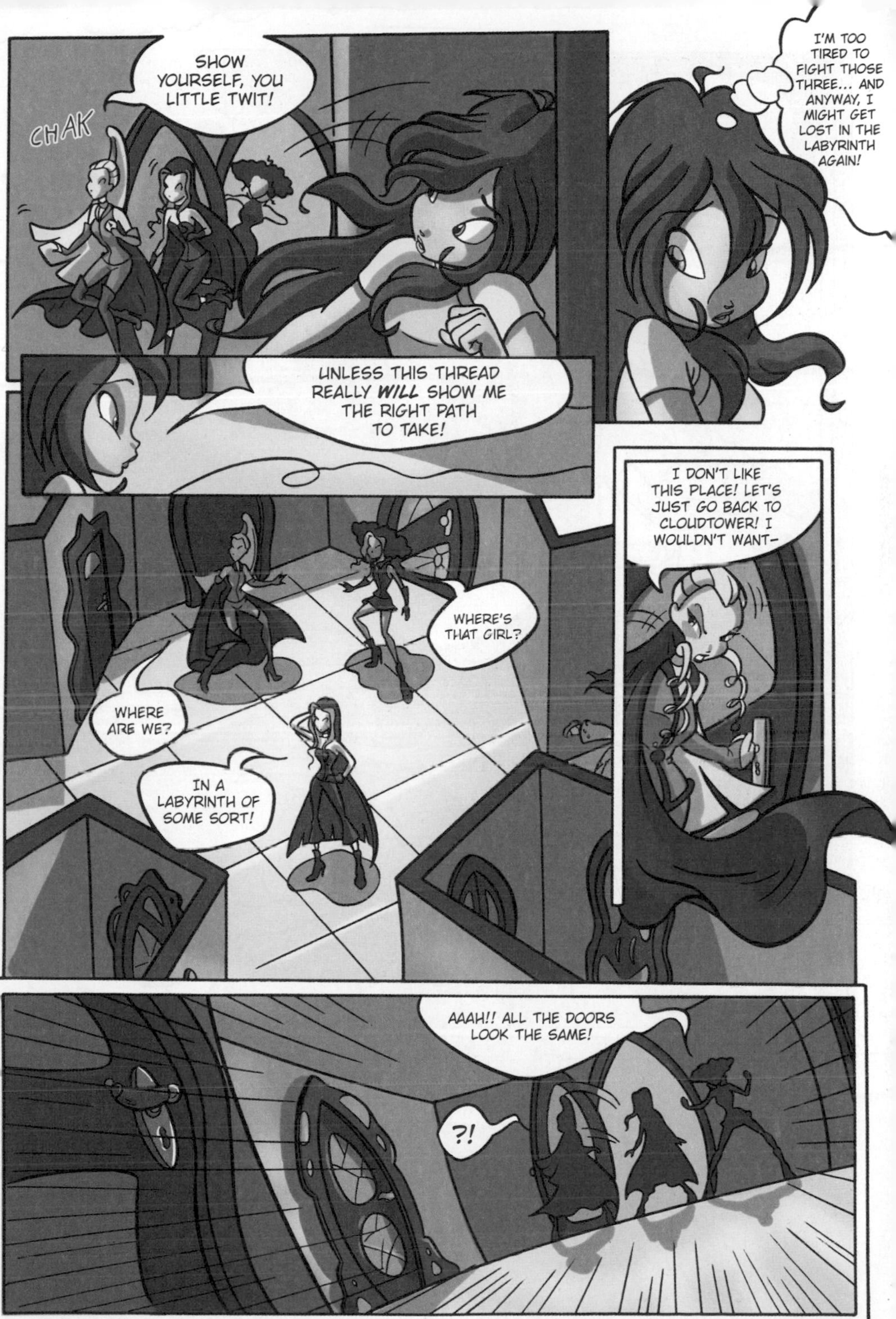
SHOW YOURSELF, YOU LITTLE TWIT!
CHAK
I'M TOO TIRED TO FIGHT THOSE THREE... AND ANYWAY, I MIGHT GET LOST IN THE LABYRINTH AGAIN!
UNLESS THIS THREAD REALLY WILL SHOW ME THE RIGHT PATH TO TAKE!
WHERE'S THAT GIRL?
WHERE ARE WE?
IN A LABYRINTH OF SOME SORT!
I DON'T LIKE THIS PLACE! LET'S JUST GO BACK TO CLOUDTOWER! I WOULDN'T WANT-
AAAH!! ALL THE DOORS LOOK THE SAME!
?!

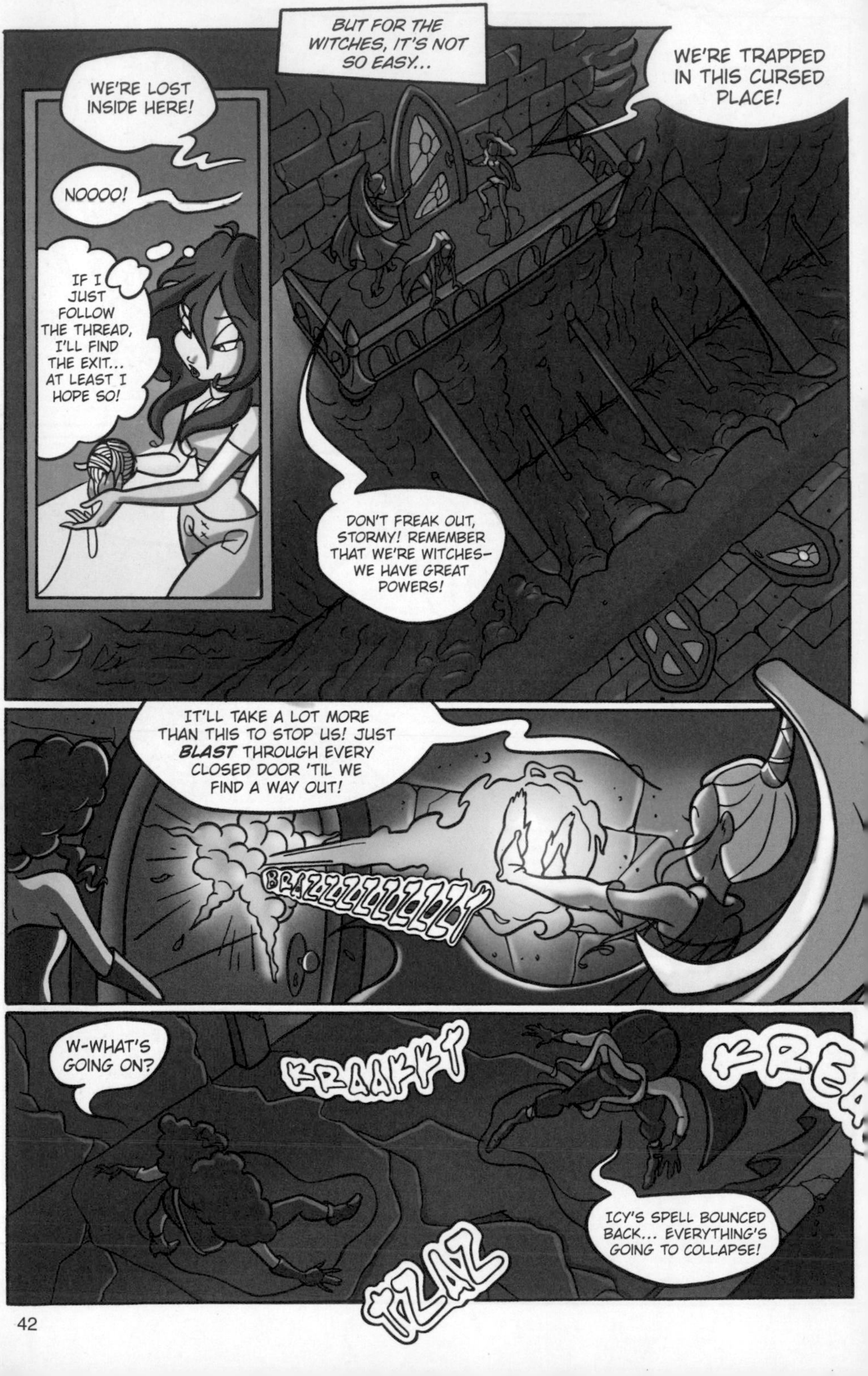

BUT FOR THE WITCHES, IT'S NOT SO EASY...
WE'RE LOST INSIDE HERE!
NOOOO!
IF I JUST FOLLOW THE THREAD, I'LL FIND THE EXIT... AT LEAST I HOPE SO!
WE'RE TRAPPED IN THIS CURSED PLACE!
DON'T FREAK OUT, STORMY! REMEMBER THAT WE'RE WITCHES- WE HAVE GREAT POWERS!
IT'LL TAKE A LOT MORE THAN THIS TO STOP US! JUST BLAST THROUGH EVERY CLOSED DOOR 'TIL WE FIND A WAY OUT!
BRAZZZZZZZZZZT
W-WHAT'S GOING ON?
KRAAKKT
ICY'S SPELL BOUNCED BACK... EVERYTHING'S GOING TO COLLAPSE!
TZAAZ

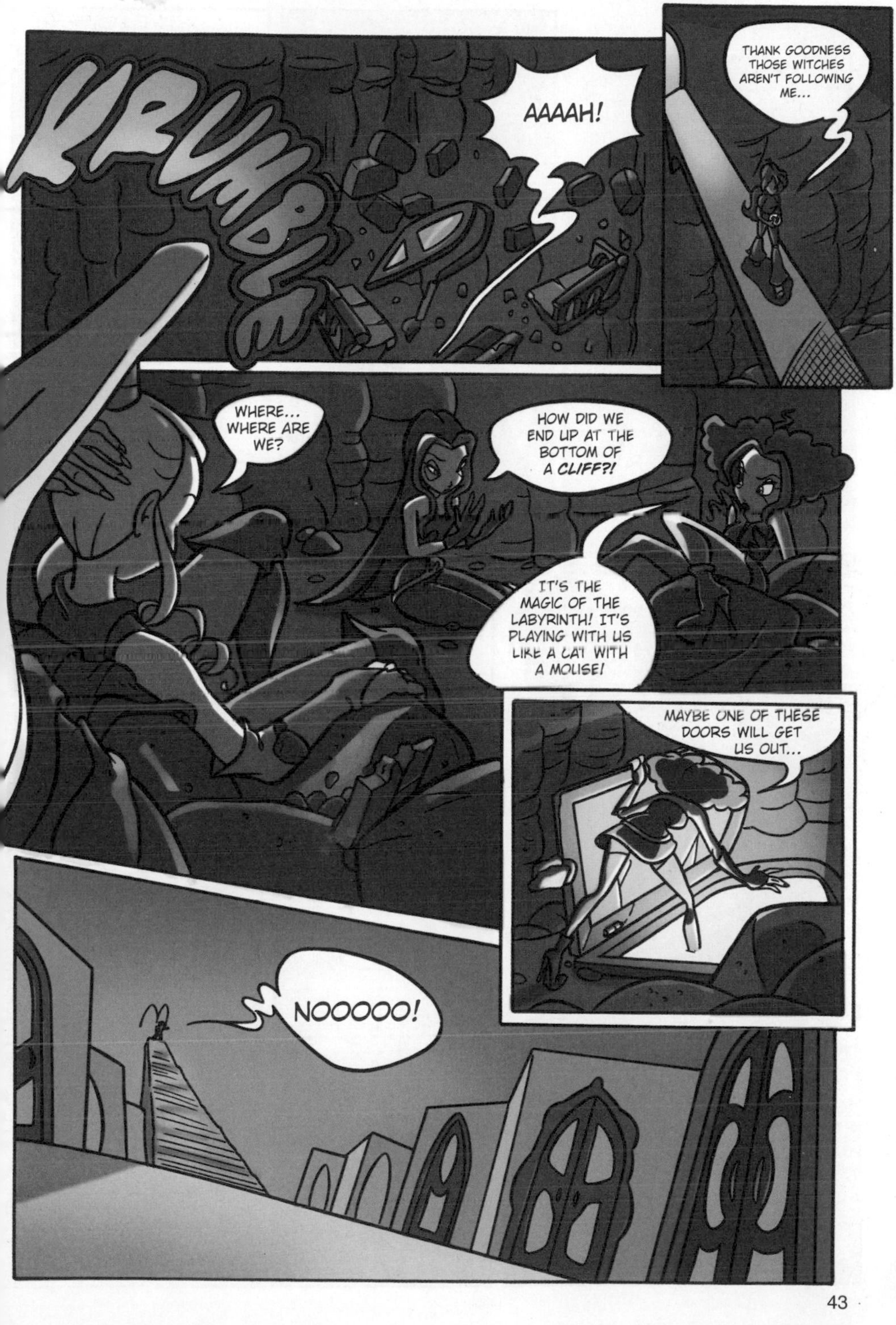
KRUMBLE
AAAAH!
THANK GOODNESS THOSE WITCHES AREN'T FOLLOWING ME...
WHERE... WHERE ARE WE?
HOW DID WE END UP AT THE BOTTOM OF A CLIFF?!
IT'S THE MAGIC OF THE LABYRINTH! IT'S PLAYING WITH US LIKE A CAT WITH A MOUSE!
MAYBE ONE OF THESE DOORS WILL GET US OUT...
NOOOOO!

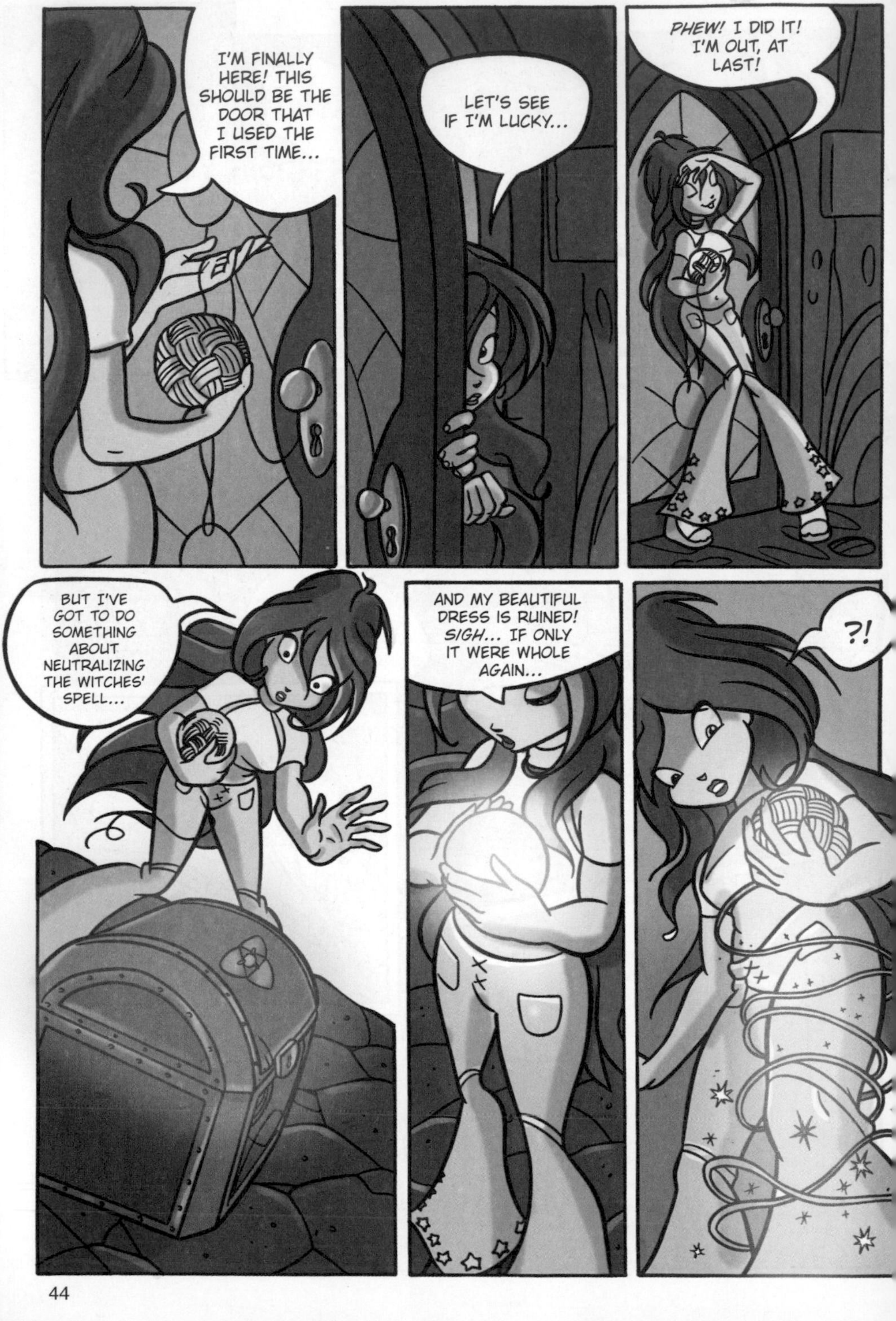

I'M FINALLY HERE! THIS SHOULD BE THE DOOR THAT I USED THE FIRST TIME...
LET'S SEE IF I'M LUCKY...
PHEW! I DID IT! I'M OUT, AT LAST!
BUT I'VE GOT TO DO SOMETHING ABOUT NEUTRALIZING THE WITCHES' SPELL...
AND MY BEAUTIFUL DRESS IS RUINED! *SIGH*... IF ONLY IT WERE WHOLE AGAIN...
?!

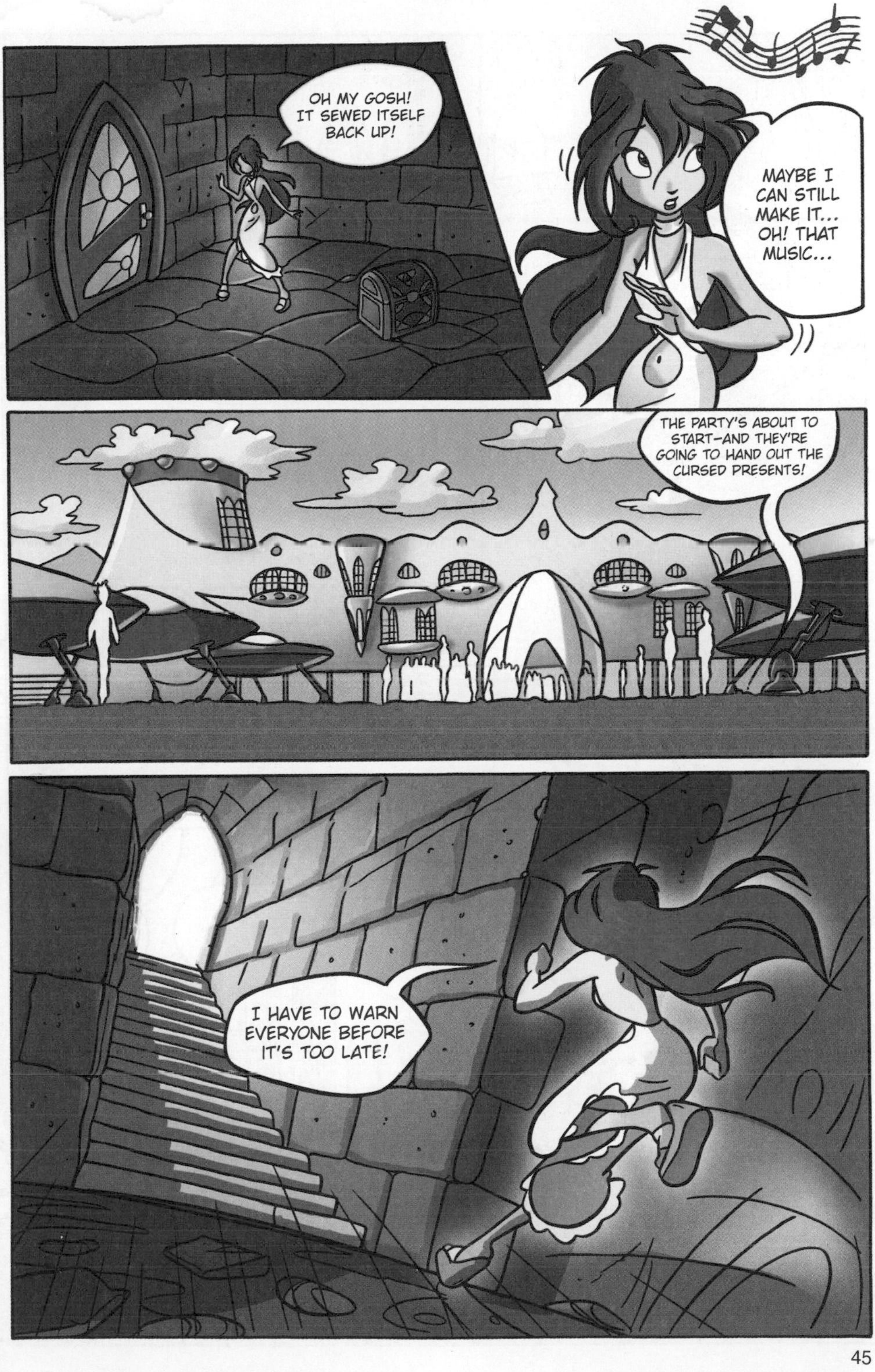
OH MY GOSH! IT SEWED ITSELF BACK UP!
MAYBE I CAN STILL MAKE IT... OH! THAT MUSIC...
THE PARTY'S ABOUT TO START—AND THEY'RE GOING TO HAND OUT THE CURSED PRESENTS!
I HAVE TO WARN EVERYONE BEFORE IT'S TOO LATE!

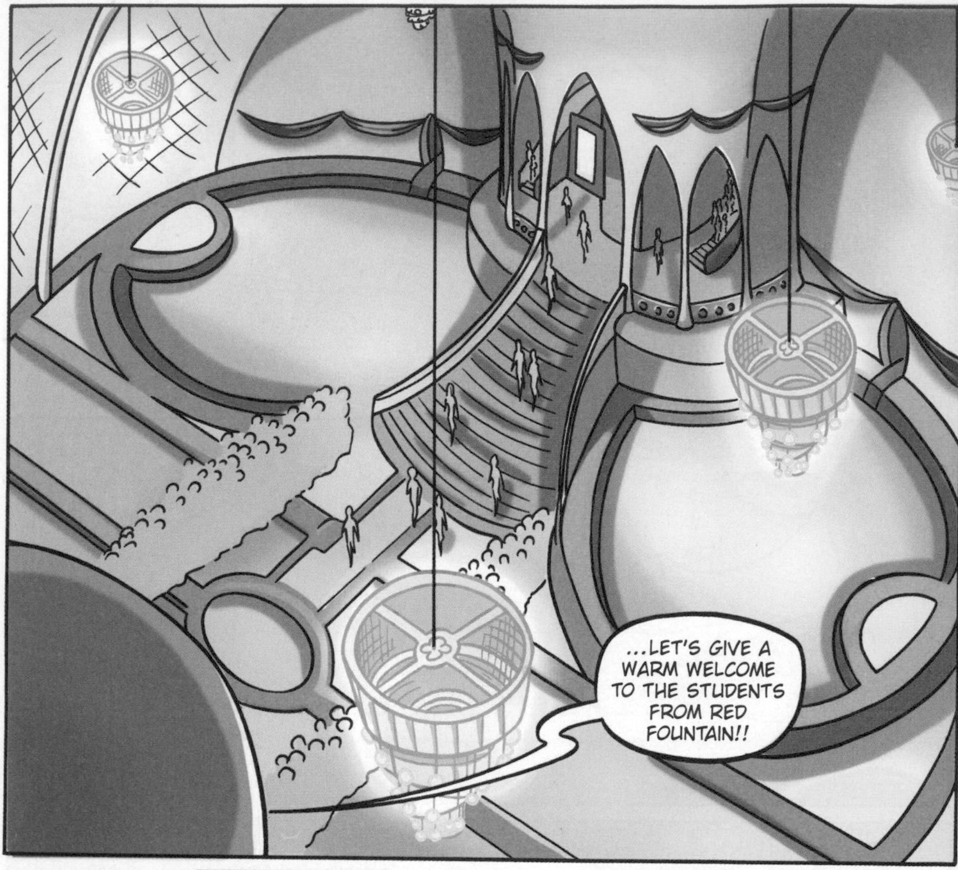
...LET'S GIVE A WARM WELCOME TO THE STUDENTS FROM RED FOUNTAIN!!

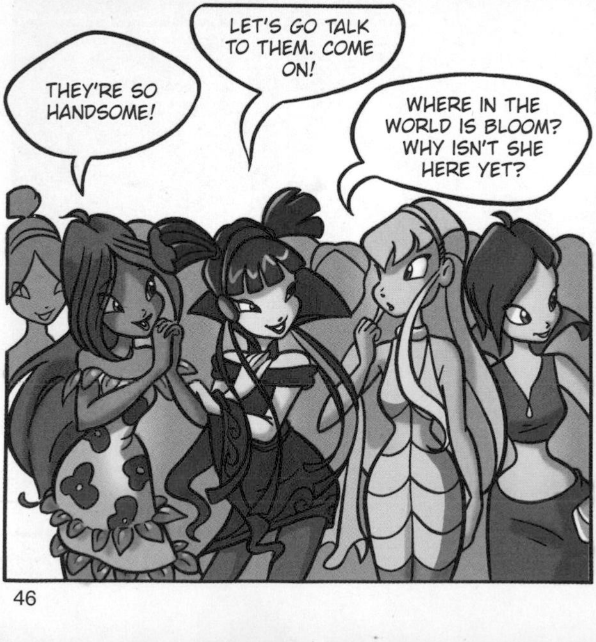
THEY'RE SO HANDSOME!
LET'S GO TALK TO THEM. COME ON!
WHERE IN THE WORLD IS BLOOM? WHY ISN'T SHE HERE YET?

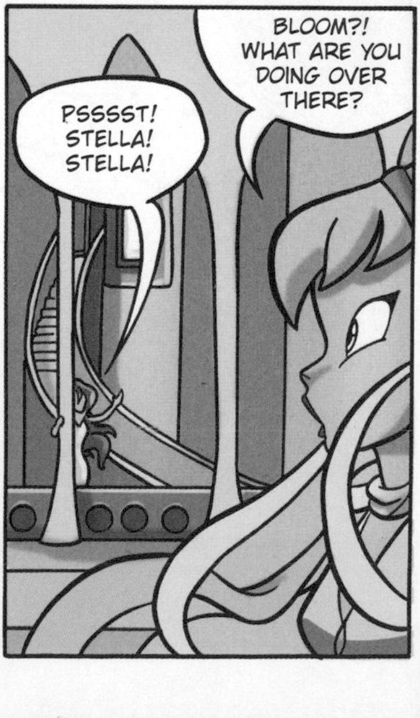
PSSSST! STELLA! STELLA!
BLOOM?! WHAT ARE YOU DOING OVER THERE?

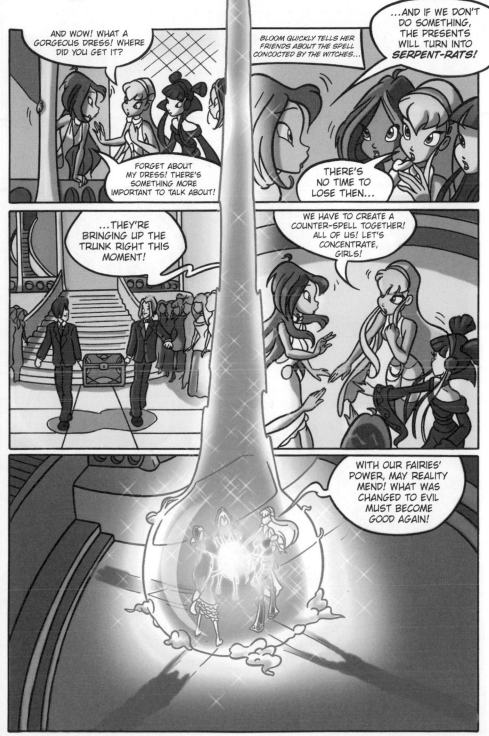

AND WOW! WHAT A GORGEOUS DRESS! WHERE DID YOU GET IT?

FORGET ABOUT MY DRESS! THERE'S SOMETHING MORE IMPORTANT TO TALK ABOUT!

BLOOM QUICKLY TELLS HER FRIENDS ABOUT THE SPELL CONCOCTED BY THE WITCHES...

...AND IF WE DON'T DO SOMETHING, THE PRESENTS WILL TURN INTO *SERPENT-RATS!*

THERE'S NO TIME TO LOSE THEN...

...THEY'RE BRINGING UP THE TRUNK RIGHT THIS MOMENT!

WE HAVE TO CREATE A COUNTER-SPELL TOGETHER! ALL OF US! LET'S CONCENTRATE, GIRLS!

WITH OUR FAIRIES' POWER, MAY REALITY MEND! WHAT WAS CHANGED TO EVIL MUST BECOME GOOD AGAIN!

47

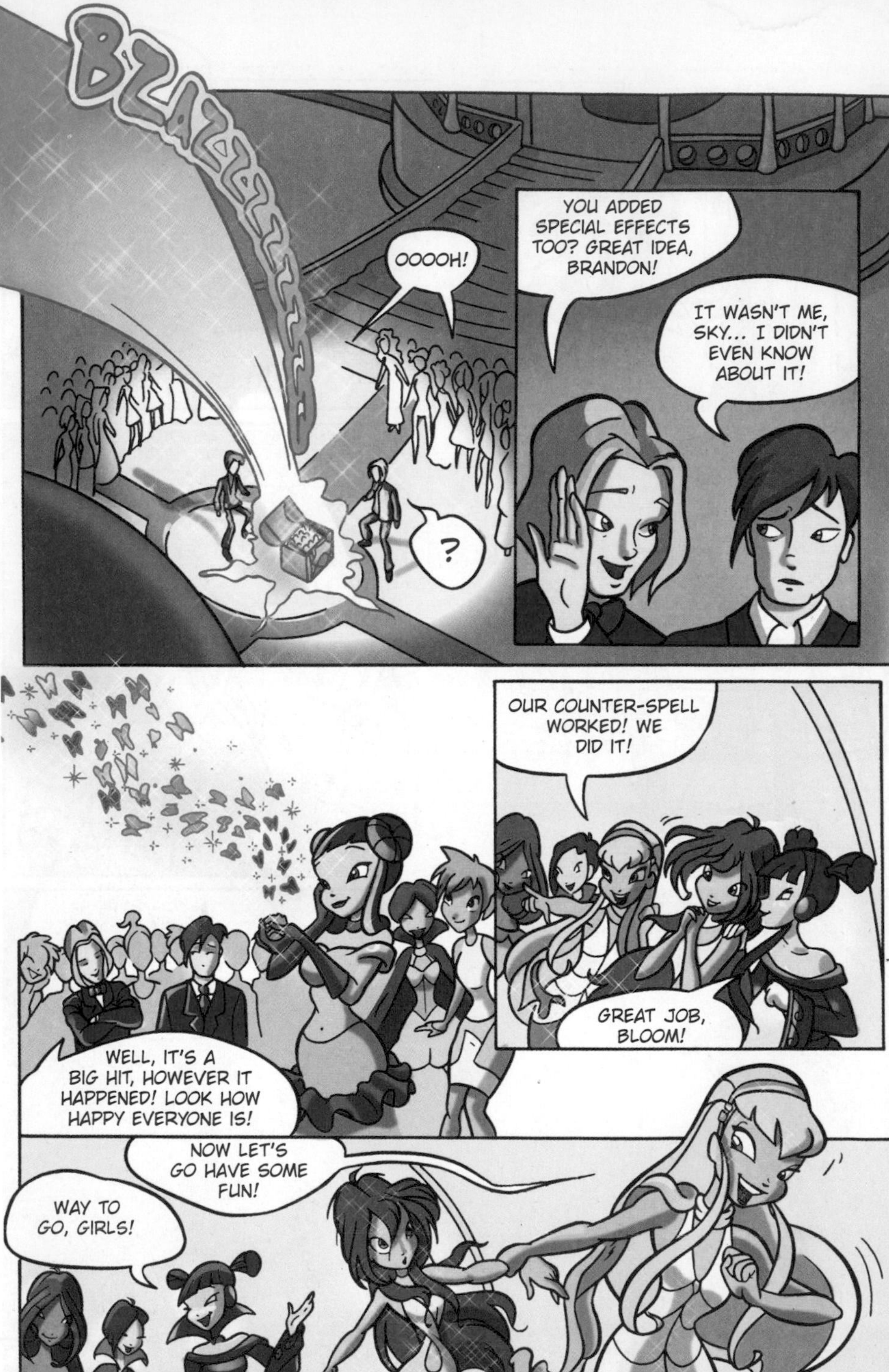
BZAZZZZZZZZZ
OOOOH!
?
YOU ADDED SPECIAL EFFECTS TOO? GREAT IDEA, BRANDON!
IT WASN'T ME, SKY... I DIDN'T EVEN KNOW ABOUT IT!
OUR COUNTER-SPELL WORKED! WE DID IT!
GREAT JOB, BLOOM!
WELL, IT'S A BIG HIT, HOWEVER IT HAPPENED! LOOK HOW HAPPY EVERYONE IS!
NOW LET'S GO HAVE SOME FUN!
WAY TO GO, GIRLS!

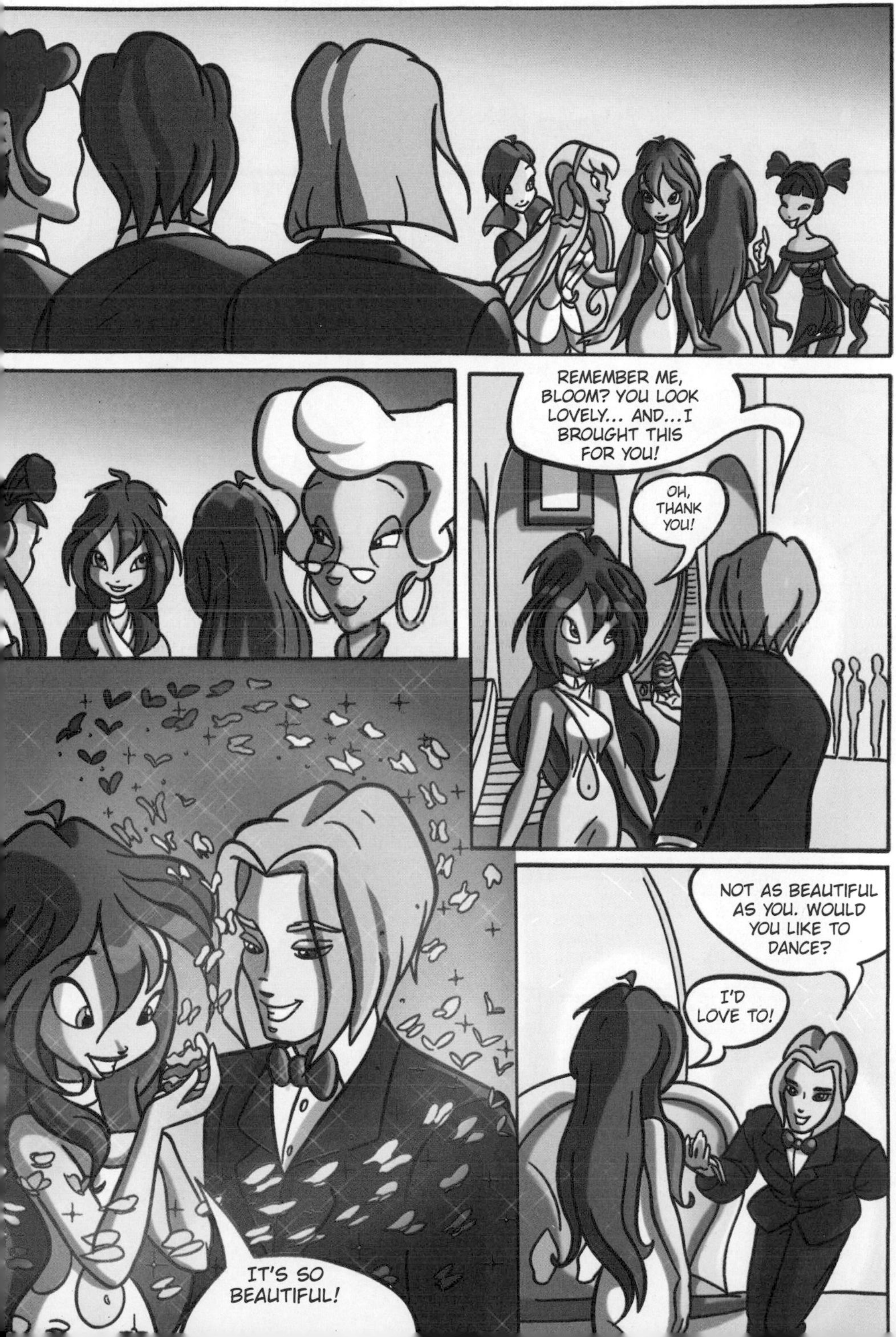
REMEMBER ME, BLOOM? YOU LOOK LOVELY... AND...I BROUGHT THIS FOR YOU!
OH, THANK YOU!
IT'S SO BEAUTIFUL!
NOT AS BEAUTIFUL AS YOU. WOULD YOU LIKE TO DANCE?
I'D LOVE TO!

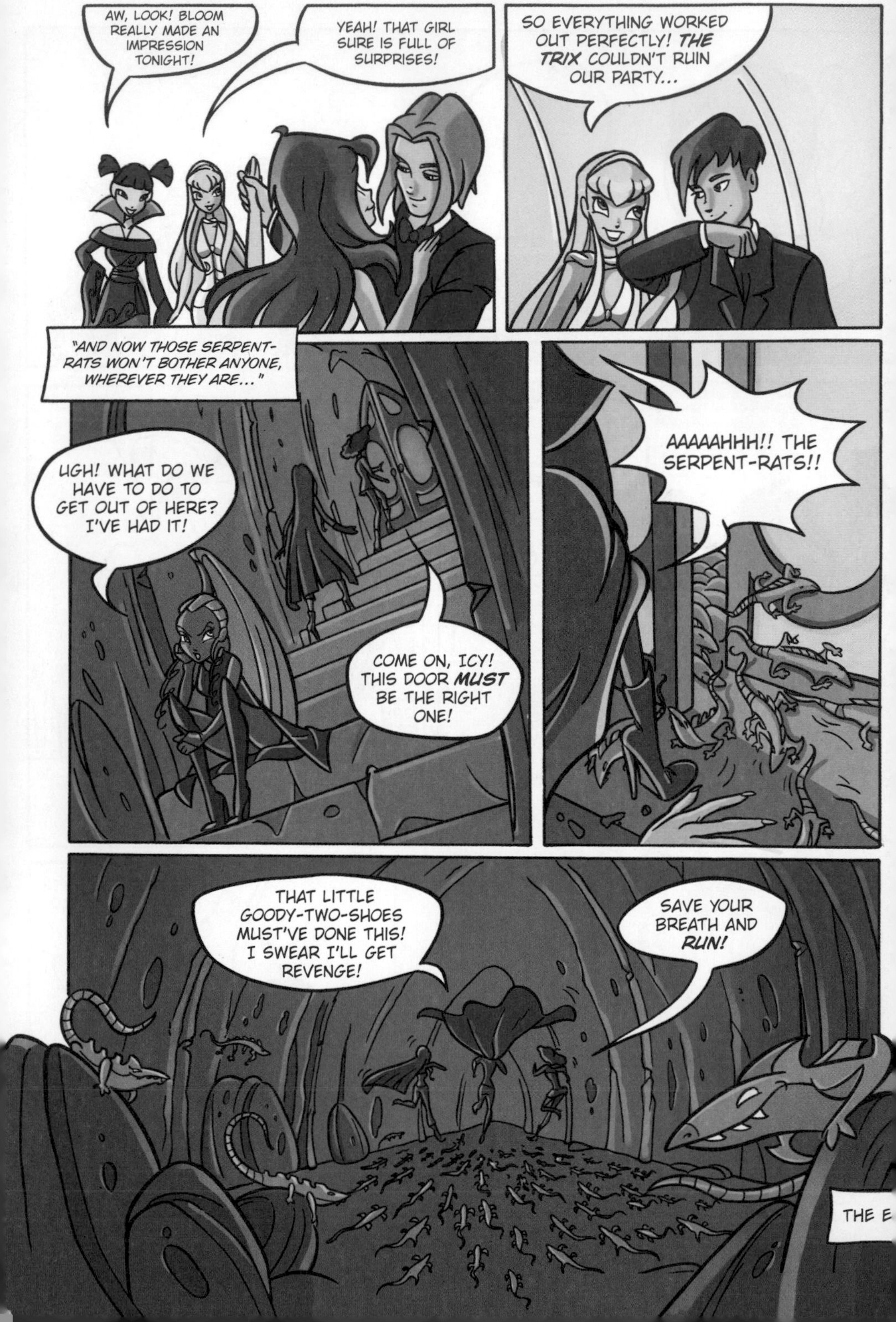
AW, LOOK! BLOOM REALLY MADE AN IMPRESSION TONIGHT!
YEAH! THAT GIRL SURE IS FULL OF SURPRISES!
SO EVERYTHING WORKED OUT PERFECTLY! THE TRIX COULDN'T RUIN OUR PARTY...
"AND NOW THOSE SERPENT-RATS WON'T BOTHER ANYONE, WHEREVER THEY ARE..."
UGH! WHAT DO WE HAVE TO DO TO GET OUT OF HERE? I'VE HAD IT!
COME ON, ICY! THIS DOOR MUST BE THE RIGHT ONE!
AAAAAHHH!! THE SERPENT-RATS!!
THAT LITTLE GOODY-TWO-SHOES MUST'VE DONE THIS! I SWEAR I'LL GET REVENGE!
SAVE YOUR BREATH AND RUN!
THE E

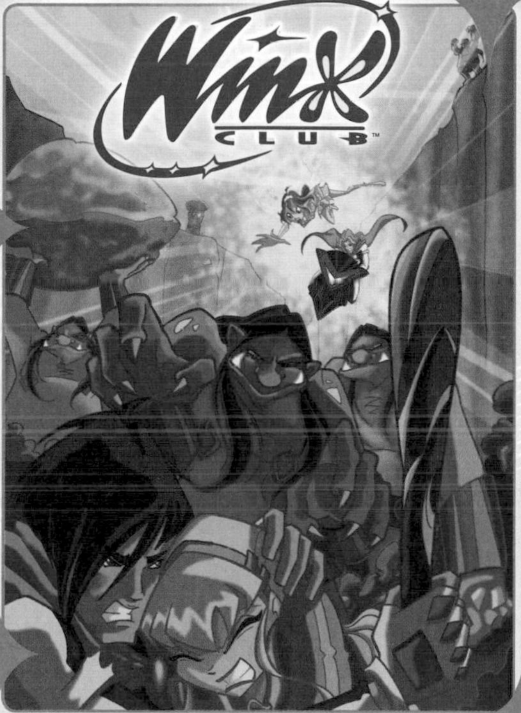
Winx
CLUB

The Boys from Red Fountain

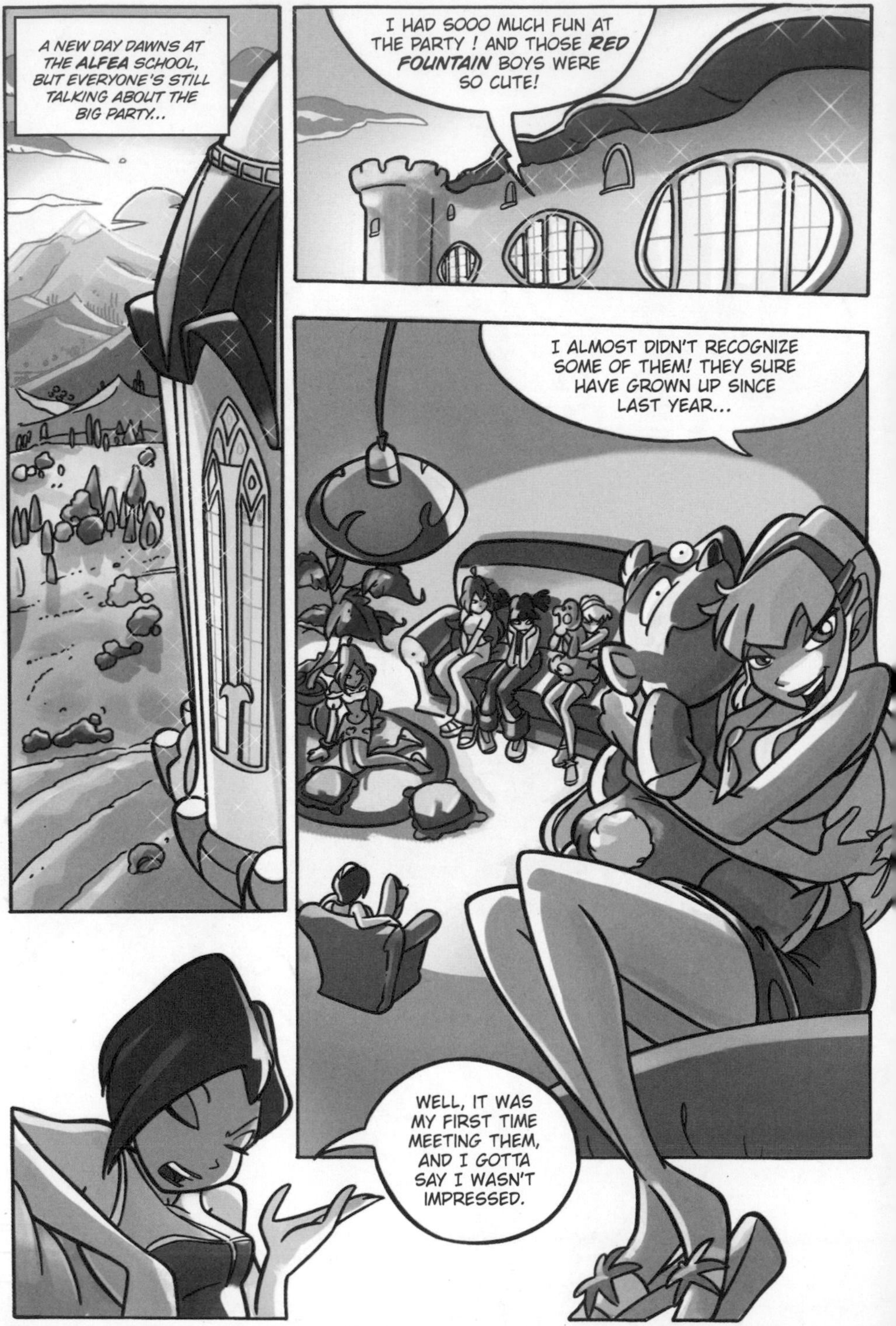
A NEW DAY DAWNS AT THE ALFEA SCHOOL, BUT EVERYONE'S STILL TALKING ABOUT THE BIG PARTY...
I HAD SOOO MUCH FUN AT THE PARTY ! AND THOSE RED FOUNTAIN BOYS WERE SO CUTE!
I ALMOST DIDN'T RECOGNIZE SOME OF THEM! THEY SURE HAVE GROWN UP SINCE LAST YEAR...
WELL, IT WAS MY FIRST TIME MEETING THEM, AND I GOTTA SAY I WASN'T IMPRESSED.

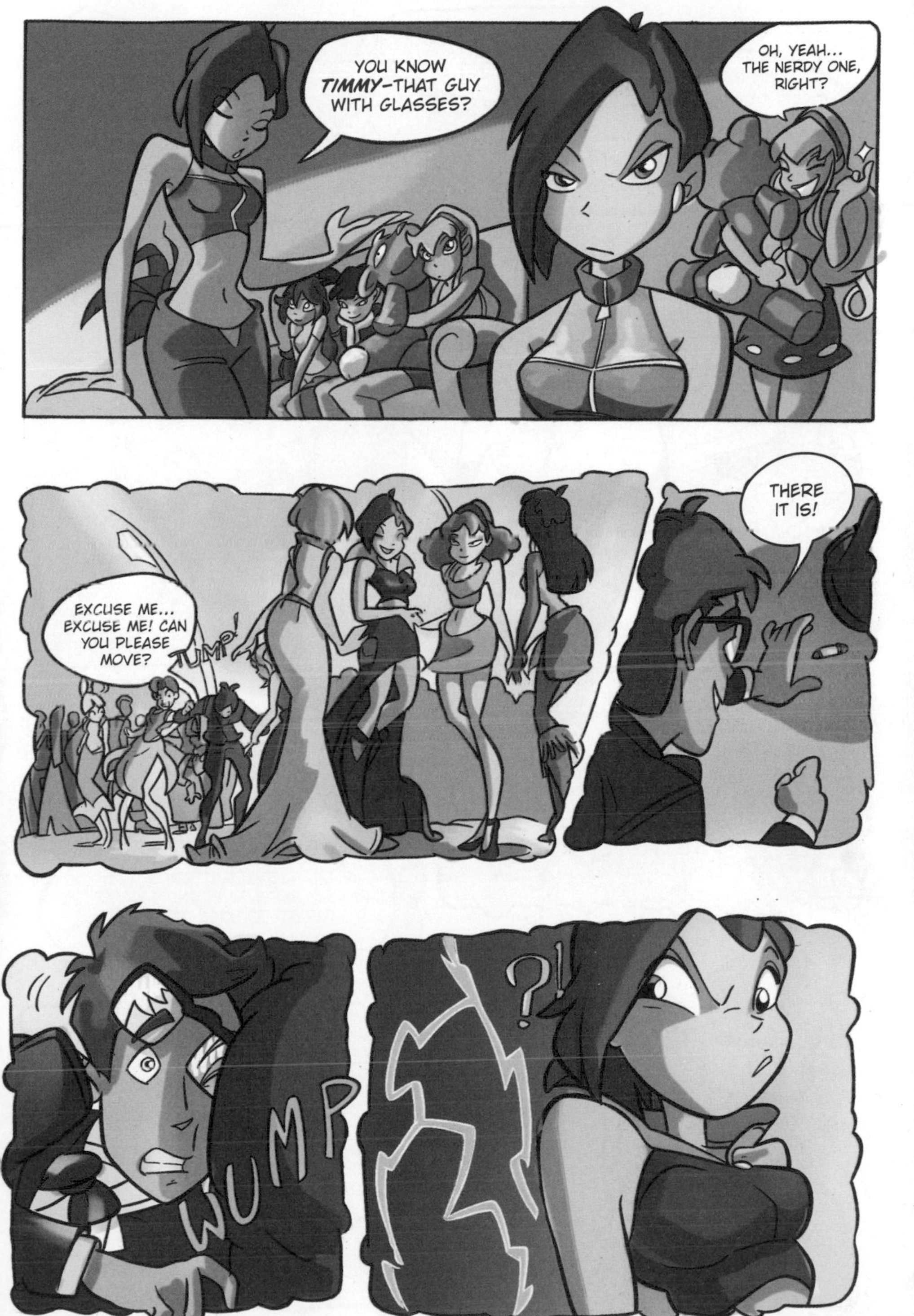
YOU KNOW TIMMY–THAT GUY WITH GLASSES?
OH, YEAH... THE NERDY ONE, RIGHT?
EXCUSE ME... EXCUSE ME! CAN YOU PLEASE MOVE?
TUMP!
THERE IT IS!
WUMP
?!

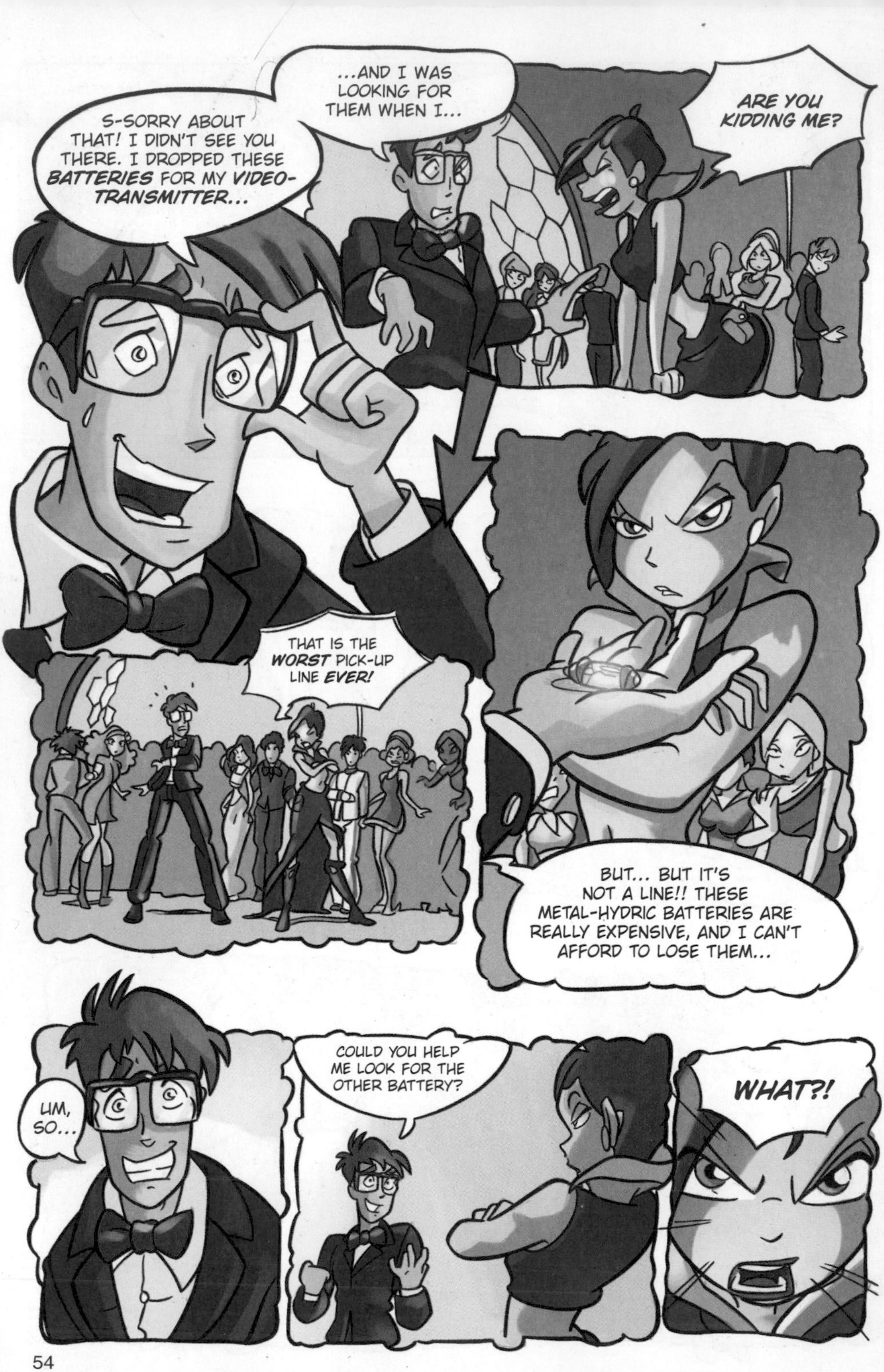
S-SORRY ABOUT THAT! I DIDN'T SEE YOU THERE. I DROPPED THESE BATTERIES FOR MY VIDEO-TRANSMITTER...
...AND I WAS LOOKING FOR THEM WHEN I...
ARE YOU KIDDING ME?
THAT IS THE WORST PICK-UP LINE EVER!
BUT... BUT IT'S NOT A LINE!! THESE METAL-HYDRIC BATTERIES ARE REALLY EXPENSIVE, AND I CAN'T AFFORD TO LOSE THEM...
UM, SO...
COULD YOU HELP ME LOOK FOR THE OTHER BATTERY?
WHAT?!

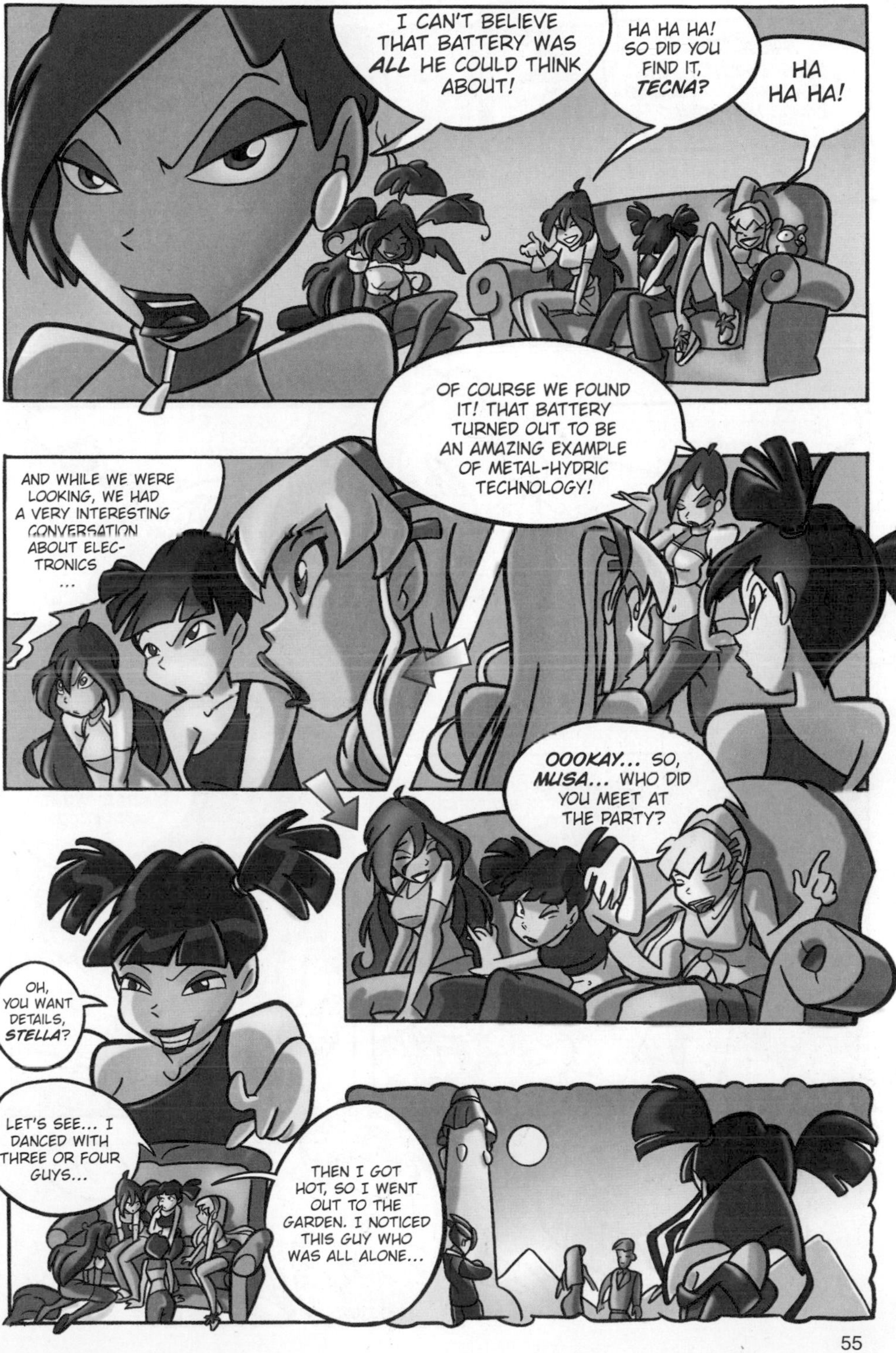

I CAN'T BELIEVE THAT BATTERY WAS **ALL** HE COULD THINK ABOUT!
HA HA HA! SO DID YOU FIND IT, **TECNA**?
HA HA HA!
OF COURSE WE FOUND IT! THAT BATTERY TURNED OUT TO BE AN AMAZING EXAMPLE OF METAL-HYDRIC TECHNOLOGY!
AND WHILE WE WERE LOOKING, WE HAD A VERY INTERESTING CONVERSATION ABOUT ELEC- TRONICS ...
OOOKAY... SO, **MUSA...** WHO DID YOU MEET AT THE PARTY?
OH, YOU WANT DETAILS, **STELLA**?
LET'S SEE... I DANCED WITH THREE OR FOUR GUYS...
THEN I GOT HOT, SO I WENT OUT TO THE GARDEN. I NOTICED THIS GUY WHO WAS ALL ALONE...

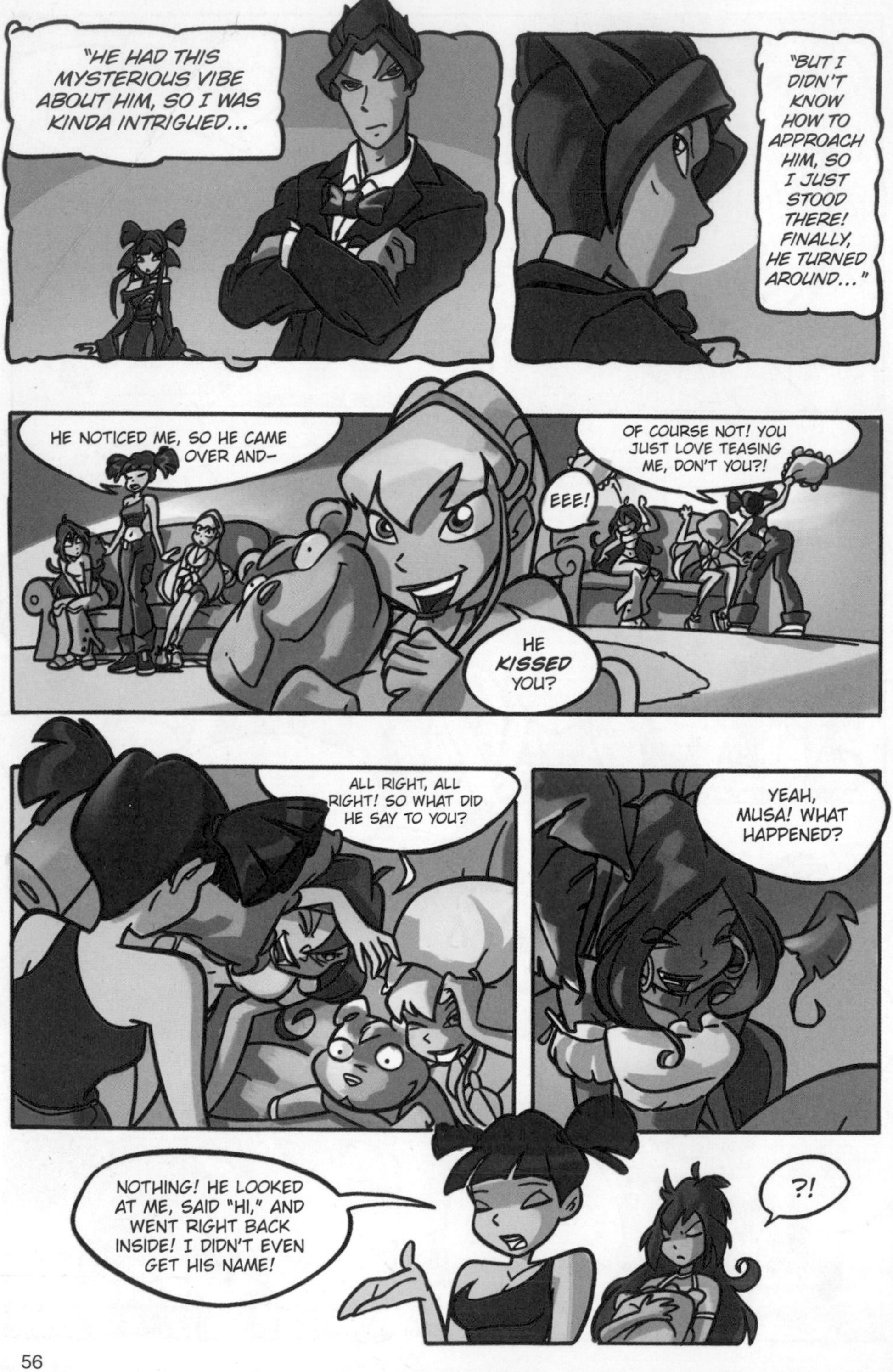
"HE HAD THIS MYSTERIOUS VIBE ABOUT HIM, SO I WAS KINDA INTRIGUED...
"BUT I DIDN'T KNOW HOW TO APPROACH HIM, SO I JUST STOOD THERE! FINALLY, HE TURNED AROUND..."
HE NOTICED ME, SO HE CAME OVER AND-
HE KISSED YOU?
EEE!
OF COURSE NOT! YOU JUST LOVE TEASING ME, DON'T YOU?!
ALL RIGHT, ALL RIGHT! SO WHAT DID HE SAY TO YOU?
YEAH, MUSA! WHAT HAPPENED?
NOTHING! HE LOOKED AT ME, SAID "HI," AND WENT RIGHT BACK INSIDE! I DIDN'T EVEN GET HIS NAME!
?!

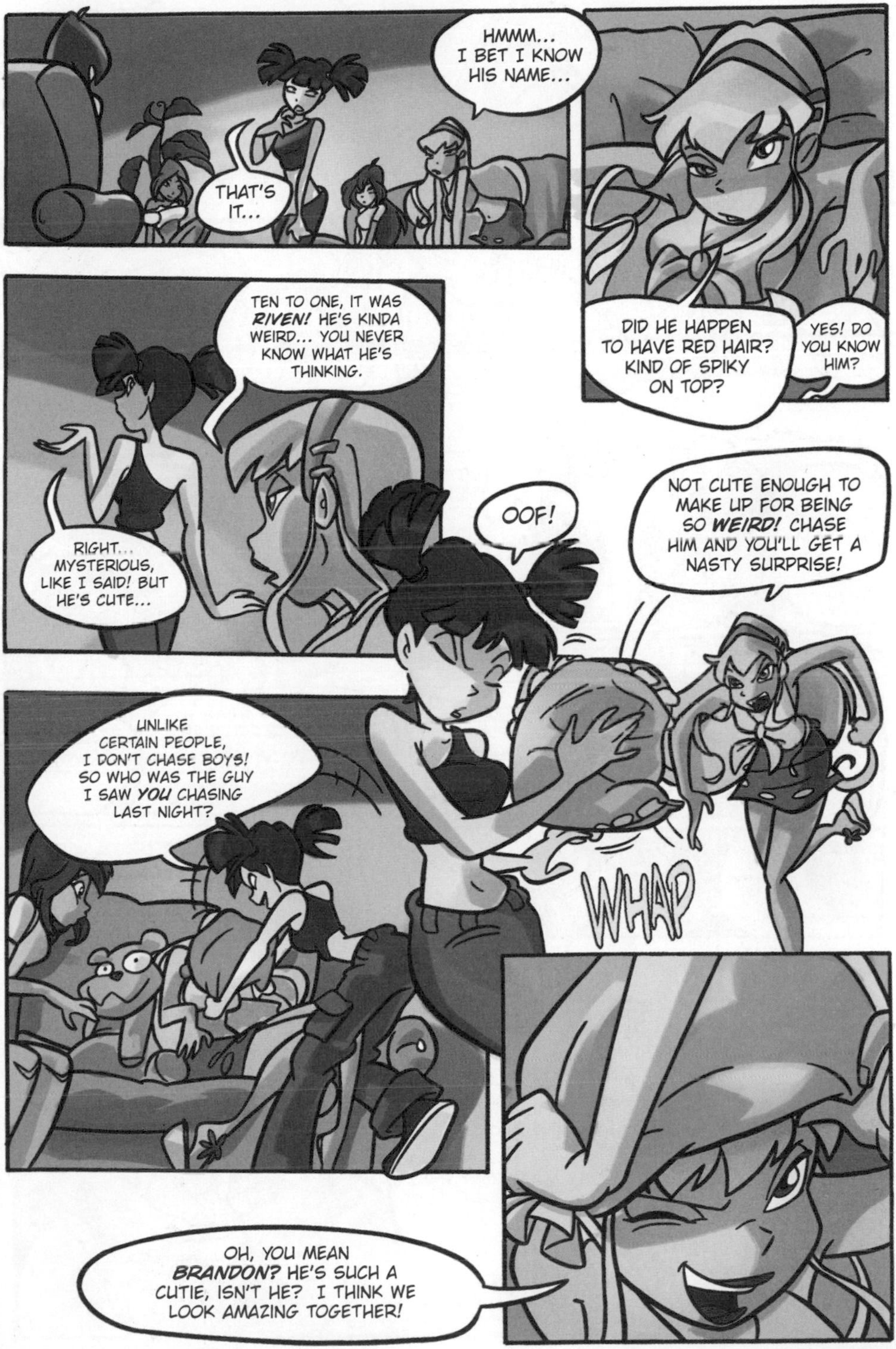
HMMM... I BET I KNOW HIS NAME...
THAT'S IT...
DID HE HAPPEN TO HAVE RED HAIR? KIND OF SPIKY ON TOP?
YES! DO YOU KNOW HIM?
TEN TO ONE, IT WAS *RIVEN!* HE'S KINDA WEIRD... YOU NEVER KNOW WHAT HE'S THINKING.
RIGHT... MYSTERIOUS, LIKE I SAID! BUT HE'S CUTE...
OOF!
NOT CUTE ENOUGH TO MAKE UP FOR BEING SO *WEIRD!* CHASE HIM AND YOU'LL GET A NASTY SURPRISE!
WHAP
UNLIKE CERTAIN PEOPLE, I DON'T CHASE BOYS! SO WHO WAS THE GUY I SAW *YOU* CHASING LAST NIGHT?
OH, YOU MEAN *BRANDON?* HE'S SUCH A CUTIE, ISN'T HE? I THINK WE LOOK AMAZING TOGETHER!

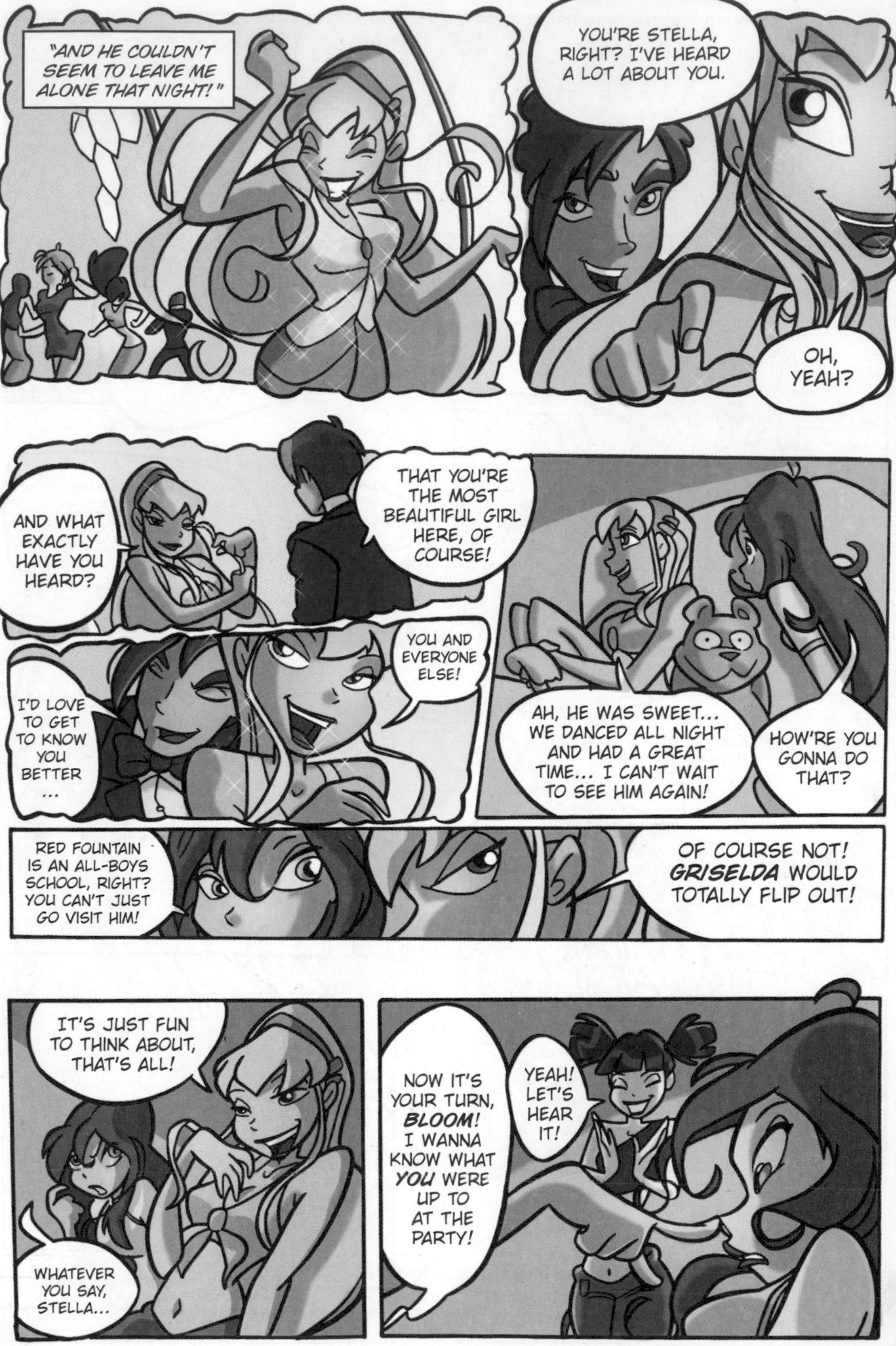
"AND HE COULDN'T SEEM TO LEAVE ME ALONE THAT NIGHT!"
YOU'RE STELLA, RIGHT? I'VE HEARD A LOT ABOUT YOU.
OH, YEAH?
AND WHAT EXACTLY HAVE YOU HEARD?
THAT YOU'RE THE MOST BEAUTIFUL GIRL HERE, OF COURSE!
I'D LOVE TO GET TO KNOW YOU BETTER ...
YOU AND EVERYONE ELSE!
AH, HE WAS SWEET... WE DANCED ALL NIGHT AND HAD A GREAT TIME... I CAN'T WAIT TO SEE HIM AGAIN!
HOW'RE YOU GONNA DO THAT?
RED FOUNTAIN IS AN ALL-BOYS SCHOOL, RIGHT? YOU CAN'T JUST GO VISIT HIM!
OF COURSE NOT! GRISELDA WOULD TOTALLY FLIP OUT!
IT'S JUST FUN TO THINK ABOUT, THAT'S ALL!
WHATEVER YOU SAY, STELLA...
NOW IT'S YOUR TURN, BLOOM! I WANNA KNOW WHAT YOU WERE UP TO AT THE PARTY!
YEAH! LET'S HEAR IT!

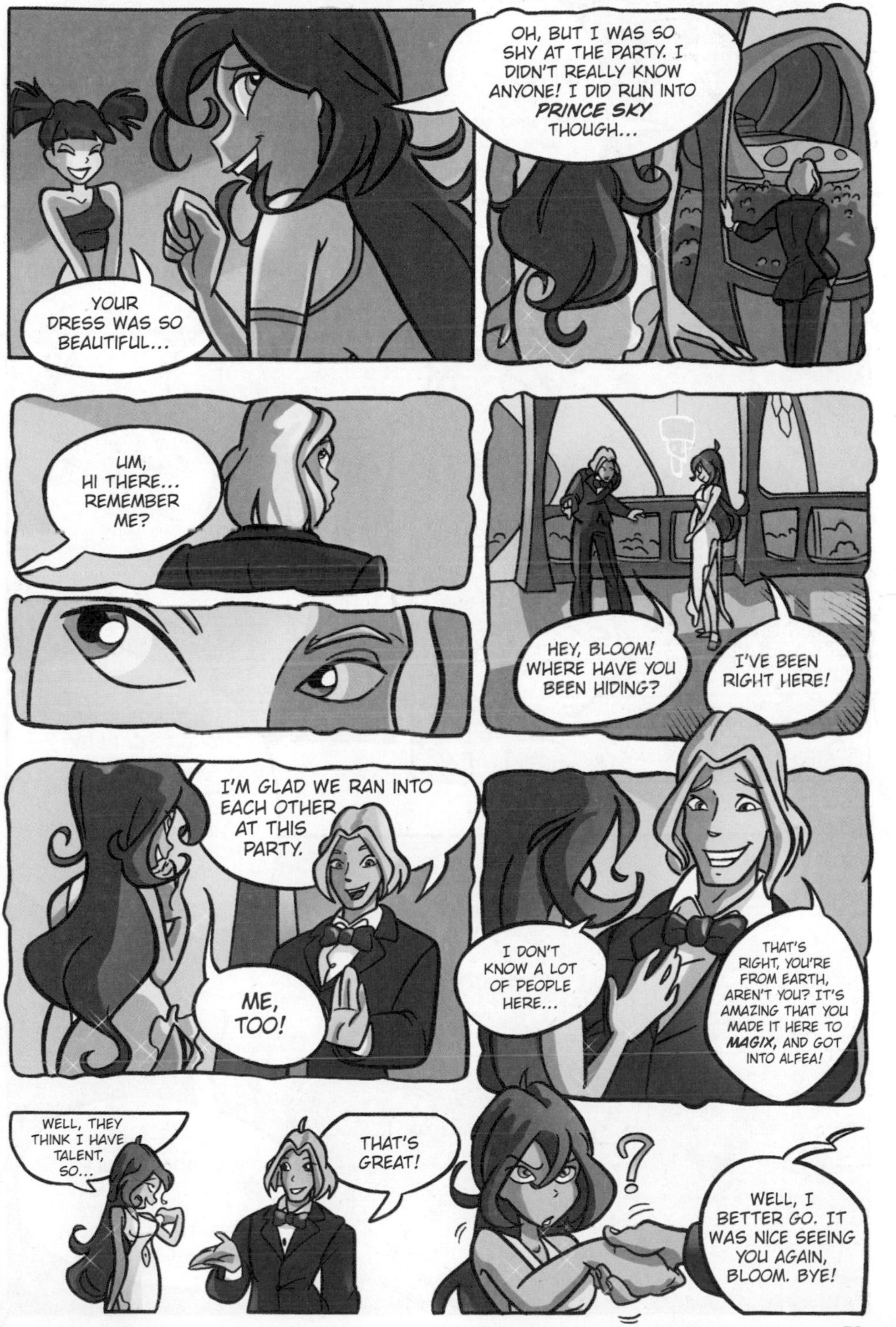
YOUR DRESS WAS SO BEAUTIFUL...
OH, BUT I WAS SO SHY AT THE PARTY. I DIDN'T REALLY KNOW ANYONE! I DID RUN INTO PRINCE SKY THOUGH...
UM, HI THERE... REMEMBER ME?
HEY, BLOOM! WHERE HAVE YOU BEEN HIDING?
I'VE BEEN RIGHT HERE!
I'M GLAD WE RAN INTO EACH OTHER AT THIS PARTY.
ME, TOO!
I DON'T KNOW A LOT OF PEOPLE HERE...
THAT'S RIGHT, YOU'RE FROM EARTH, AREN'T YOU? IT'S AMAZING THAT YOU MADE IT HERE TO MAGIX, AND GOT INTO ALFEA!
WELL, THEY THINK I HAVE TALENT, SO...
THAT'S GREAT!
?
WELL, I BETTER GO. IT WAS NICE SEEING YOU AGAIN, BLOOM. BYE!

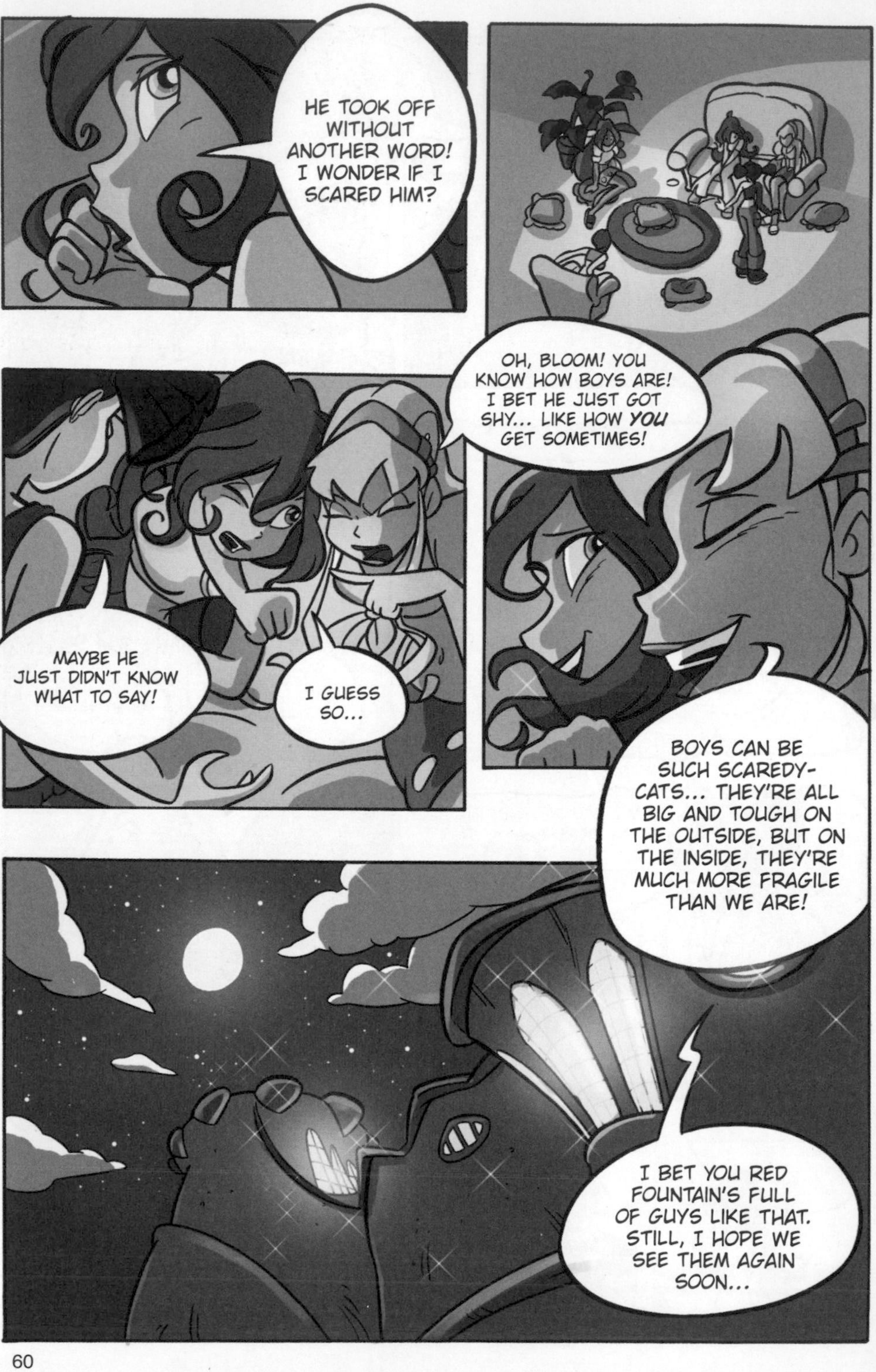
HE TOOK OFF WITHOUT ANOTHER WORD! I WONDER IF I SCARED HIM?
OH, BLOOM! YOU KNOW HOW BOYS ARE! I BET HE JUST GOT SHY... LIKE HOW YOU GET SOMETIMES!
MAYBE HE JUST DIDN'T KNOW WHAT TO SAY!
I GUESS SO...
BOYS CAN BE SUCH SCAREDY-CATS... THEY'RE ALL BIG AND TOUGH ON THE OUTSIDE, BUT ON THE INSIDE, THEY'RE MUCH MORE FRAGILE THAN WE ARE!
I BET YOU RED FOUNTAIN'S FULL OF GUYS LIKE THAT. STILL, I HOPE WE SEE THEM AGAIN SOON...

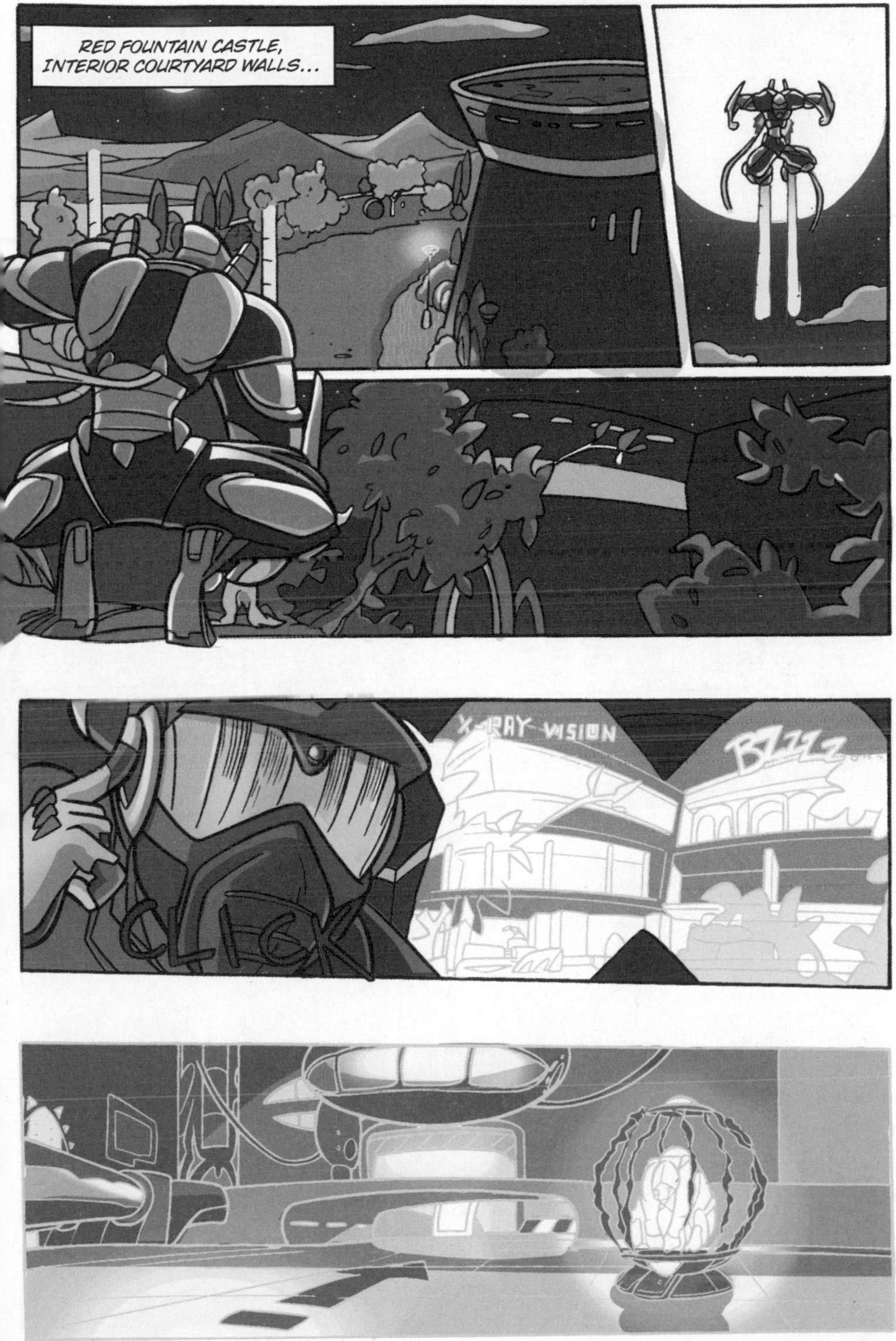
RED FOUNTAIN CASTLE,
INTERIOR COURTYARD WALLS...
CLICK
X-RAY VISION
BZZZZ...

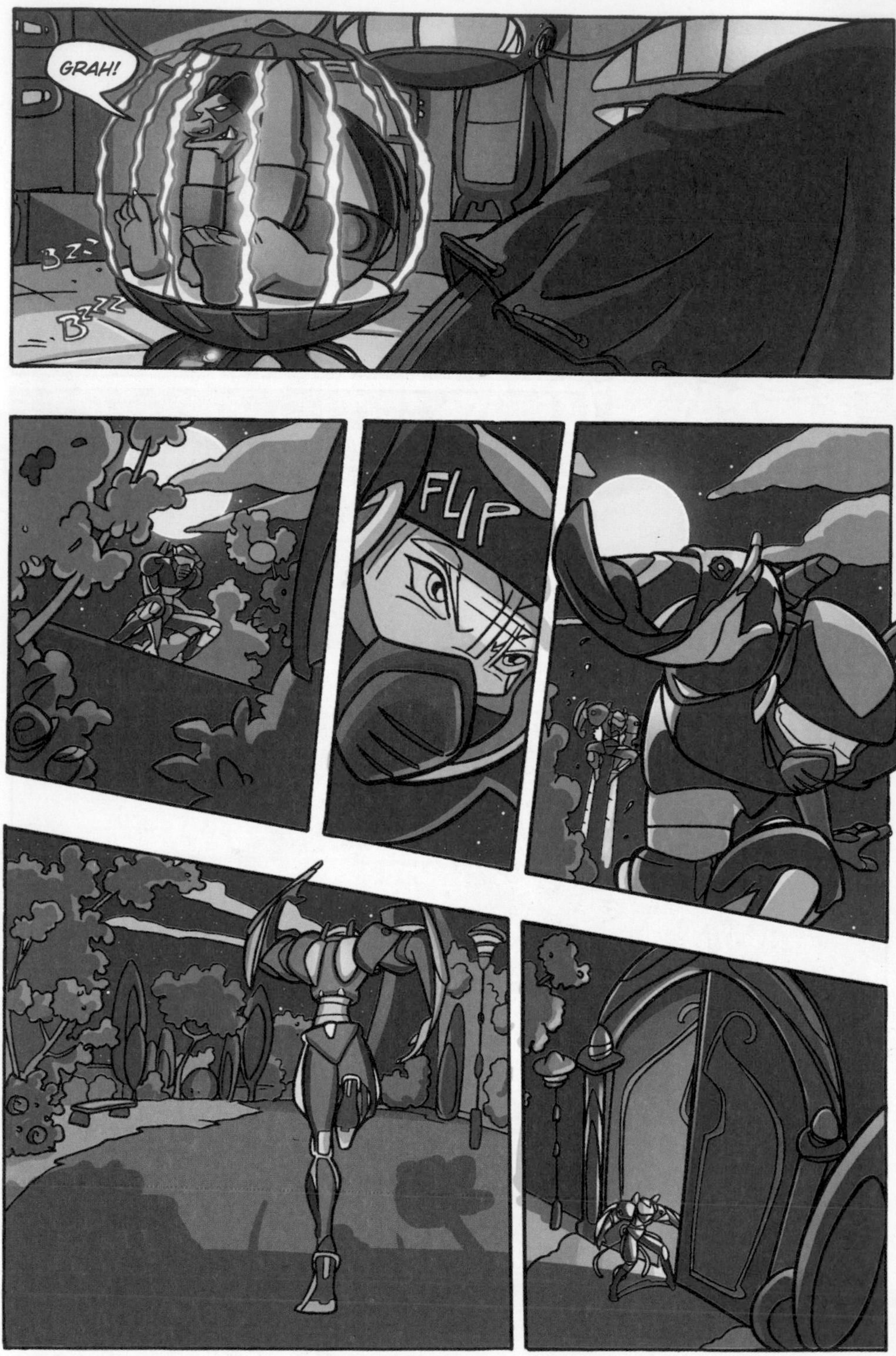
GRAH!
BZZ
BZZZ
FLIP

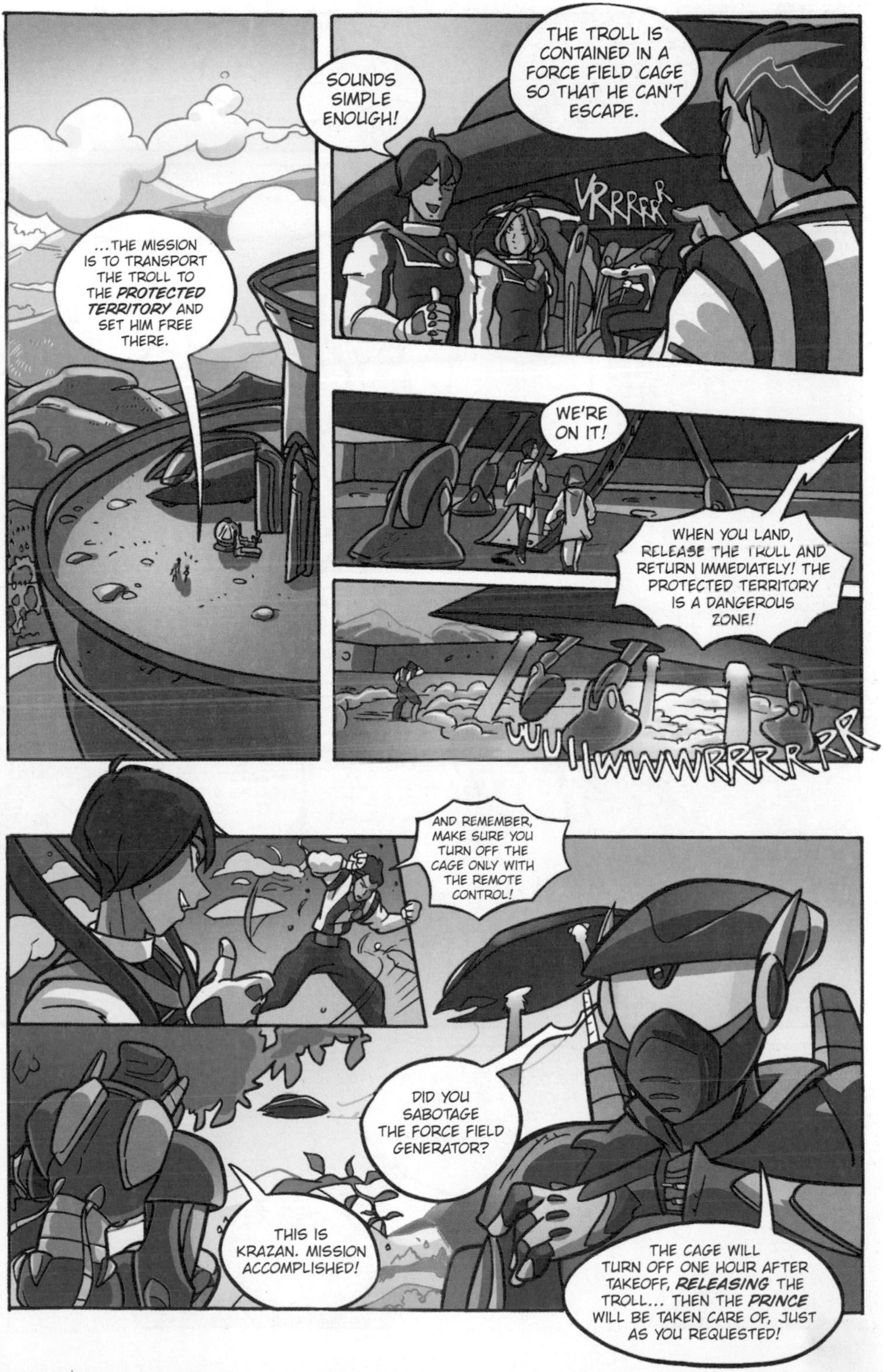
...THE MISSION IS TO TRANSPORT THE TROLL TO THE *PROTECTED TERRITORY* AND SET HIM FREE THERE.
SOUNDS SIMPLE ENOUGH!
THE TROLL IS CONTAINED IN A FORCE FIELD CAGE SO THAT HE CAN'T ESCAPE.
VRRRRRR
WE'RE ON IT!
WHEN YOU LAND, RELEASE THE TROLL AND RETURN IMMEDIATELY! THE PROTECTED TERRITORY IS A DANGEROUS ZONE!
WUUIIWWWWRRRRRRR
AND REMEMBER, MAKE SURE YOU TURN OFF THE CAGE ONLY WITH THE REMOTE CONTROL!
DID YOU SABOTAGE THE FORCE FIELD GENERATOR?
THIS IS KRAZAN. MISSION ACCOMPLISHED!
THE CAGE WILL TURN OFF ONE HOUR AFTER TAKEOFF, *RELEASING* THE TROLL... THEN THE *PRINCE* WILL BE TAKEN CARE OF, JUST AS YOU REQUESTED!

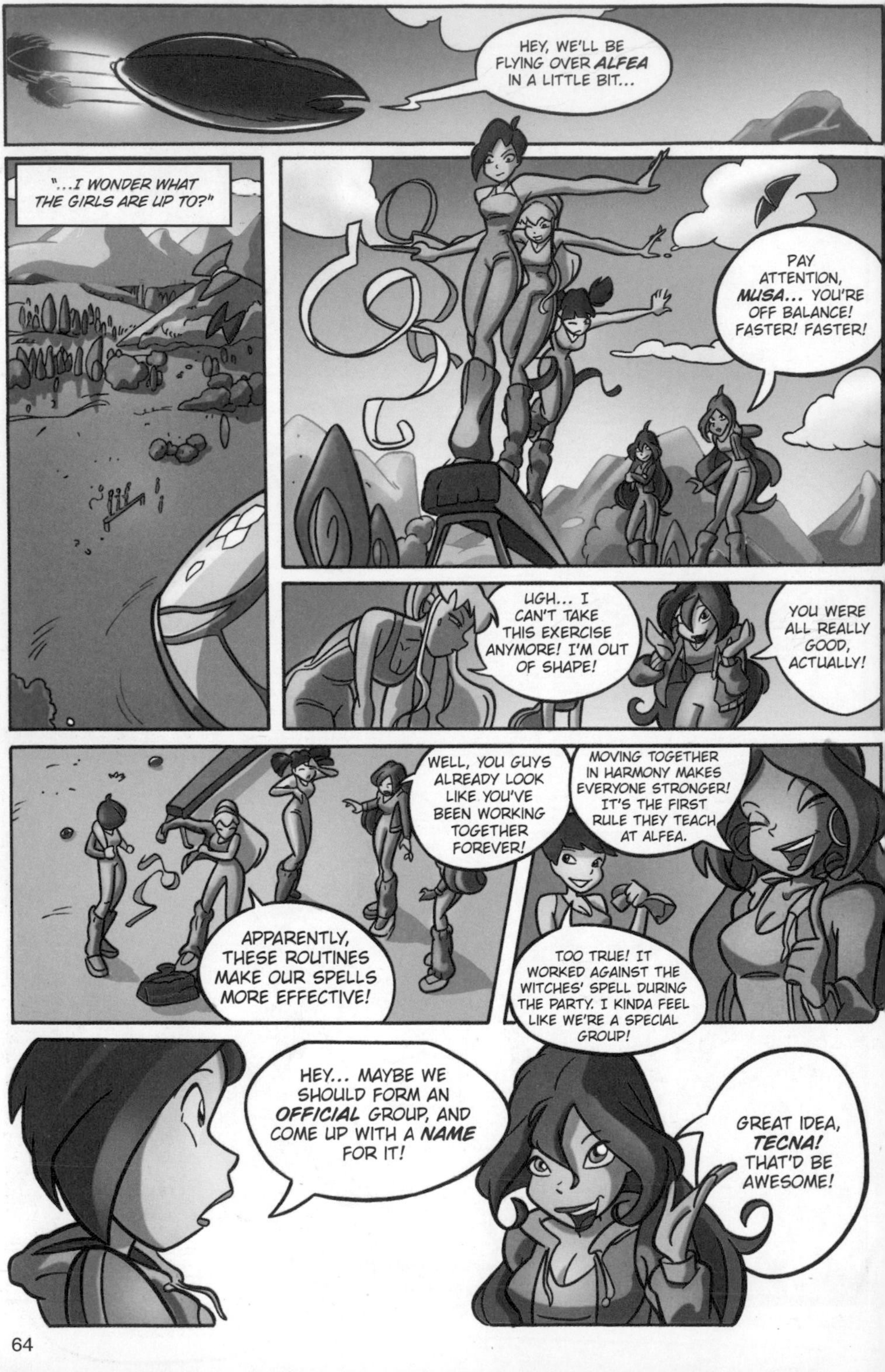
HEY, WE'LL BE FLYING OVER ALFEA IN A LITTLE BIT...
"...I WONDER WHAT THE GIRLS ARE UP TO?"
PAY ATTENTION, MUSA... YOU'RE OFF BALANCE! FASTER! FASTER!
UGH... I CAN'T TAKE THIS EXERCISE ANYMORE! I'M OUT OF SHAPE!
YOU WERE ALL REALLY GOOD, ACTUALLY!
WELL, YOU GUYS ALREADY LOOK LIKE YOU'VE BEEN WORKING TOGETHER FOREVER!
APPARENTLY, THESE ROUTINES MAKE OUR SPELLS MORE EFFECTIVE!
MOVING TOGETHER IN HARMONY MAKES EVERYONE STRONGER! IT'S THE FIRST RULE THEY TEACH AT ALFEA.
TOO TRUE! IT WORKED AGAINST THE WITCHES' SPELL DURING THE PARTY. I KINDA FEEL LIKE WE'RE A SPECIAL GROUP!
HEY... MAYBE WE SHOULD FORM AN OFFICIAL GROUP, AND COME UP WITH A NAME FOR IT!
GREAT IDEA, TECNA! THAT'D BE AWESOME!

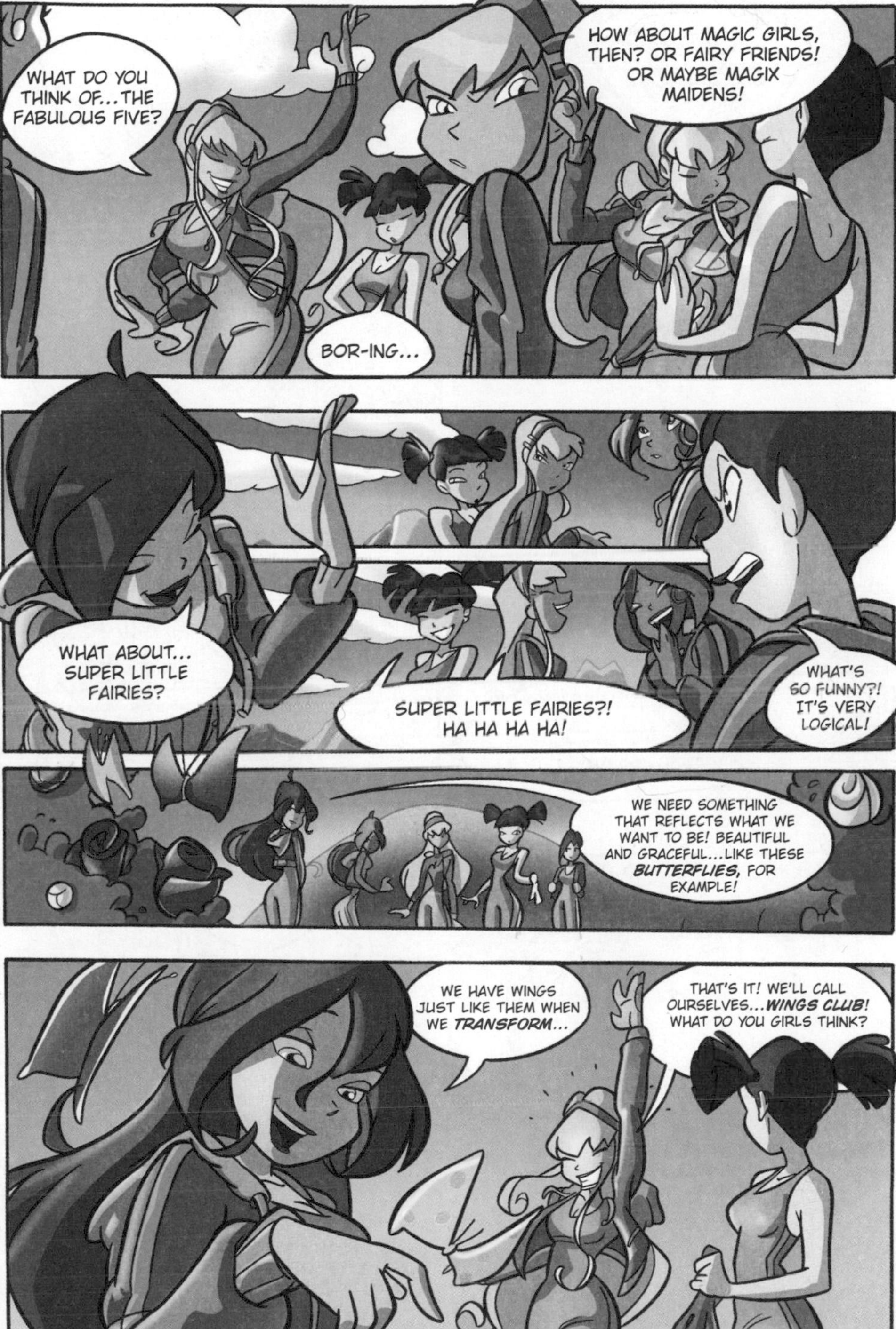
WHAT DO YOU THINK OF...THE FABULOUS FIVE?
BOR-ING...
HOW ABOUT MAGIC GIRLS, THEN? OR FAIRY FRIENDS! OR MAYBE MAGIX MAIDENS!
WHAT ABOUT... SUPER LITTLE FAIRIES?
SUPER LITTLE FAIRIES?! HA HA HA HA!
WHAT'S SO FUNNY?! IT'S VERY LOGICAL!
WE NEED SOMETHING THAT REFLECTS WHAT WE WANT TO BE! BEAUTIFUL AND GRACEFUL...LIKE THESE BUTTERFLIES, FOR EXAMPLE!
WE HAVE WINGS JUST LIKE THEM WHEN WE TRANSFORM...
THAT'S IT! WE'LL CALL OURSELVES...WINGS CLUB! WHAT DO YOU GIRLS THINK?

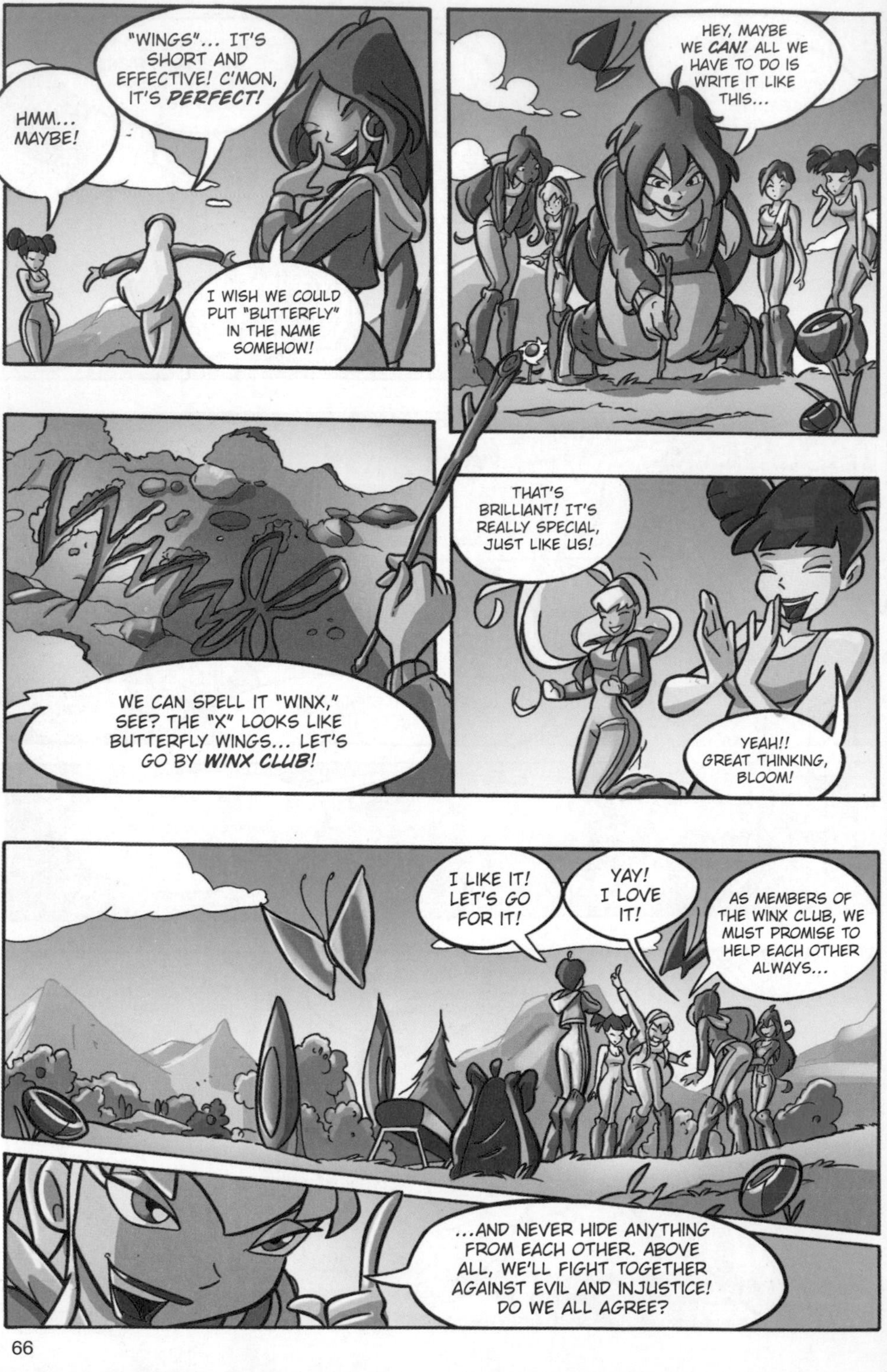
"WINGS"... IT'S SHORT AND EFFECTIVE! C'MON, IT'S PERFECT!
HMM... MAYBE!
I WISH WE COULD PUT "BUTTERFLY" IN THE NAME SOMEHOW!
HEY, MAYBE WE CAN! ALL WE HAVE TO DO IS WRITE IT LIKE THIS...
WE CAN SPELL IT "WINX," SEE? THE "X" LOOKS LIKE BUTTERFLY WINGS... LET'S GO BY WINX CLUB!
THAT'S BRILLIANT! IT'S REALLY SPECIAL, JUST LIKE US!
YEAH!! GREAT THINKING, BLOOM!
I LIKE IT! LET'S GO FOR IT!
YAY! I LOVE IT!
AS MEMBERS OF THE WINX CLUB, WE MUST PROMISE TO HELP EACH OTHER ALWAYS...
...AND NEVER HIDE ANYTHING FROM EACH OTHER. ABOVE ALL, WE'LL FIGHT TOGETHER AGAINST EVIL AND INJUSTICE! DO WE ALL AGREE?

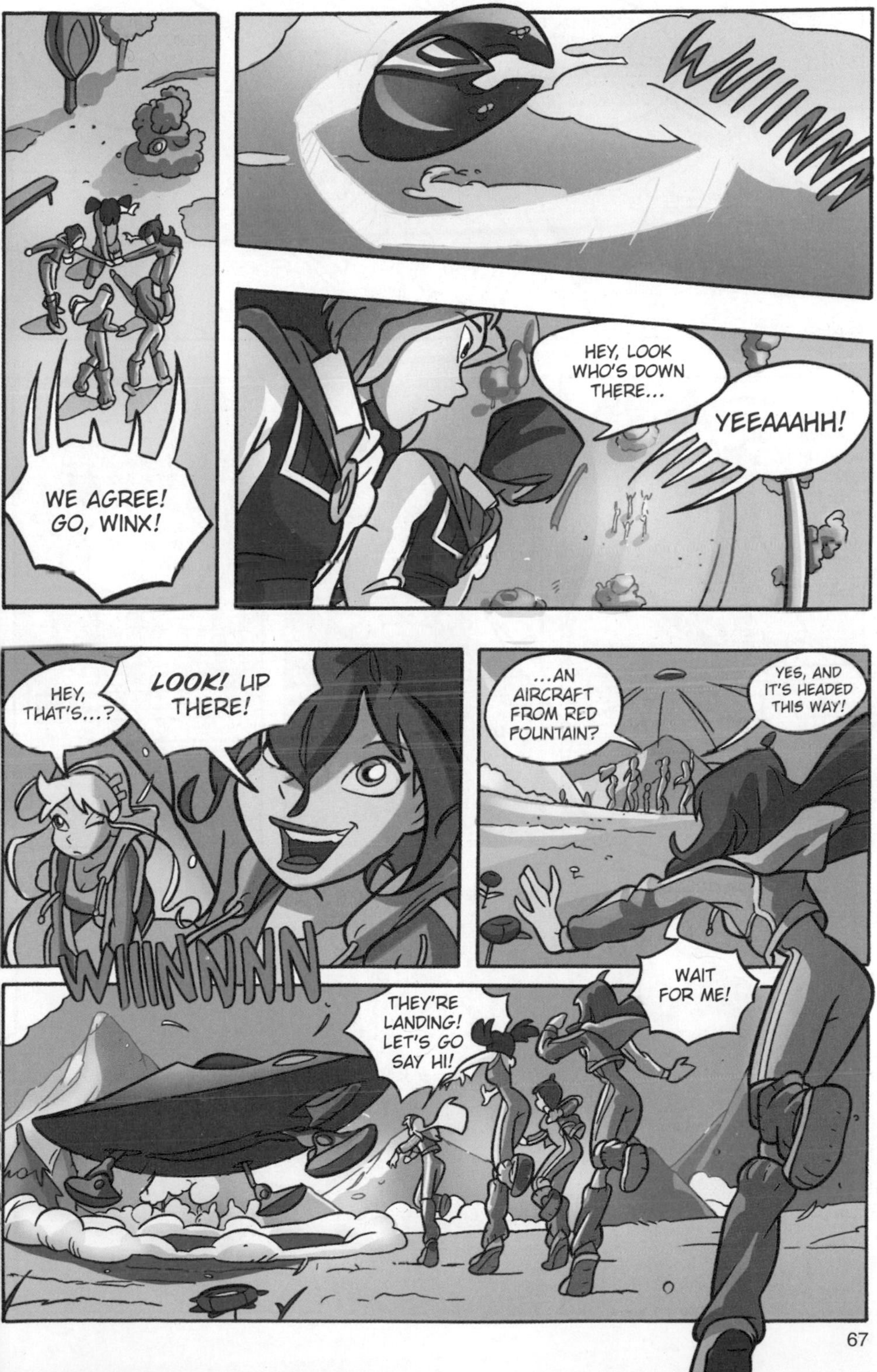
WUIIINNN
WE AGREE! GO, WINX!
HEY, LOOK WHO'S DOWN THERE...
YEEAAAHH!
HEY, THAT'S...?
LOOK! UP THERE!
...AN AIRCRAFT FROM RED FOUNTAIN?
YES, AND IT'S HEADED THIS WAY!
WIIINNNN
THEY'RE LANDING! LET'S GO SAY HI!
WAIT FOR ME!

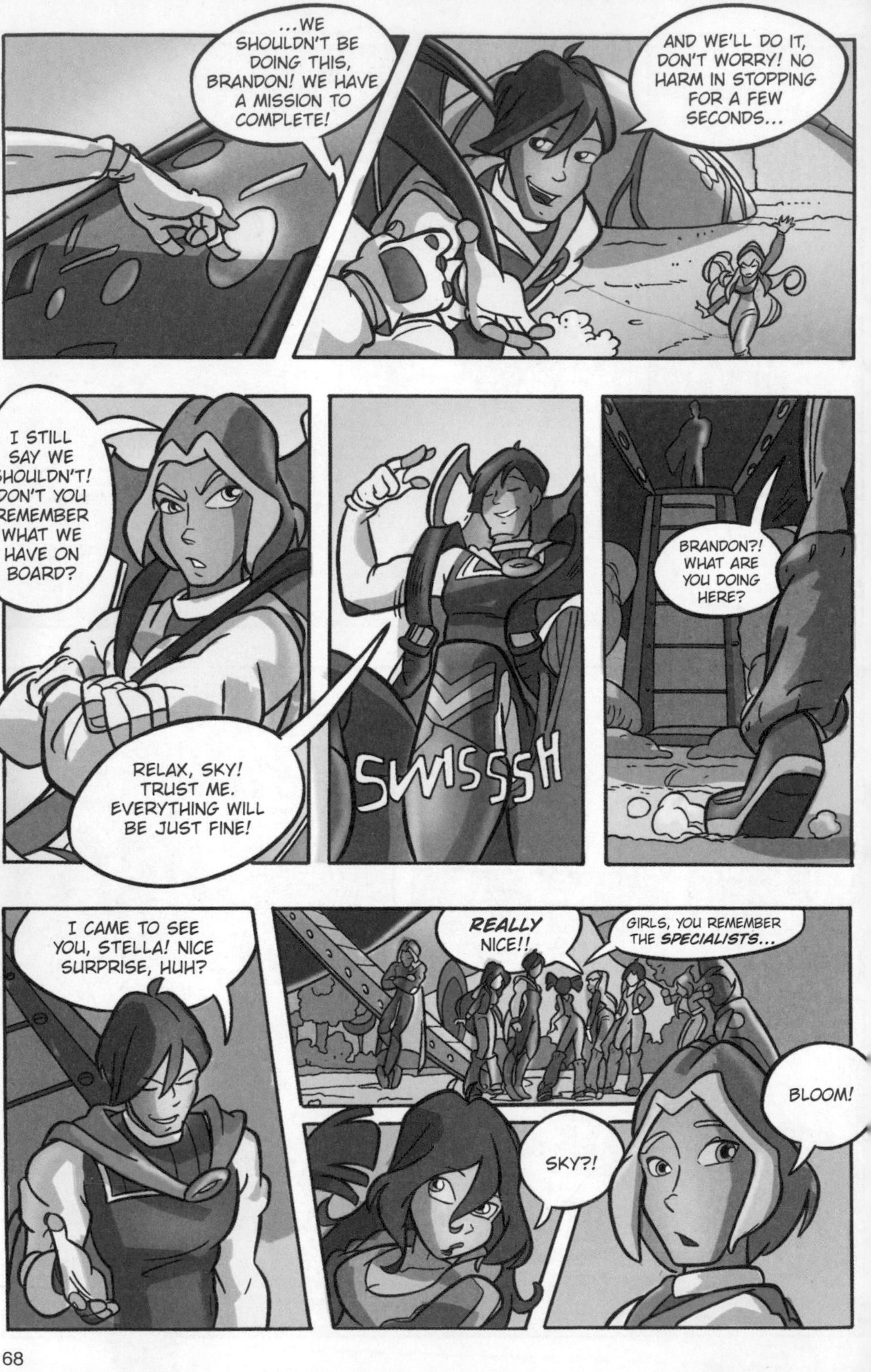
...WE SHOULDN'T BE DOING THIS, BRANDON! WE HAVE A MISSION TO COMPLETE!
AND WE'LL DO IT, DON'T WORRY! NO HARM IN STOPPING FOR A FEW SECONDS...
I STILL SAY WE SHOULDN'T! DON'T YOU REMEMBER WHAT WE HAVE ON BOARD?
RELAX, SKY! TRUST ME. EVERYTHING WILL BE JUST FINE!
SWISSSH
BRANDON?! WHAT ARE YOU DOING HERE?
I CAME TO SEE YOU, STELLA! NICE SURPRISE, HUH?
REALLY NICE!!
GIRLS, YOU REMEMBER THE ***SPECIALISTS...***
SKY?!
BLOOM!

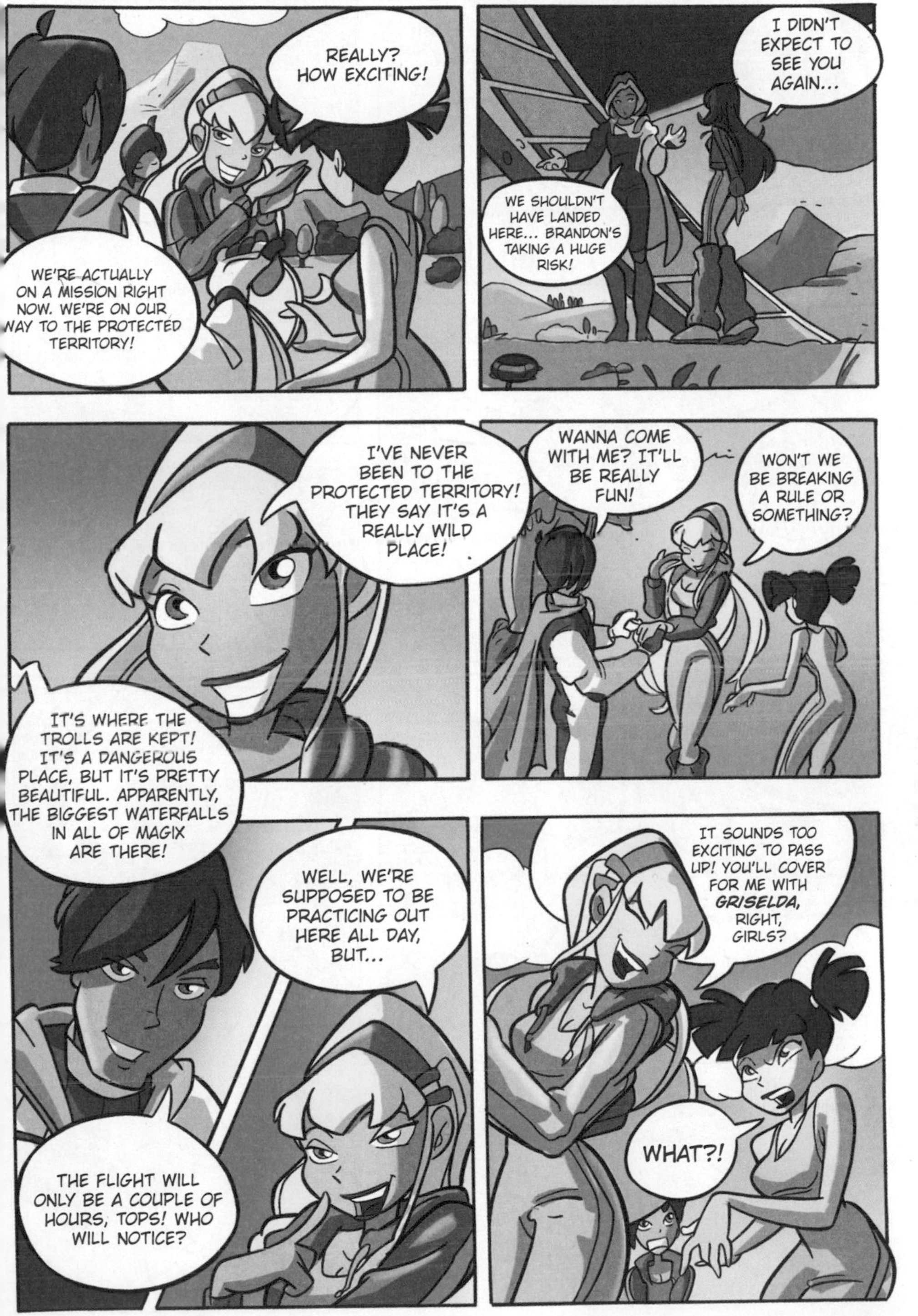
REALLY? HOW EXCITING!
WE'RE ACTUALLY ON A MISSION RIGHT NOW. WE'RE ON OUR WAY TO THE PROTECTED TERRITORY!
I DIDN'T EXPECT TO SEE YOU AGAIN...
WE SHOULDN'T HAVE LANDED HERE... BRANDON'S TAKING A HUGE RISK!
I'VE NEVER BEEN TO THE PROTECTED TERRITORY! THEY SAY IT'S A REALLY WILD PLACE!
IT'S WHERE THE TROLLS ARE KEPT! IT'S A DANGEROUS PLACE, BUT IT'S PRETTY BEAUTIFUL. APPARENTLY, THE BIGGEST WATERFALLS IN ALL OF MAGIX ARE THERE!
WANNA COME WITH ME? IT'LL BE REALLY FUN!
WON'T WE BE BREAKING A RULE OR SOMETHING?
WELL, WE'RE SUPPOSED TO BE PRACTICING OUT HERE ALL DAY, BUT...
THE FLIGHT WILL ONLY BE A COUPLE OF HOURS, TOPS! WHO WILL NOTICE?
IT SOUNDS TOO EXCITING TO PASS UP! YOU'LL COVER FOR ME WITH GRISELDA, RIGHT, GIRLS?
WHAT?!

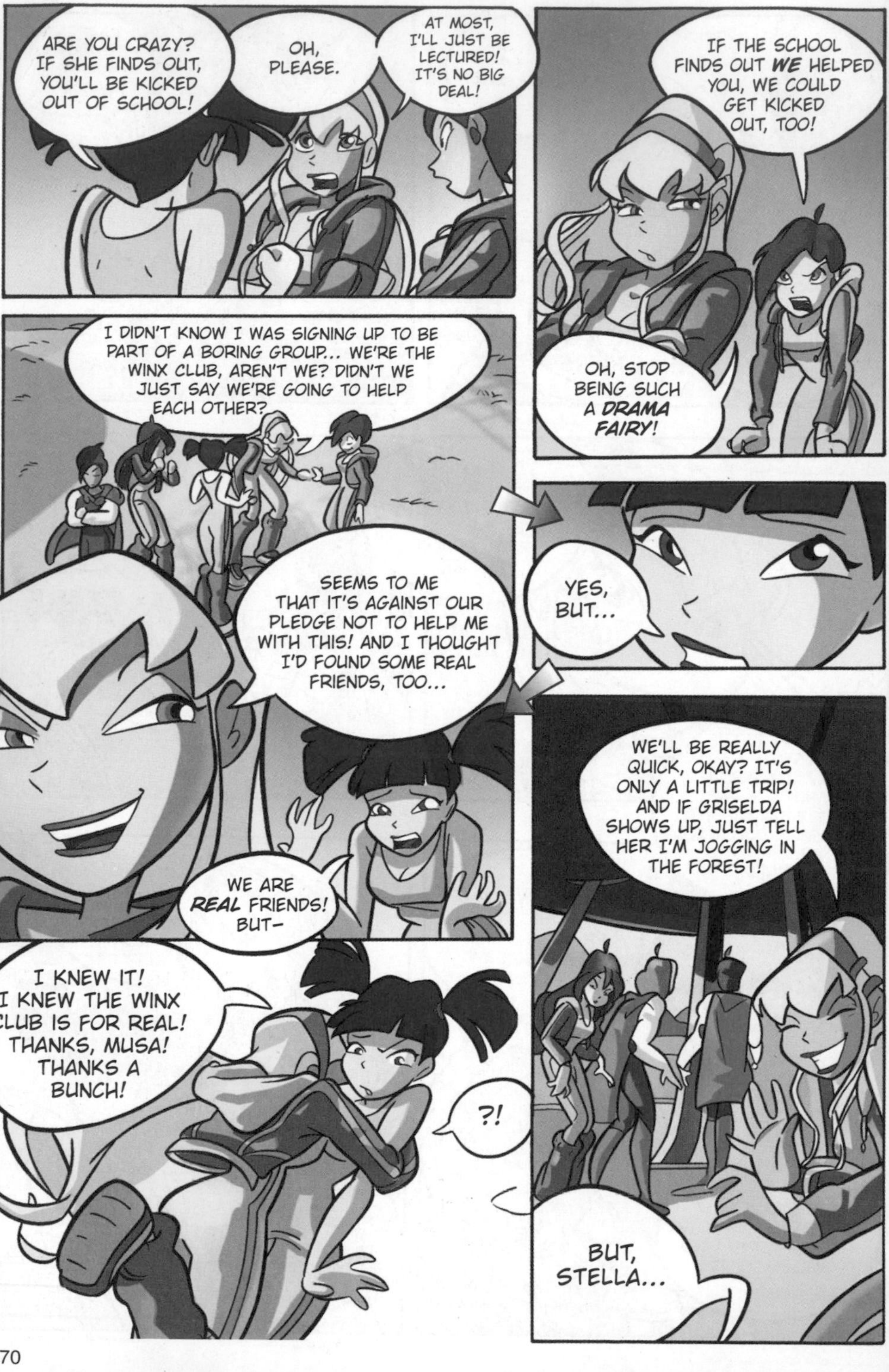
ARE YOU CRAZY? IF SHE FINDS OUT, YOU'LL BE KICKED OUT OF SCHOOL!
OH, PLEASE.
AT MOST, I'LL JUST BE LECTURED! IT'S NO BIG DEAL!
IF THE SCHOOL FINDS OUT WE HELPED YOU, WE COULD GET KICKED OUT, TOO!
OH, STOP BEING SUCH A DRAMA FAIRY!
I DIDN'T KNOW I WAS SIGNING UP TO BE PART OF A BORING GROUP... WE'RE THE WINX CLUB, AREN'T WE? DIDN'T WE JUST SAY WE'RE GOING TO HELP EACH OTHER?
YES, BUT...
SEEMS TO ME THAT IT'S AGAINST OUR PLEDGE NOT TO HELP ME WITH THIS! AND I THOUGHT I'D FOUND SOME REAL FRIENDS, TOO...
WE ARE REAL FRIENDS! BUT–
WE'LL BE REALLY QUICK, OKAY? IT'S ONLY A LITTLE TRIP! AND IF GRISELDA SHOWS UP, JUST TELL HER I'M JOGGING IN THE FOREST!
I KNEW IT! I KNEW THE WINX CLUB IS FOR REAL! THANKS, MUSA! THANKS A BUNCH!
?!
BUT, STELLA...

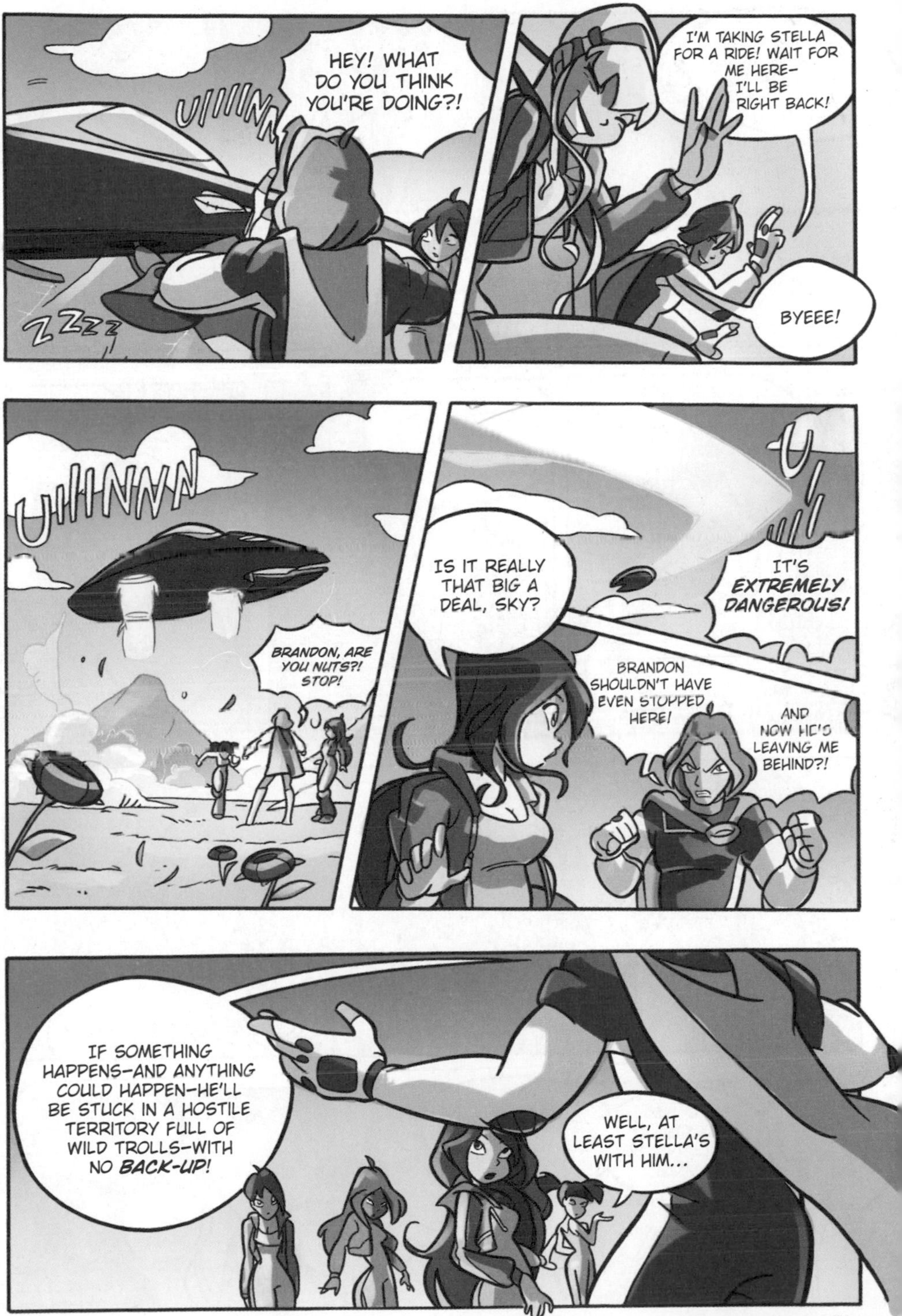
UIIIINN
HEY! WHAT DO YOU THINK YOU'RE DOING?!
ZZZZ
I'M TAKING STELLA FOR A RIDE! WAIT FOR ME HERE– I'LL BE RIGHT BACK!
BYEEE!
UIIINNN
BRANDON, ARE YOU NUTS?! STOP!
IS IT REALLY THAT BIG A DEAL, SKY?
IT'S EXTREMELY DANGEROUS!
BRANDON SHOULDN'T HAVE EVEN STOPPED HERE!
AND NOW HE'S LEAVING ME BEHIND?!
IF SOMETHING HAPPENS–AND ANYTHING COULD HAPPEN–HE'LL BE STUCK IN A HOSTILE TERRITORY FULL OF WILD TROLLS–WITH NO BACK-UP!
WELL, AT LEAST STELLA'S WITH HIM...

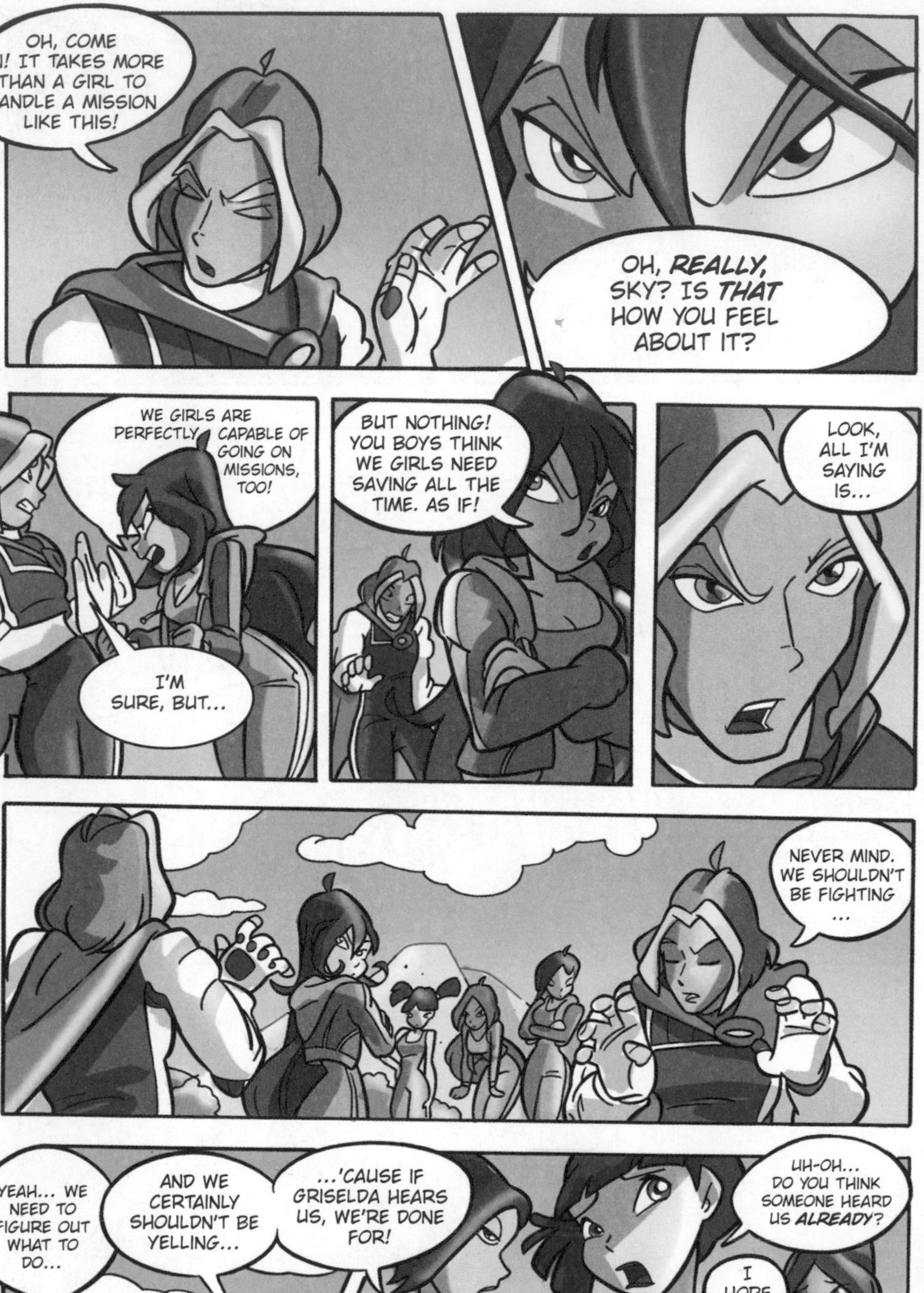

OH, COME ON! IT TAKES MORE THAN A GIRL TO HANDLE A MISSION LIKE THIS!
OH, REALLY, SKY? IS THAT HOW YOU FEEL ABOUT IT?
WE GIRLS ARE PERFECTLY CAPABLE OF GOING ON MISSIONS, TOO!
I'M SURE, BUT...
BUT NOTHING! YOU BOYS THINK WE GIRLS NEED SAVING ALL THE TIME. AS IF!
LOOK, ALL I'M SAYING IS...
NEVER MIND. WE SHOULDN'T BE FIGHTING ...
YEAH... WE NEED TO FIGURE OUT WHAT TO DO...
AND WE CERTAINLY SHOULDN'T BE YELLING...
...'CAUSE IF GRISELDA HEARS US, WE'RE DONE FOR!
UH-OH... DO YOU THINK SOMEONE HEARD US ALREADY?
I HOPE NOT...

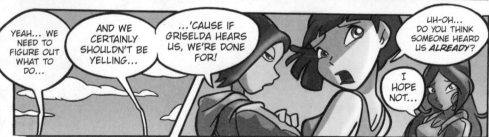

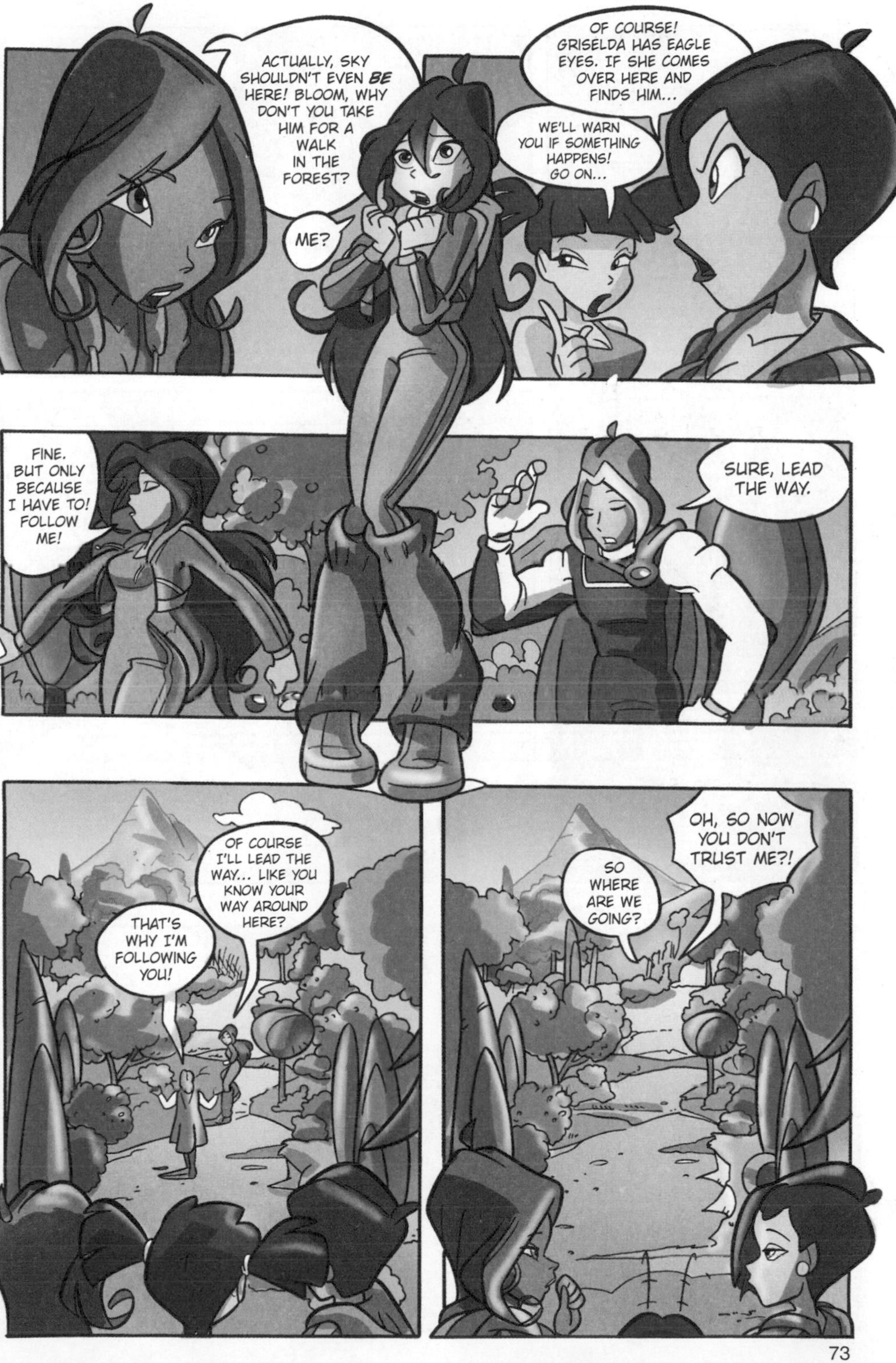
ACTUALLY, SKY SHOULDN'T EVEN *BE* HERE! BLOOM, WHY DON'T YOU TAKE HIM FOR A WALK IN THE FOREST?
ME?
OF COURSE! GRISELDA HAS EAGLE EYES. IF SHE COMES OVER HERE AND FINDS HIM...
WE'LL WARN YOU IF SOMETHING HAPPENS! GO ON...
FINE. BUT ONLY BECAUSE I HAVE TO! FOLLOW ME!
SURE, LEAD THE WAY.
OF COURSE I'LL LEAD THE WAY... LIKE YOU KNOW YOUR WAY AROUND HERE?
THAT'S WHY I'M FOLLOWING YOU!
OH, SO NOW YOU DON'T TRUST ME?!
SO WHERE ARE WE GOING?

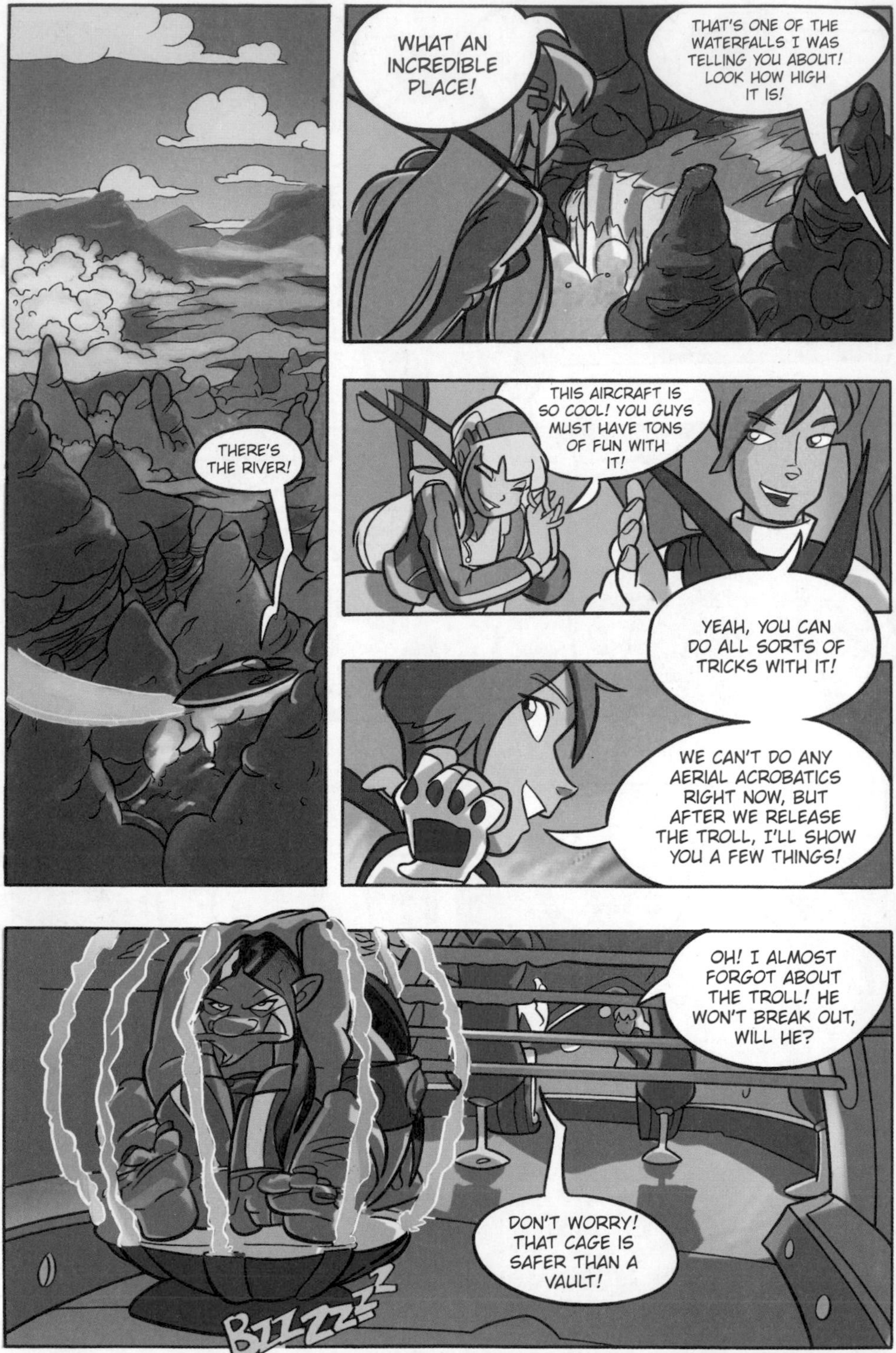
THERE'S THE RIVER!
WHAT AN INCREDIBLE PLACE!
THAT'S ONE OF THE WATERFALLS I WAS TELLING YOU ABOUT! LOOK HOW HIGH IT IS!
THIS AIRCRAFT IS SO COOL! YOU GUYS MUST HAVE TONS OF FUN WITH IT!
YEAH, YOU CAN DO ALL SORTS OF TRICKS WITH IT!
WE CAN'T DO ANY AERIAL ACROBATICS RIGHT NOW, BUT AFTER WE RELEASE THE TROLL, I'LL SHOW YOU A FEW THINGS!
OH! I ALMOST FORGOT ABOUT THE TROLL! HE WON'T BREAK OUT, WILL HE?
DON'T WORRY! THAT CAGE IS SAFER THAN A VAULT!
BZZZZZZ

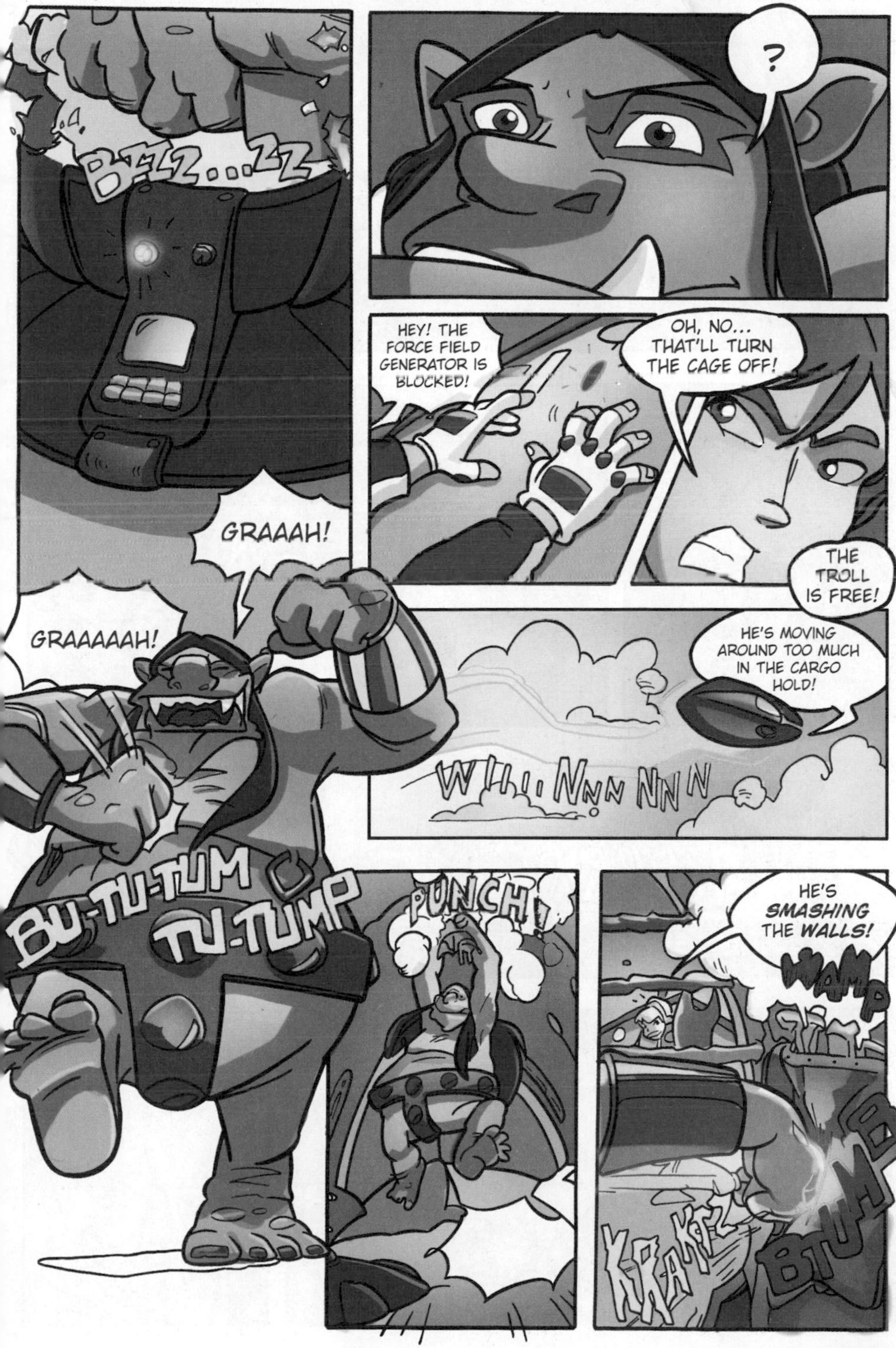
BZZZ...ZZ
?
HEY! THE FORCE FIELD GENERATOR IS BLOCKED!
OH, NO... THAT'LL TURN THE CAGE OFF!
GRAAAH!
THE TROLL IS FREE!
GRAAAAAH!
HE'S MOVING AROUND TOO MUCH IN THE CARGO HOLD!
WIII NNN NNN
BU-TU-TUM TU-TUMP
PUNCH!
HE'S *SMASHING* THE *WALLS*!
WAMP
KRAKK
BTUMB

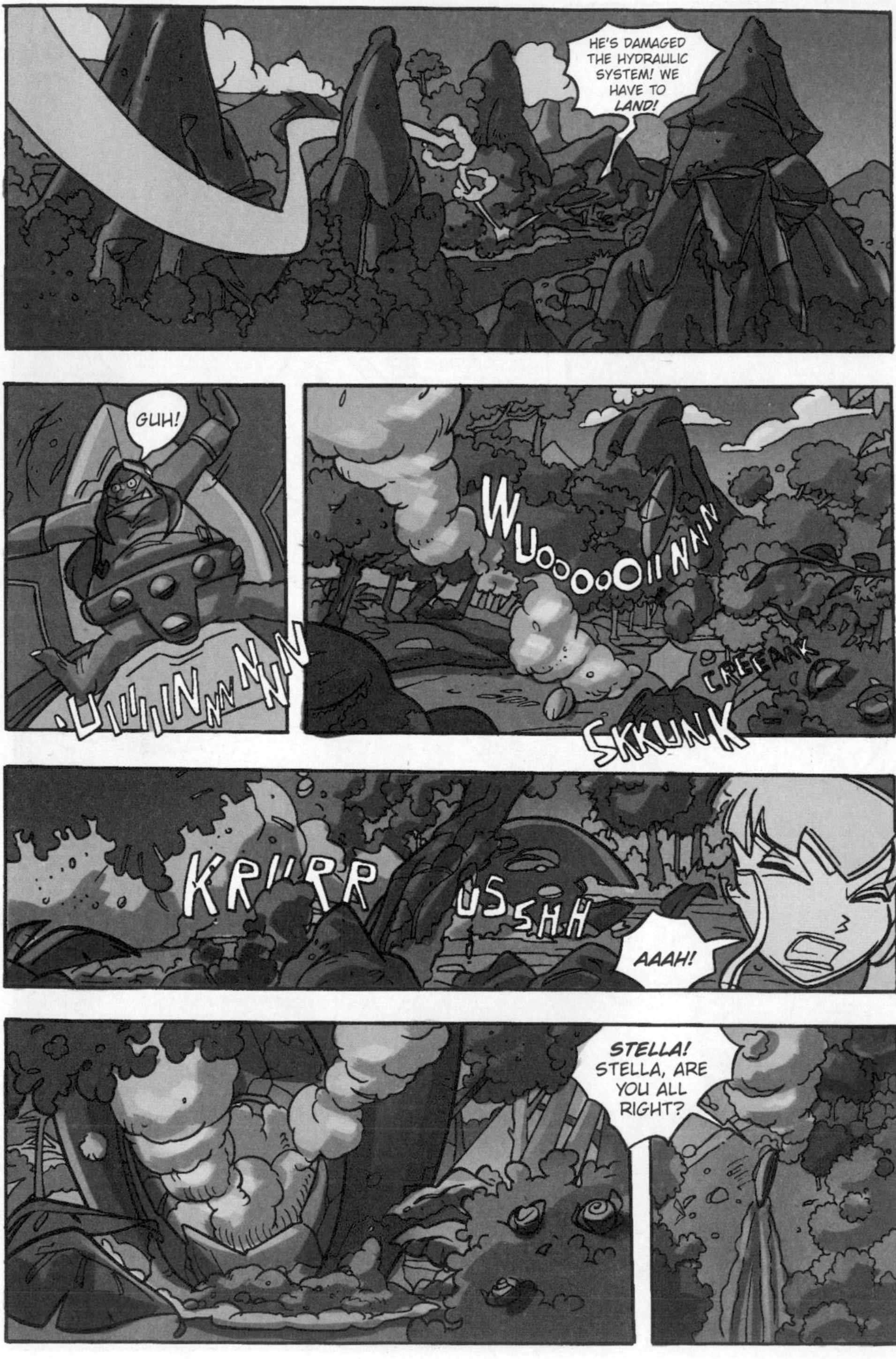

HE'S DAMAGED THE HYDRAULIC SYSTEM! WE HAVE TO LAND!
GUH!
UIIIIINNNNNN
WUOOOOOIINNN
CREEAAK
SKKUNK
KRIIRR
USSHH
AAAH!
STELLA! STELLA, ARE YOU ALL RIGHT?

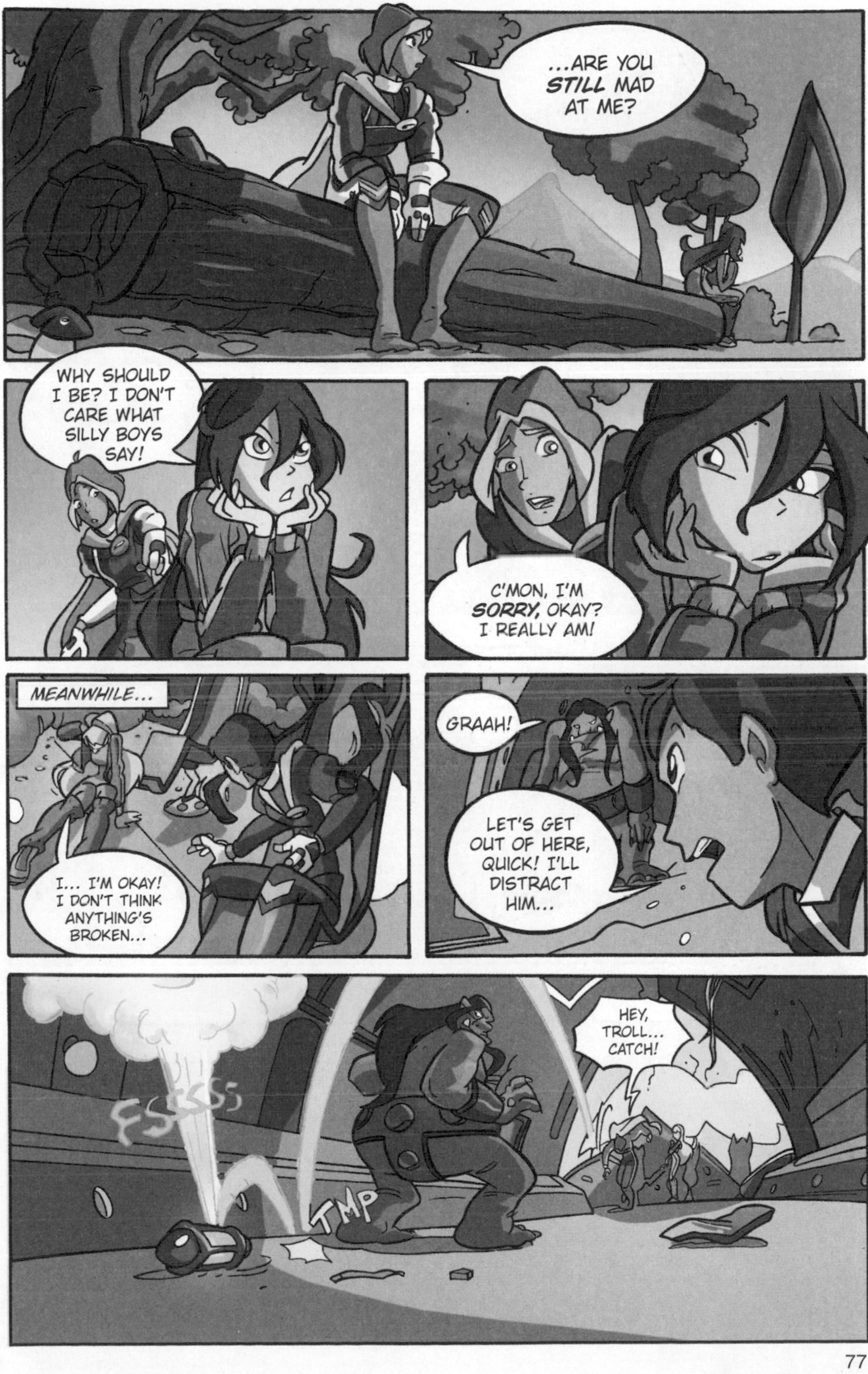
...ARE YOU STILL MAD AT ME?
WHY SHOULD I BE? I DON'T CARE WHAT SILLY BOYS SAY!
C'MON, I'M SORRY, OKAY? I REALLY AM!
MEANWHILE...
I... I'M OKAY! I DON'T THINK ANYTHING'S BROKEN...
GRAAH!
LET'S GET OUT OF HERE, QUICK! I'LL DISTRACT HIM...
HEY, TROLL... CATCH!
FSSSS
TMP

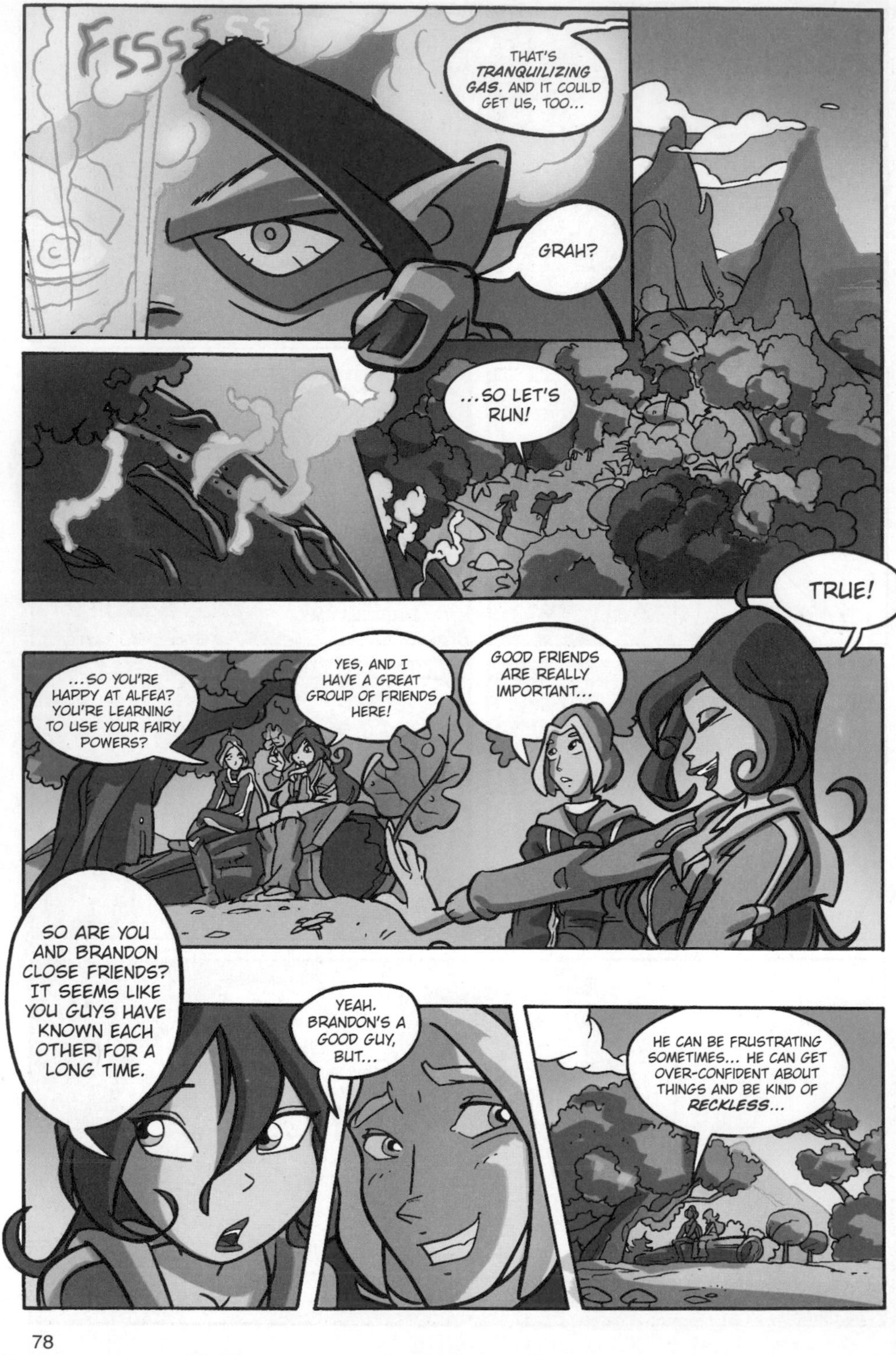
FSSSSSS
THAT'S TRANQUILIZING GAS. AND IT COULD GET US, TOO...
GRAH?
...SO LET'S RUN!
...SO YOU'RE HAPPY AT ALFEA? YOU'RE LEARNING TO USE YOUR FAIRY POWERS?
YES, AND I HAVE A GREAT GROUP OF FRIENDS HERE!
GOOD FRIENDS ARE REALLY IMPORTANT...
TRUE!
SO ARE YOU AND BRANDON CLOSE FRIENDS? IT SEEMS LIKE YOU GUYS HAVE KNOWN EACH OTHER FOR A LONG TIME.
YEAH. BRANDON'S A GOOD GUY, BUT...
HE CAN BE FRUSTRATING SOMETIMES... HE CAN GET OVER-CONFIDENT ABOUT THINGS AND BE KIND OF RECKLESS...

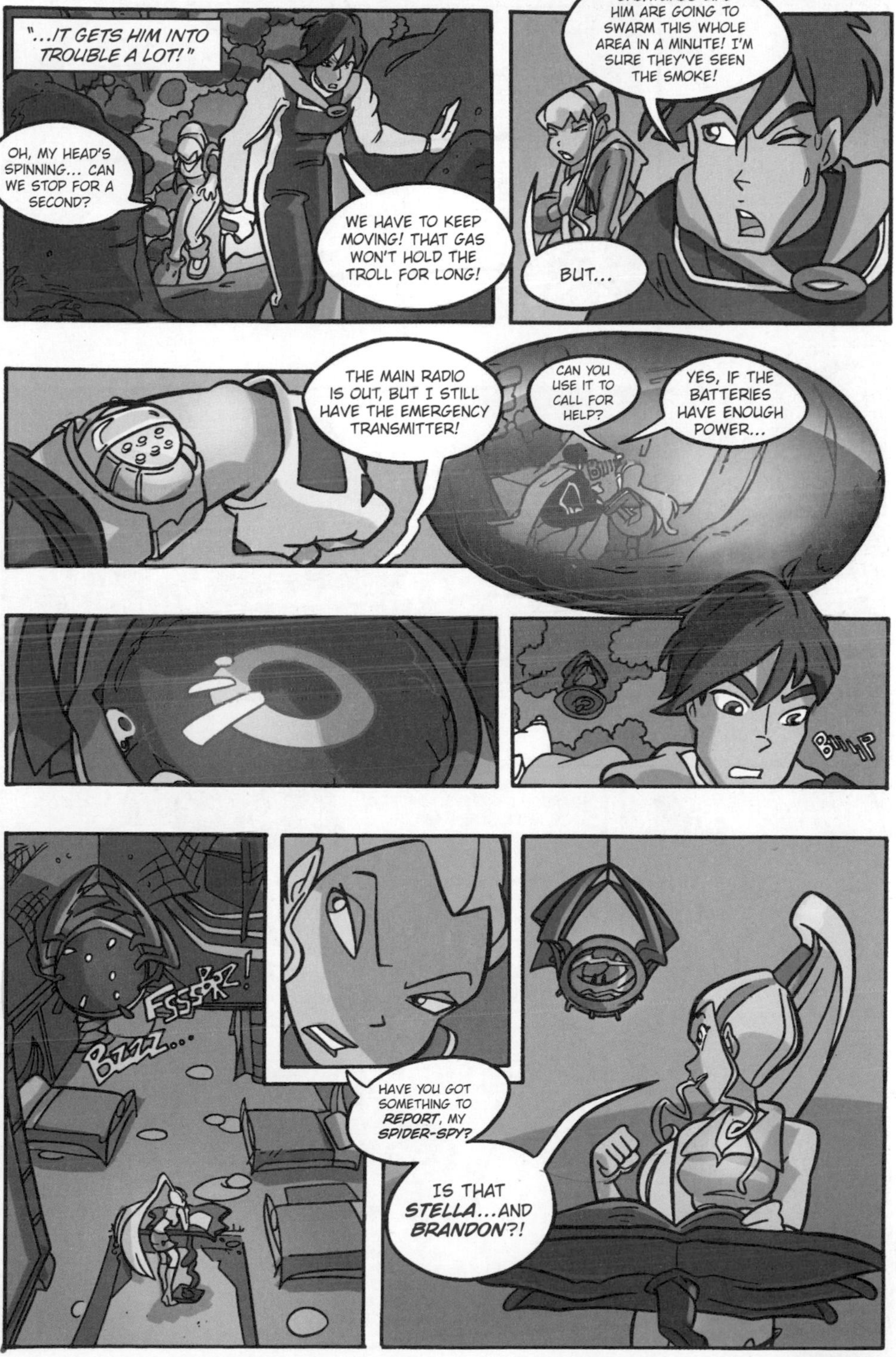
"...IT GETS HIM INTO TROUBLE A LOT!"
OH, MY HEAD'S SPINNING... CAN WE STOP FOR A SECOND?
WE HAVE TO KEEP MOVING! THAT GAS WON'T HOLD THE TROLL FOR LONG!
CREATURES LIKE HIM ARE GOING TO SWARM THIS WHOLE AREA IN A MINUTE! I'M SURE THEY'VE SEEN THE SMOKE!
BUT...
THE MAIN RADIO IS OUT, BUT I STILL HAVE THE EMERGENCY TRANSMITTER!
CAN YOU USE IT TO CALL FOR HELP?
YES, IF THE BATTERIES HAVE ENOUGH POWER...
BLIIP
FSSSBZZ!
BZZZZ...
HAVE YOU GOT SOMETHING TO REPORT, MY SPIDER-SPY?
IS THAT STELLA...AND BRANDON?!

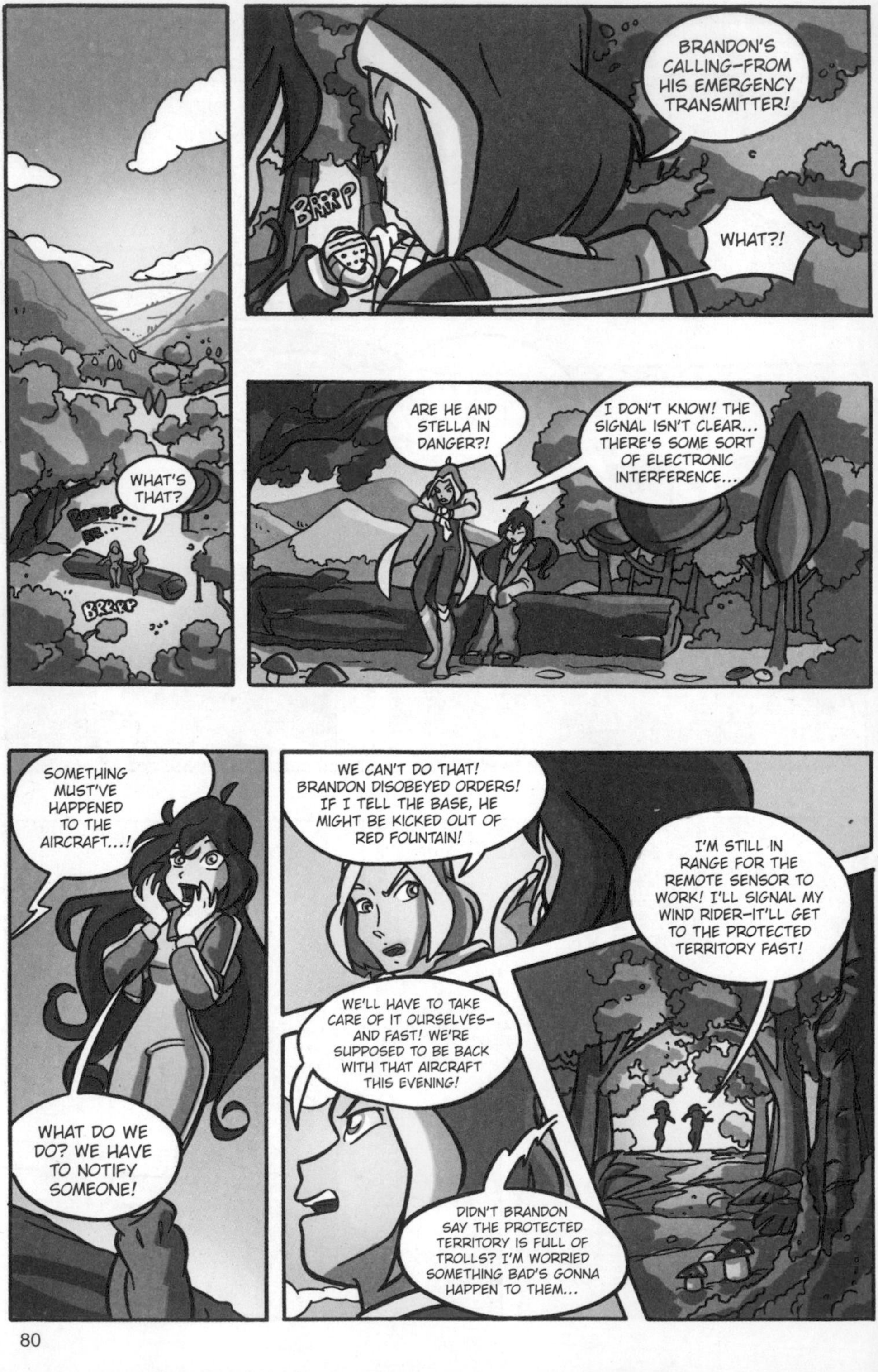
BRANDON'S CALLING—FROM HIS EMERGENCY TRANSMITTER!
WHAT?!
WHAT'S THAT?
ARE HE AND STELLA IN DANGER?!
I DON'T KNOW! THE SIGNAL ISN'T CLEAR... THERE'S SOME SORT OF ELECTRONIC INTERFERENCE...
SOMETHING MUST'VE HAPPENED TO THE AIRCRAFT...!
WHAT DO WE DO? WE HAVE TO NOTIFY SOMEONE!
WE CAN'T DO THAT! BRANDON DISOBEYED ORDERS! IF I TELL THE BASE, HE MIGHT BE KICKED OUT OF RED FOUNTAIN!
WE'LL HAVE TO TAKE CARE OF IT OURSELVES—AND FAST! WE'RE SUPPOSED TO BE BACK WITH THAT AIRCRAFT THIS EVENING!
I'M STILL IN RANGE FOR THE REMOTE SENSOR TO WORK! I'LL SIGNAL MY WIND RIDER—IT'LL GET TO THE PROTECTED TERRITORY FAST!
DIDN'T BRANDON SAY THE PROTECTED TERRITORY IS FULL OF TROLLS? I'M WORRIED SOMETHING BAD'S GONNA HAPPEN TO THEM...

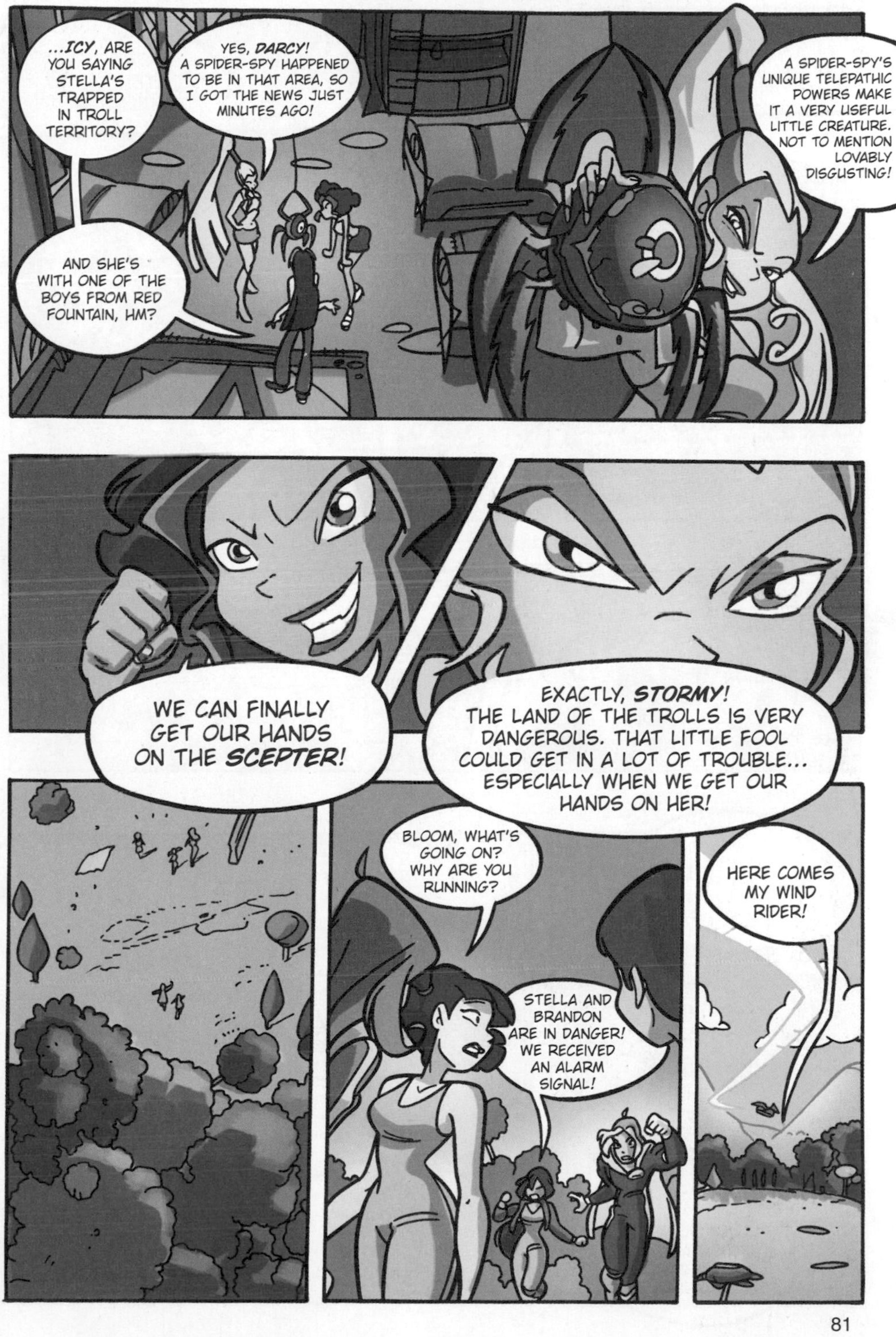
...ICY, ARE YOU SAYING STELLA'S TRAPPED IN TROLL TERRITORY?
YES, DARCY! A SPIDER-SPY HAPPENED TO BE IN THAT AREA, SO I GOT THE NEWS JUST MINUTES AGO!
AND SHE'S WITH ONE OF THE BOYS FROM RED FOUNTAIN, HM?
A SPIDER-SPY'S UNIQUE TELEPATHIC POWERS MAKE IT A VERY USEFUL LITTLE CREATURE. NOT TO MENTION LOVABLY DISGUSTING!
WE CAN FINALLY GET OUR HANDS ON THE SCEPTER!
EXACTLY, STORMY! THE LAND OF THE TROLLS IS VERY DANGEROUS. THAT LITTLE FOOL COULD GET IN A LOT OF TROUBLE... ESPECIALLY WHEN WE GET OUR HANDS ON HER!
BLOOM, WHAT'S GOING ON? WHY ARE YOU RUNNING?
STELLA AND BRANDON ARE IN DANGER! WE RECEIVED AN ALARM SIGNAL!
HERE COMES MY WIND RIDER!

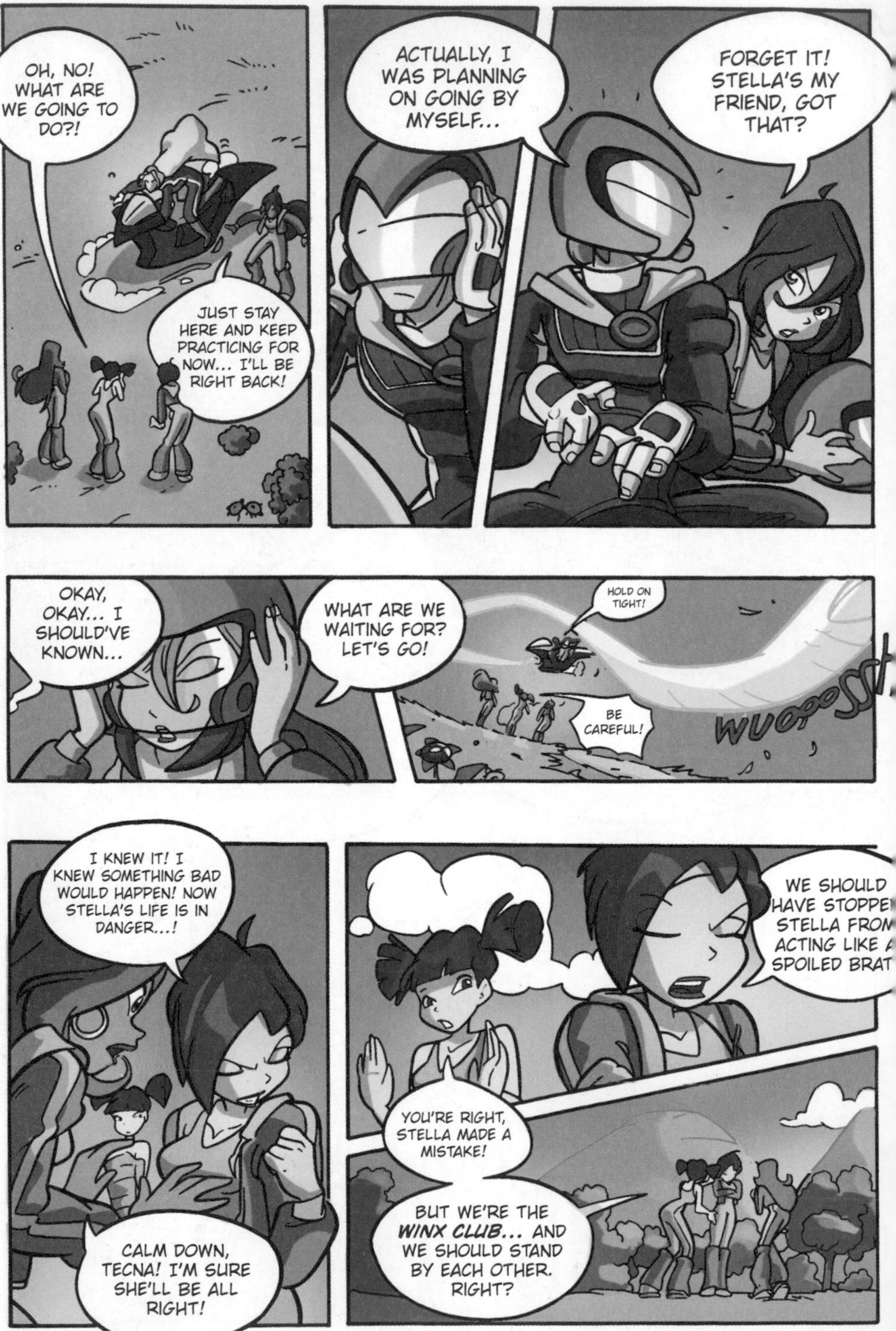
OH, NO! WHAT ARE WE GOING TO DO?!
JUST STAY HERE AND KEEP PRACTICING FOR NOW... I'LL BE RIGHT BACK!
ACTUALLY, I WAS PLANNING ON GOING BY MYSELF...
FORGET IT! STELLA'S MY FRIEND, GOT THAT?
OKAY, OKAY... I SHOULD'VE KNOWN...
WHAT ARE WE WAITING FOR? LET'S GO!
HOLD ON TIGHT!
BE CAREFUL!
WUOOOOSSH
I KNEW IT! I KNEW SOMETHING BAD WOULD HAPPEN! NOW STELLA'S LIFE IS IN DANGER...!
CALM DOWN, TECNA! I'M SURE SHE'LL BE ALL RIGHT!
WE SHOULD HAVE STOPPE STELLA FROM ACTING LIKE A SPOILED BRAT
YOU'RE RIGHT, STELLA MADE A MISTAKE!
BUT WE'RE THE WINX CLUB... AND WE SHOULD STAND BY EACH OTHER. RIGHT?

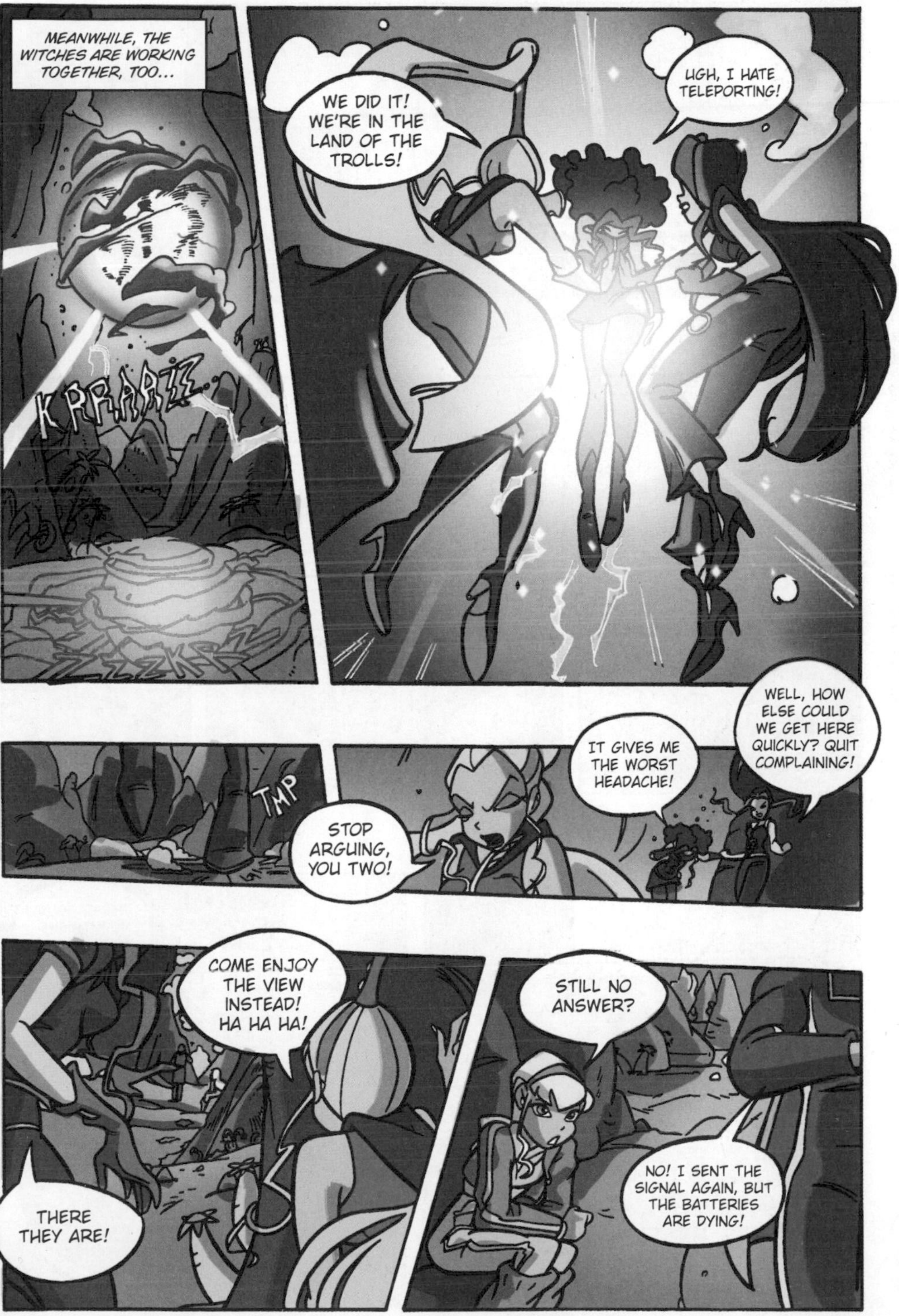
MEANWHILE, THE WITCHES ARE WORKING TOGETHER, TOO...
KRRAAZZ...
WE DID IT! WE'RE IN THE LAND OF THE TROLLS!
UGH, I HATE TELEPORTING!
TMP
IT GIVES ME THE WORST HEADACHE!
WELL, HOW ELSE COULD WE GET HERE QUICKLY? QUIT COMPLAINING!
STOP ARGUING, YOU TWO!
COME ENJOY THE VIEW INSTEAD! HA HA HA!
THERE THEY ARE!
STILL NO ANSWER?
NO! I SENT THE SIGNAL AGAIN, BUT THE BATTERIES ARE DYING!

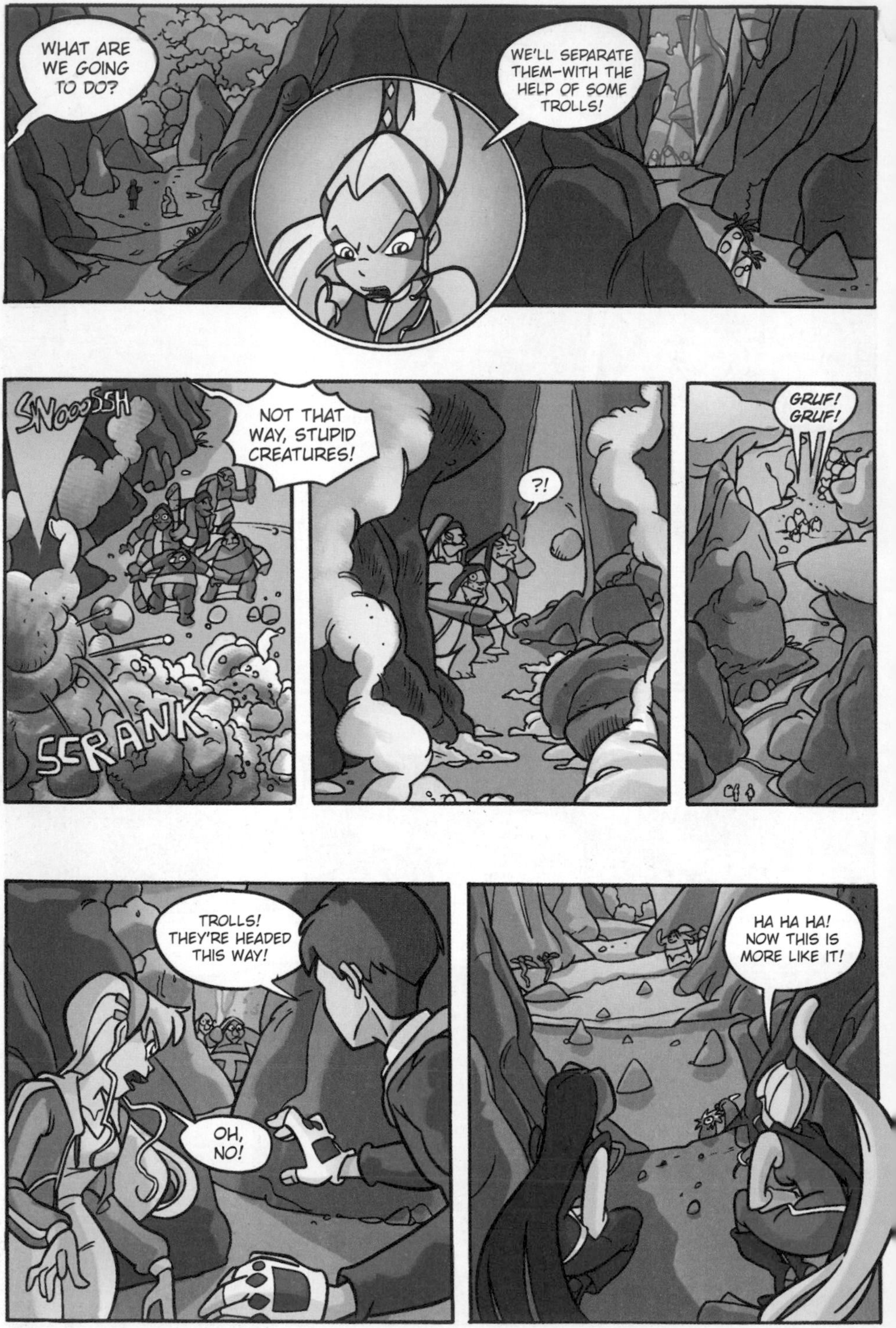
WHAT ARE WE GOING TO DO?
WE'LL SEPARATE THEM—WITH THE HELP OF SOME TROLLS!
SWOOOSSH
NOT THAT WAY, STUPID CREATURES!
SCRANK
?!
GRUF! GRUF!
TROLLS! THEY'RE HEADED THIS WAY!
OH, NO!
HA HA HA! NOW THIS IS MORE LIKE IT!

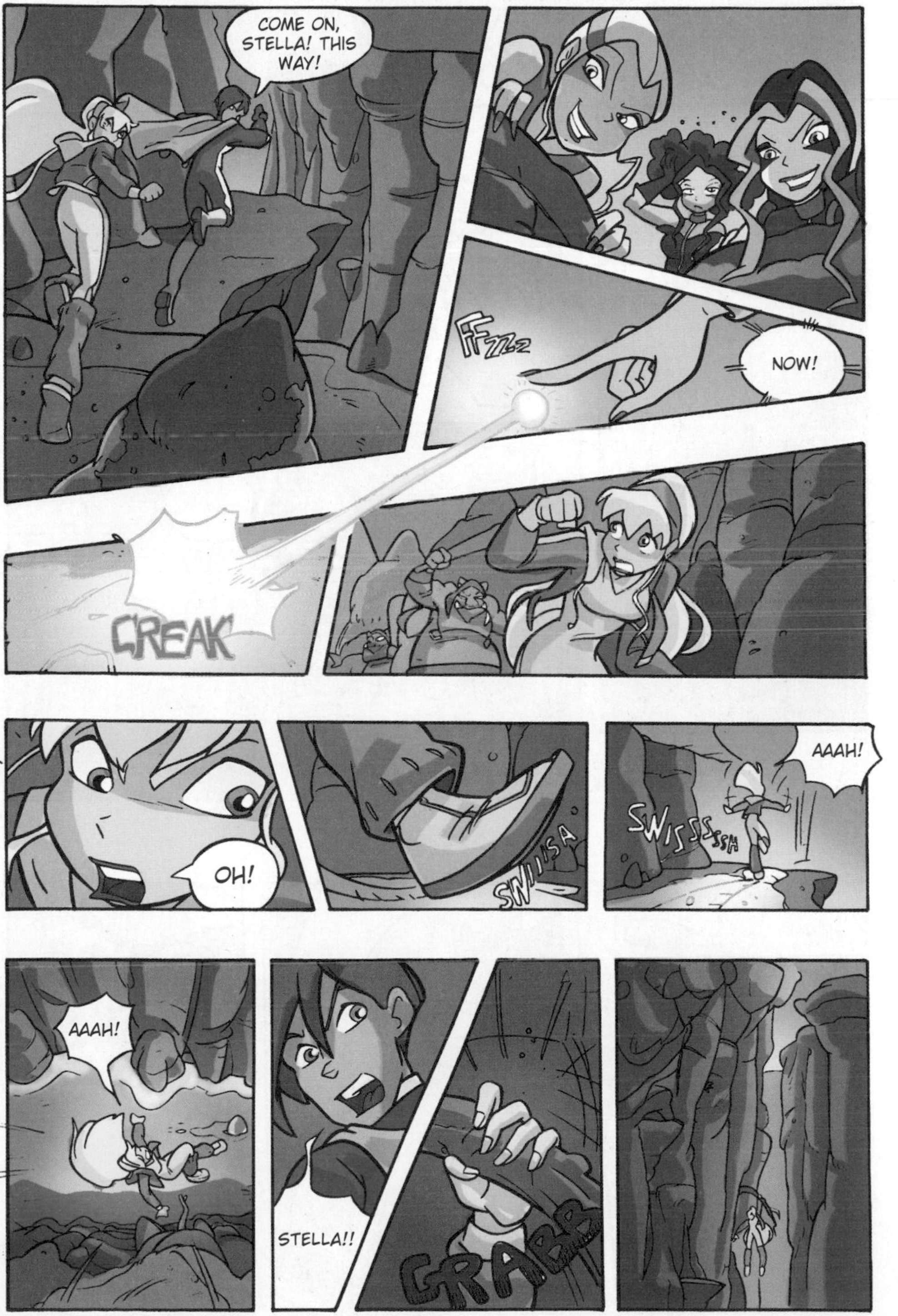
COME ON, STELLA! THIS WAY!
FFZZZ
NOW!
CREAK
OH!
SWIISA
SWISSSSSH
AAAH!
AAAH!
STELLA!!
GRABB

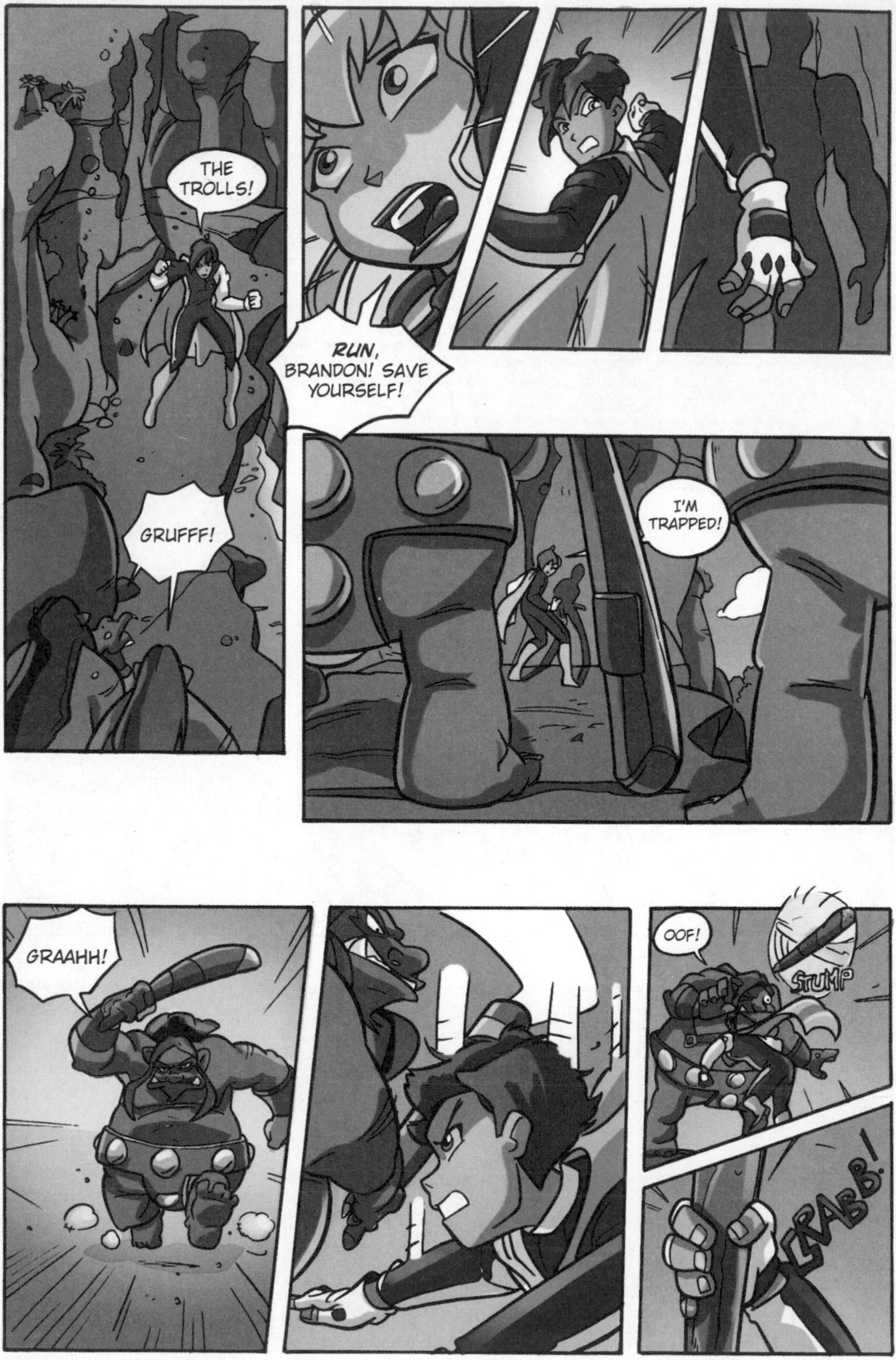
THE TROLLS!
RUN, BRANDON! SAVE YOURSELF!
GRUFFF!
I'M TRAPPED!
GRAAHH!
OOF!
STUMP
GRABB!

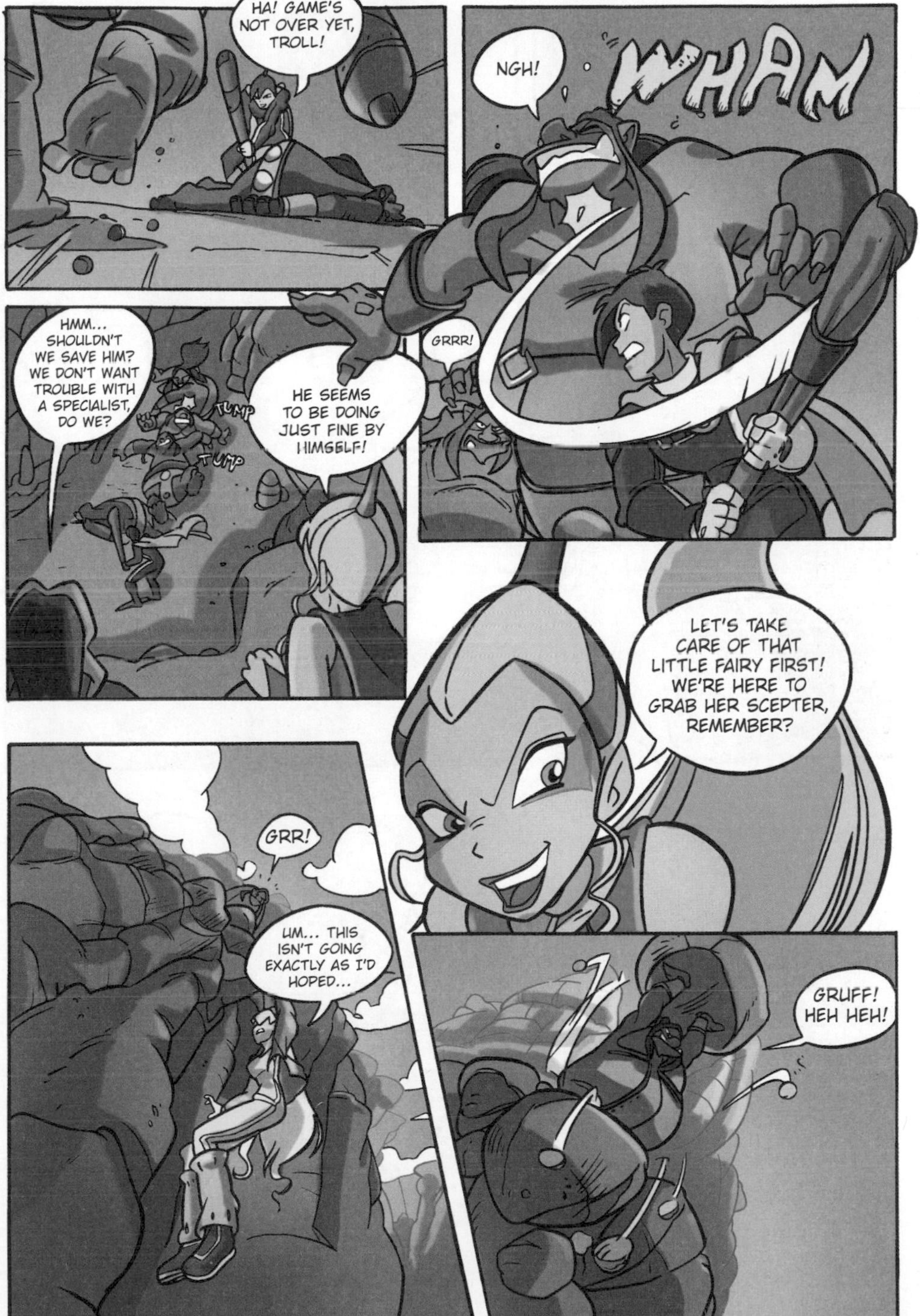

HA! GAME'S NOT OVER YET, TROLL!
NGH!
WHAM
HMM... SHOULDN'T WE SAVE HIM? WE DON'T WANT TROUBLE WITH A SPECIALIST, DO WE?
TUMP
TUMP
HE SEEMS TO BE DOING JUST FINE BY HIMSELF!
GRRR!
LET'S TAKE CARE OF THAT LITTLE FAIRY FIRST! WE'RE HERE TO GRAB HER SCEPTER, REMEMBER?
GRR!
UM... THIS ISN'T GOING EXACTLY AS I'D HOPED...
GRUFF! HEH HEH!

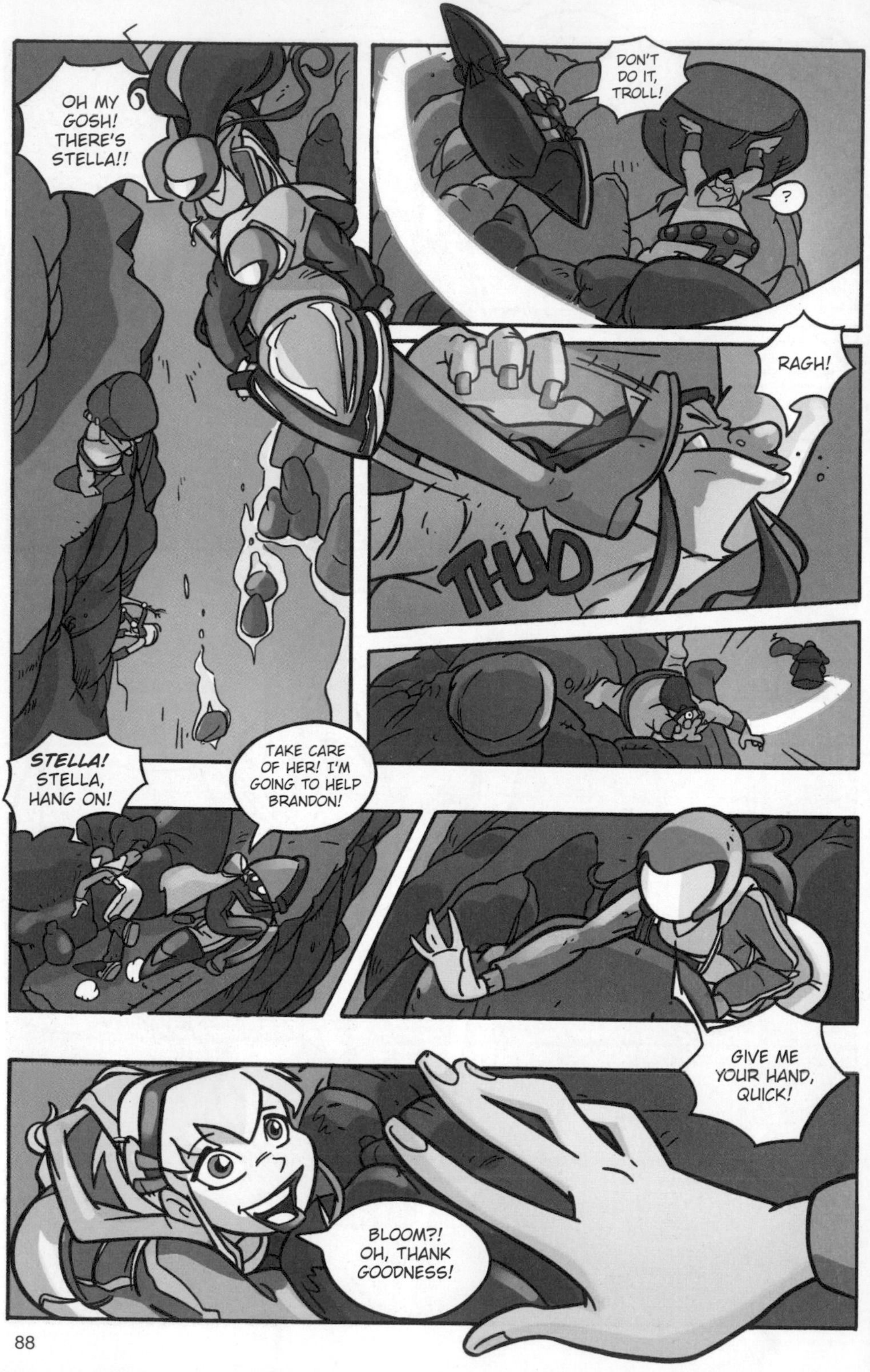
OH MY GOSH! THERE'S STELLA!!
DON'T DO IT, TROLL!
?
RAGH!
THUD
STELLA! STELLA, HANG ON!
TAKE CARE OF HER! I'M GOING TO HELP BRANDON!
GIVE ME YOUR HAND, QUICK!
BLOOM?! OH, THANK GOODNESS!

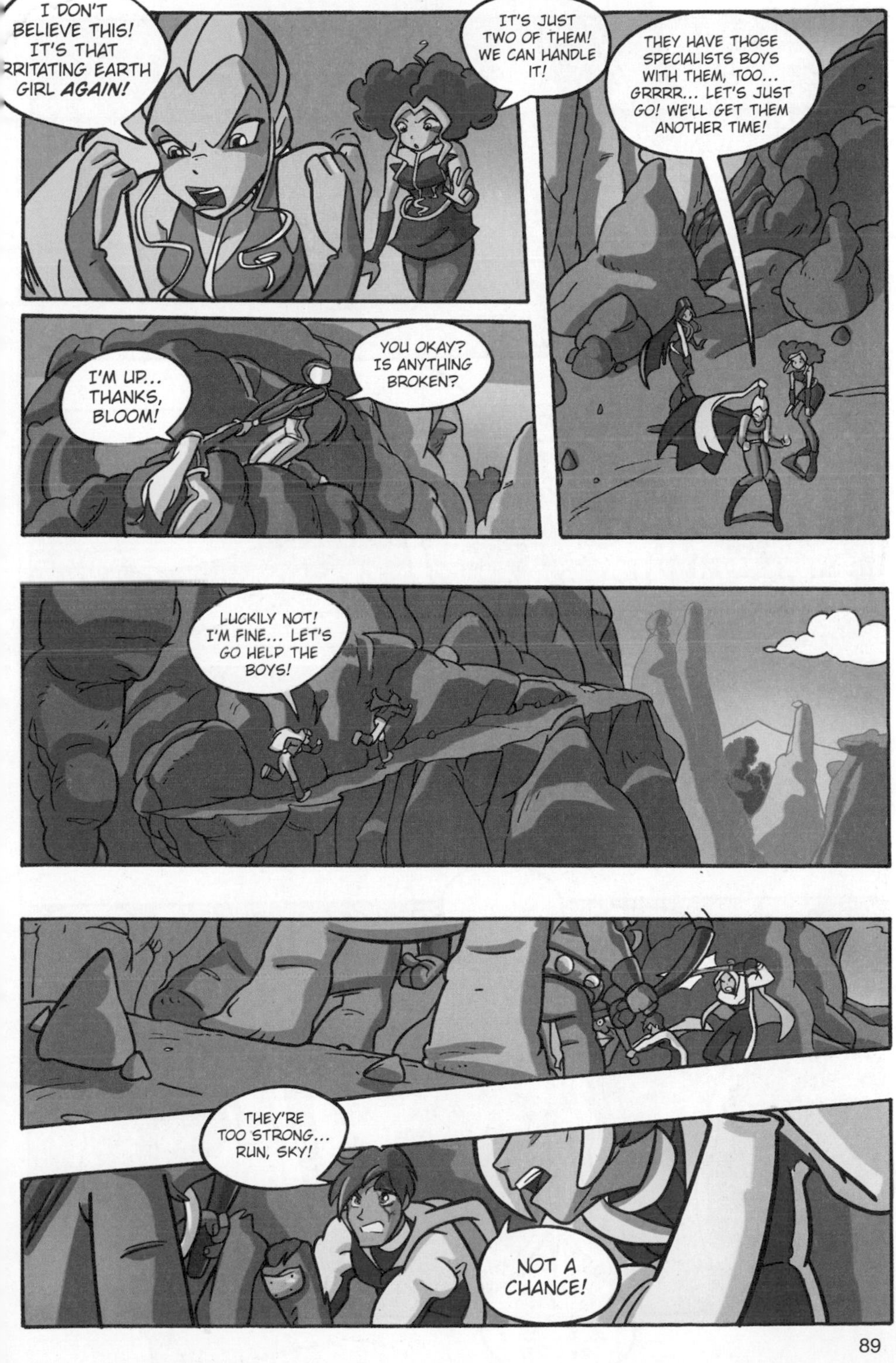
I DON'T BELIEVE THIS! IT'S THAT RRITATING EARTH GIRL AGAIN!
IT'S JUST TWO OF THEM! WE CAN HANDLE IT!
THEY HAVE THOSE SPECIALISTS BOYS WITH THEM, TOO... GRRRR... LET'S JUST GO! WE'LL GET THEM ANOTHER TIME!
YOU OKAY? IS ANYTHING BROKEN?
I'M UP... THANKS, BLOOM!
LUCKILY NOT! I'M FINE... LET'S GO HELP THE BOYS!
THEY'RE TOO STRONG... RUN, SKY!
NOT A CHANCE!

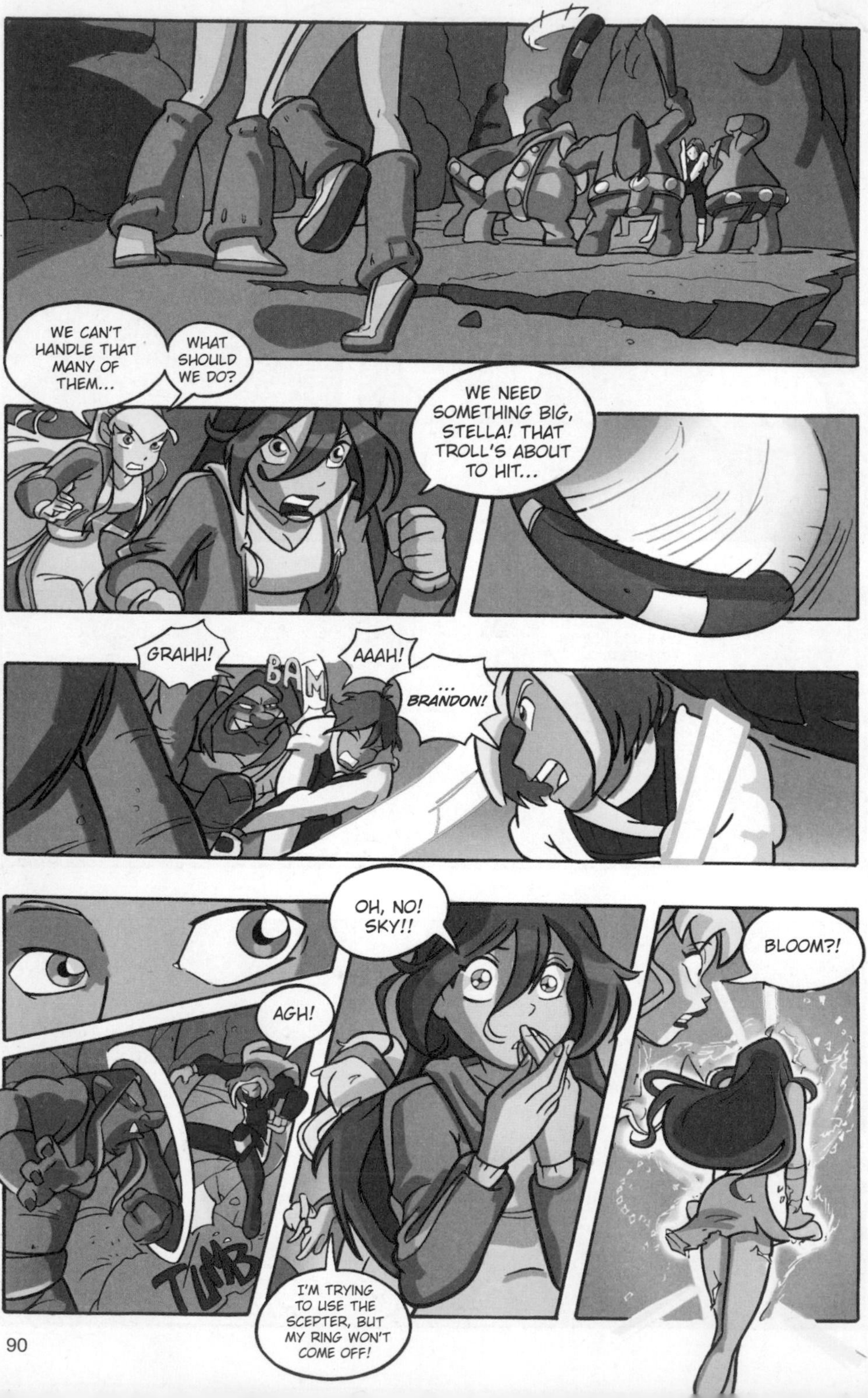
WE CAN'T HANDLE THAT MANY OF THEM...
WHAT SHOULD WE DO?
WE NEED SOMETHING BIG, STELLA! THAT TROLL'S ABOUT TO HIT...
GRAHH!
BAM
AAAH!
... BRANDON!
OH, NO! SKY!!
BLOOM?!
AGH!
TUMB
I'M TRYING TO USE THE SCEPTER, BUT MY RING WON'T COME OFF!

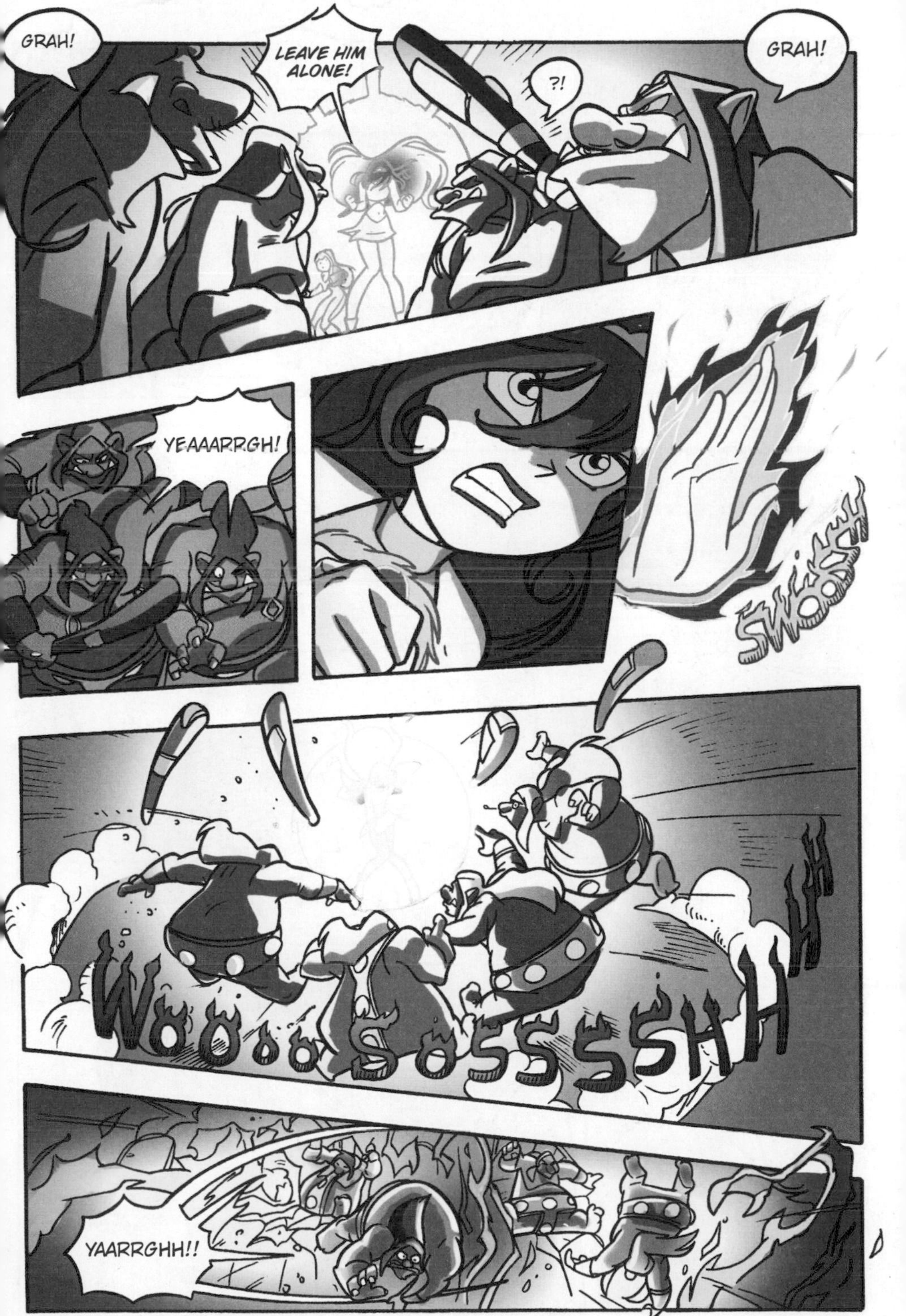
GRAH!
LEAVE HIM ALONE!
?!
GRAH!
YEAAARRGH!
SWOOSH
WOOOOSSSSSHHH
YAARRGHH!!

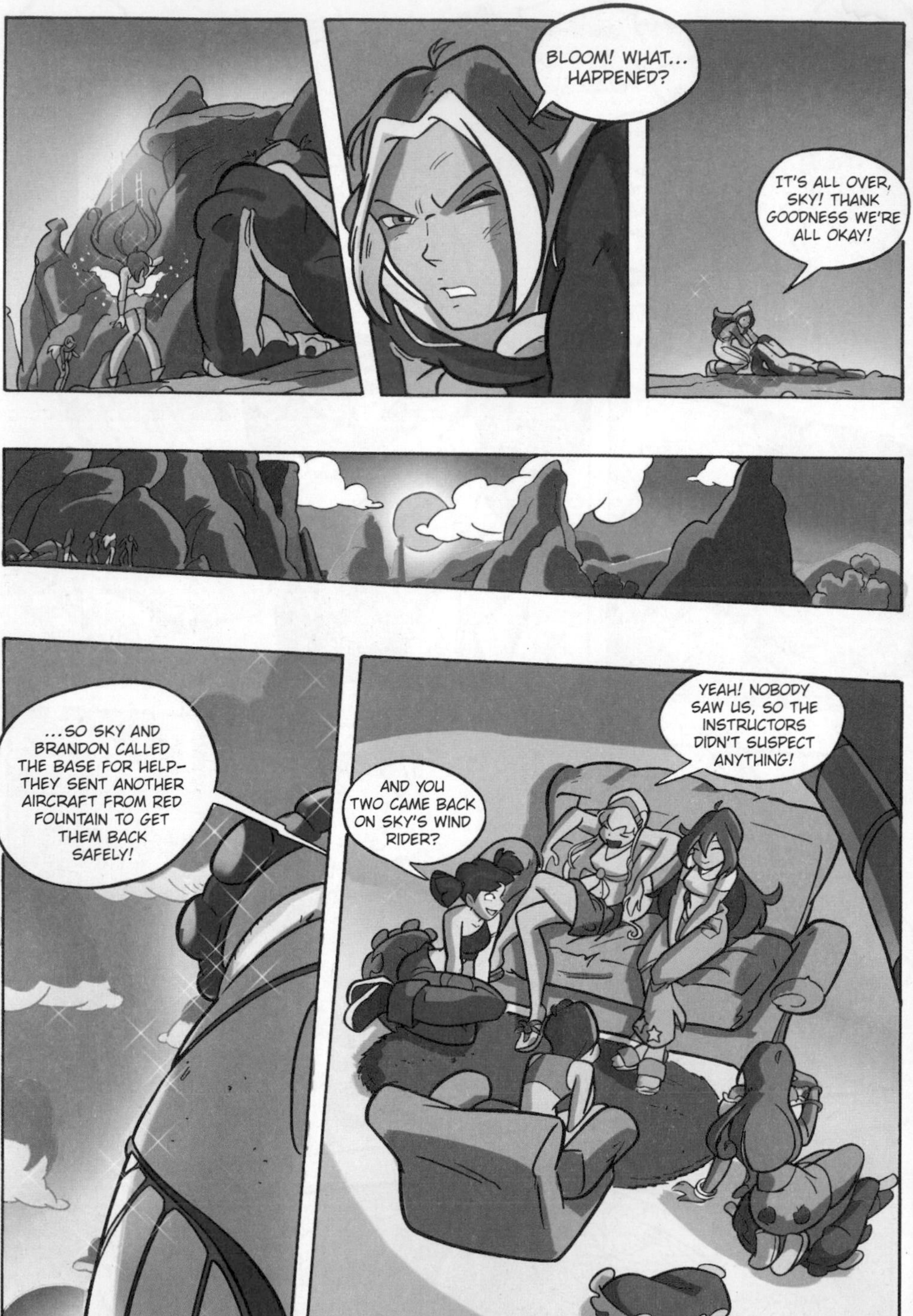
BLOOM! WHAT... HAPPENED?
IT'S ALL OVER, SKY! THANK GOODNESS WE'RE ALL OKAY!
...SO SKY AND BRANDON CALLED THE BASE FOR HELP-THEY SENT ANOTHER AIRCRAFT FROM RED FOUNTAIN TO GET THEM BACK SAFELY!
YEAH! NOBODY SAW US, SO THE INSTRUCTORS DIDN'T SUSPECT ANYTHING!
AND YOU TWO CAME BACK ON SKY'S WIND RIDER?

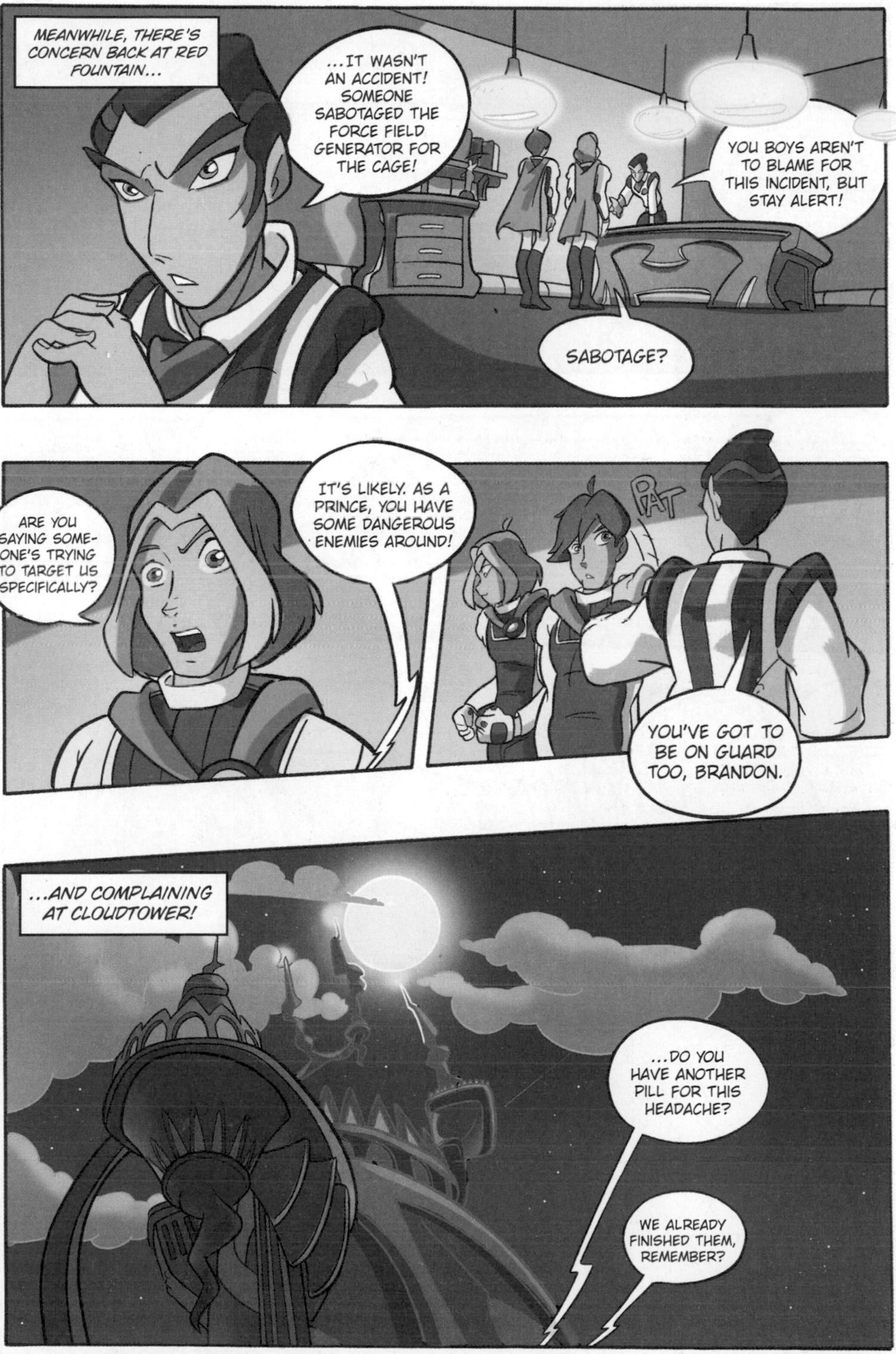

MEANWHILE, THERE'S CONCERN BACK AT RED FOUNTAIN...
...IT WASN'T AN ACCIDENT! SOMEONE SABOTAGED THE FORCE FIELD GENERATOR FOR THE CAGE!
YOU BOYS AREN'T TO BLAME FOR THIS INCIDENT, BUT STAY ALERT!
SABOTAGE?
ARE YOU SAYING SOME-ONE'S TRYING TO TARGET US SPECIFICALLY?
IT'S LIKELY. AS A PRINCE, YOU HAVE SOME DANGEROUS ENEMIES AROUND!
PAT
YOU'VE GOT TO BE ON GUARD TOO, BRANDON.
...AND COMPLAINING AT CLOUDTOWER!
...DO YOU HAVE ANOTHER PILL FOR THIS HEADACHE?
WE ALREADY FINISHED THEM, REMEMBER?

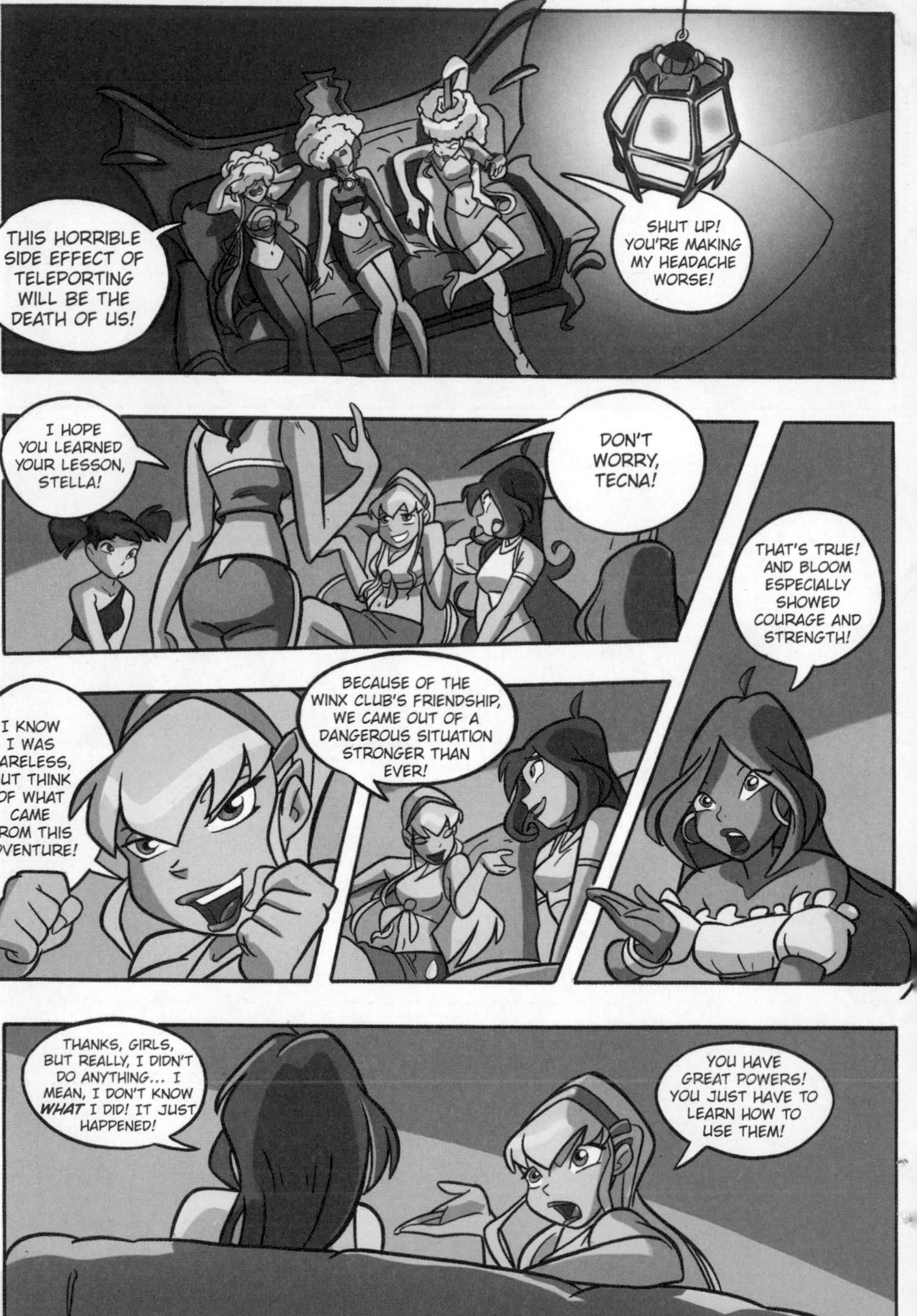
THIS HORRIBLE SIDE EFFECT OF TELEPORTING WILL BE THE DEATH OF US!
SHUT UP! YOU'RE MAKING MY HEADACHE WORSE!
I HOPE YOU LEARNED YOUR LESSON, STELLA!
DON'T WORRY, TECNA!
THAT'S TRUE! AND BLOOM ESPECIALLY SHOWED COURAGE AND STRENGTH!
I KNOW I WAS CARELESS, BUT THINK OF WHAT CAME FROM THIS ADVENTURE!
BECAUSE OF THE WINX CLUB'S FRIENDSHIP, WE CAME OUT OF A DANGEROUS SITUATION STRONGER THAN EVER!
THANKS, GIRLS, BUT REALLY, I DIDN'T DO ANYTHING... I MEAN, I DON'T KNOW ***WHAT*** I DID! IT JUST HAPPENED!
YOU HAVE GREAT POWERS! YOU JUST HAVE TO LEARN HOW TO USE THEM!

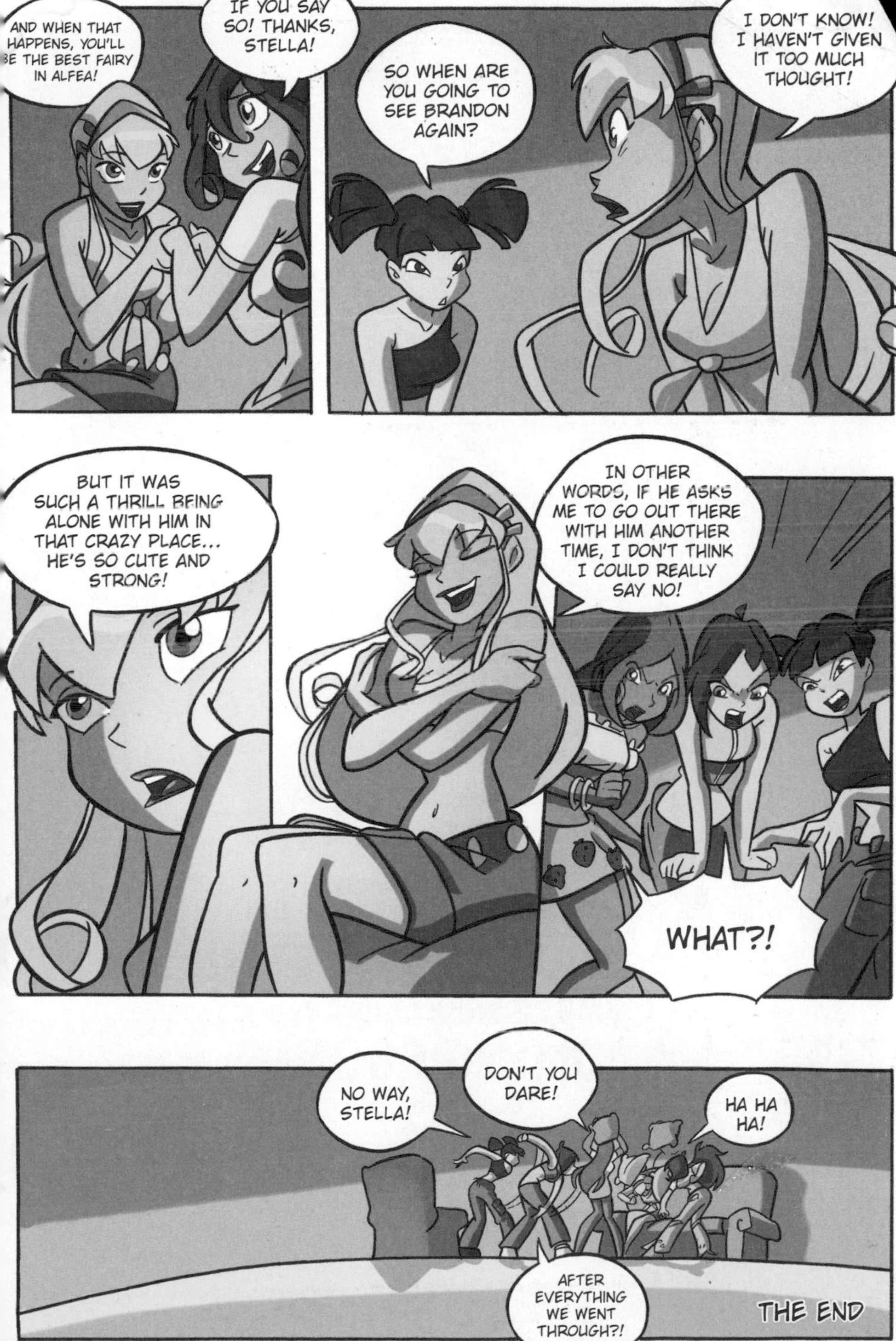
AND WHEN THAT HAPPENS, YOU'LL BE THE BEST FAIRY IN ALFEA!
IF YOU SAY SO! THANKS, STELLA!
SO WHEN ARE YOU GOING TO SEE BRANDON AGAIN?
I DON'T KNOW! I HAVEN'T GIVEN IT TOO MUCH THOUGHT!
BUT IT WAS SUCH A THRILL BEING ALONE WITH HIM IN THAT CRAZY PLACE... HE'S SO CUTE AND STRONG!
IN OTHER WORDS, IF HE ASKS ME TO GO OUT THERE WITH HIM ANOTHER TIME, I DON'T THINK I COULD REALLY SAY NO!
WHAT?!
NO WAY, STELLA!
DON'T YOU DARE!
HA HA HA!
AFTER EVERYTHING WE WENT THROUGH?!
THE END

Now Available

Winx Club
1
Bloom's Discovery
As seen on nickelodeon

Look for MORE Winx Club Adventures
COMING SOON!

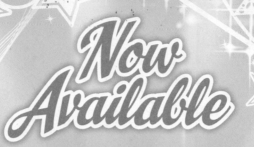

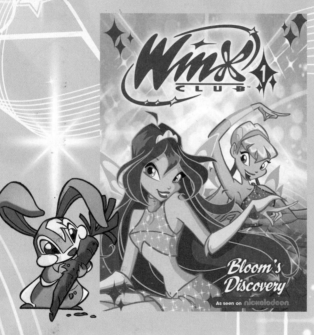